Against Whom?

by the same author

FORTUNE'S FINGER
UNDER THE SKIN
DEVIL'S DUE
INNOCENCE AND EXPERIENCE
THE LIFELINE
OLD WINE
WITHIN THE CUP
PRIVATE WORLDS
LONDON PRIDE
THE MORTAL STORM
MASKS AND FACES
HEART OF A CHILD

SEARCH FOR A SOUL
THE CHALLENGE

ALFRED ADLER

AGAINST WHOM?

by   *PB*

PHYLLIS
BOTTOME

FABER AND FABER
24 Russell Square
London

First published in mcmliv
by Faber and Faber Limited
24 *Russell Square London W.C.*1
Printed in Great Britain by
Purnell and Sons Limited
Paulton (Somerset) and London

To my friend

BRIAN

in appreciation and affection

★

'Realism is the spiritual victory
over ego-centricity'

NICOLAS BERDYAEV

1

When Father Bretherton woke he found himself balanced on golden air. The bed he was lying on had the softness of a cloud and the resilience of heather. He was not out of doors, but keen persuasive air streamed over him with delicate lightness. The air and the altitude did half the work of his menaced lungs for him; but he still had to do the other half.

Three peaks, newly covered with a light powdering of snow, glittering like javelins, shot up into a fathomless blue dome. He did not have to lift his head to see them. His heart beat feebly, all his limbs ached, and his head swam, but none of these familiar symptoms disturbed him unduly. He felt that his illness was simply a condition that required a certain amount of attention. Pain to Father Bretherton was not a personal affront, nor even an insuperable obstacle. It was a signpost as yet unread, pointing towards life, or towards death. Like Hotspur, Father Bretherton felt that he owed God a death; but it was none of his business which debt— the longer one of life, or the more abrupt one of death —might be required of him. What troubled him a little was whether he had been asleep, and dreamed of the girl who had come in, after the nurse had left him, or whether she had been a real girl?

She looked like Nefertiti, the long-dead Queen of Egypt; and if she were real then she was unmistakably the same girl to whom he had given his sleeper in the train the night before. His Father Superior would have been severely angry with him for giving up a necessary luxury paid for by the community; but he hadn't been able to help offering it to her. Even her mother's bullying voice, determined to use her anxiety for her daughter as a weapon, and almost disappointed that Father Bretherton had so instantly relinquished his right, had contained more humanity than Nefertiti's proud acceptance untouched by gratitude.

The child—for she was little more than a child—had a heart-shaped face, set on a slender stem like a flower; her hollowed cheeks were so white that they might have been carved out of a snowflake. Yet her beauty had not impressed Father Bretherton as much as her danger. He knew that pride—riding for a fall—shatters even the strongest; and this child looked built out of pride, and wholly vulnerable.

In his dream, the girl had come into his room. But was it a dream?—for in the pauses of his long sustained wakefulness, he knew that his body sometimes slept, though his mind refused to subside into unconsciousness with it. The girl had moved quietly and, with a determination that overcame physical weakness, straight to his bedside. "Please," she said, leaning over him, "don't tell any of Them that I took your sleeper! Everything is all wrong here—and I'm miserable. I wanted my tea downstairs in the lounge, and they tried to make me go to my room—you know nurses!—I mightn't have got any for ages, and not a proper tea then, the *real* tea was downstairs, and people I wanted to look at—and I didn't intend to wait—why should I? So I called a waiter and he brought me tea—and then —and then—I don't believe he was a waiter—but the doctor, the chief doctor of the Sanatorium!"

Her horror made her shake all over; it was so strange,

6

so dreadful for her new life, to begin like that! Father Bretherton felt how she'd been perhaps dreaming of an heroic start—and now this had been checked, they would think her troublesome—a bother—and selfish to have taken his berth, and made him sit up in the passage all night, though there had been that wonderful sleeping-car conductor, who brought him coffee, and helped him when he fainted.

"Of course I won't tell them!" he said quietly. "But hadn't you better go straight back to bed? You look too weak to stand."

She had said, in the dream, "Yes, I'm tired; but you've got a better room than I have: it's a corner one. I don't think it's fair!"

This evidently annoyed her again; she was very easily annoyed, but so weak that she clung to his bed to keep herself from falling; then she must have gone back, for the dream ended.

Had she slept, poor child? And could she see the same mountains, covered with waves of spreading gold, and hushed by the ministry of frost, that his contented eyes now rested on? The pine trees stretched in un-ending ranks, climbing as high as they could reach up the mountain's side; beyond them were empty golden spaces where nothing grew at all—except silence. There was no wind to gossip through the pine trees that cast blue shadows, and were garlanded by heavy wreaths of snow.

How unlike, how utterly unlike his home in West Africa, where he had often in the squatters' dump out-side the wicked dirty Port had to shut his eyes to see God at all! Still, God was, wherever you looked for Him, and wherever you didn't look as well. He asked nothing of you except what He had given you. It was true that His gifts were often hidden under an accumulation of

7

rubbish, which had like some Augean stable to be regularly cleaned out before you could reach them. Father Bretherton had spent the better part of thirty-eight years cleaning out these Augean stables.

His Community, who were renowned for making good missionaries, were proud of Father Bretherton's career. Even the West African Governor, when Father Bretherton had left, said a little ruefully, "I suppose if he were not so good a Christian, I should have had less trouble with him!" And now the Governor himself had gone, and Father Bretherton's beloved, truculent, lively Africans were free to work out—or lose—their own salvation. Father Bretherton, praying steadily for them throughout his long unsteady illness, thought that they would find it. Astonishing how God worked in the face of the determined opposition of His children!

Father Bretherton's mind broke away from him again in shimmering fragments; he could not reach the end of a single thought. But fortunately he could take things very easily with God, he reminded himself, it was only men who insisted on coherence. They had their own prestige to think about, and could not afford to suffer fools gladly; but to be God's Fool was in itself an honour.

"We've done a great deal of harm to our African brothers," Father Bretherton said to God. "Indeed all the harm we could. Still I always told them not to forget—though we can't be surprised if they do—that they have also learned everything they know of order, cleanliness—even a little decency sometimes—from what we have been able to teach them. You must forgive us, Lord, how impatient we've been, because we are arrogant—as all ignorant children are arrogant —and we haven't realised how little we know about either ourselves or our brothers!"

The door opened softly, and a young nurse, in a gay

uniform of light blue and spotless white, brought in his breakfast.

It was, Father Bretherton thought, a breakfast any king might have envied. Fresh, sweet-smelling rolls, wavy pats of unadulterated golden butter, the flavour and scent of coffee freshly ground and roasted.

"I do hope you'll like it," Nurse Oliver said. "But of course after that long journey you may have had a bad night?"

"I've had a wonderful night," Father Bretherton told her, "and I never remember seeing a more beautiful breakfast!"

"You don't hear many of them speak like that," Nurse Oliver repeated to Sister Peckham after the morning rush had steadied down. "He thanks for everything, asks for nothing, and tries to do all he can to help himself."

"He knows how to behave," Sister Peckham admitted, "but his prognosis is bad—two big cavities close together. Blackwater fever and working too soon —when he ought to have been dead—after it. We shall have to watch him carefully. Even his white bell I should answer first on the floor, if I were you; the blue one I'll see to myself of course. Remember he's a priest and frightened of women; still, he gave me no trouble last night, except that he wanted to kneel to say his prayers, which he can't. He mustn't move at all for the first week anyway. Just wash him as if he were a baby—and leave nothing personal to the younger nurses. I'll give you what help you need.

"The girl next door to him is going to give us a lot of trouble, but perhaps she'll be better when her mother's gone. She's the kind that expects to be praised for being ill—they don't get better quickly whatever you do for them. Why should they, seeing they've

9

nothing to get better for! Being in bed and being catered for like any queen is her cup of tea. Here are the doctors, Nurse! Run into 24 and see that he hasn't messed up his room again. He tosses his bedclothes like hay, the moment your back's turned."

Sister Peckham did not stiffen, since stiffness was an organic part of her, as she heard the quick step of the doctors approaching down the long corridor but it was as if she rearranged her stiffness to better advantage. Her charts were all in order, the night sister's report with them; she was sorry the night sister had such slovenly handwriting, but this was beyond Sister Peckham's power to rectify. She never relaxed until she could control all that was controllable, but the margin—which she kept as narrow as possible—of the uncontrollable, she left strictly alone. She was for brief moments aware that the batteries of her being were more safely turned off than on; but she seldom acted upon this depletion of her activities; and never, when she was on duty.

From the respectful objectivity with which she now greeted her chief and his assistant colleague, it would have been impossible to guess that Sister Peckham had feelings for either of them other than professional etiquette required. Nevertheless, she loved John Mac-Taggart, her chief, with a compassionate and some-times impatient maternal passion, while for Dr. Konrad Rainer she repressed a rigid moral repulsion. She knew no actual harm of him. He was a Viennese, a physician of great skill, but with far more charm than Sister Peckham thought was good for his women patients.

Dr. MacTaggart had no charm. He was a lean, concentrated man, who clung to his profession with savage intensity. He gave each patient the utmost he had to give. But he knew no way of withholding his blunt retreats from those who made false claims on him. Nor did he allow self-pity to go unchecked in his patients. He had none at all for himself; and although he was by nature a compassionate cynic, Sister Peckham thought that he sometimes let pity stop in him, before its full uses were over. All his patients leaned on him, some of them adored him. With Konrad Rainer it was the other way round; he got adored first, and trusted—not invariably—afterwards.

Dr. MacTaggart looked at his new patients' reports first.

"Alive!" he said, with a gleam under thick eyebrows at Sister Peckham's sedate countenance. "That's something, anyhow! Well, they're both quite ill, these two. I should say, roughly speaking, one by accident and one on purpose. No doubt you already know which is which and realise that we must take equal care of both. I'll take the Padre's case myself; and Rainer, this young baggage can go to you. I haven't got her plates yet. According to the mother, we should give up all work on the rest of the Sanatorium, and concentrate entirely on her daughter's case. I've sent the mother off by car to the Dorf, this morning early. Keep her visits down, Sister. It's a pity we can't make the whole place out of bounds for relations. You needn't come in with me, Nurse Oliver. I've spent half the night with this chap already."

"You needn't come in with me either, Sister," Konrad Rainer said, with an amused, half-challenging air. Sister Peckham looked at him, returning his challenge without amusement. She couldn't go into a patient's room if the doctor didn't want her to go with him. She could only very delicately show this one by her manner that she thought her presence, where a young girl and Konrad Rainer were concerned, was highly necessary.

11

"I'll end up with this new girl," Dr. Rainer dropped casually, "and begin the other end—if the patients are ready for me, Sister?"

"The patients are always ready for you, sir," Sister Peckham said with controlled exasperation; "at any time after ten o'clock, unless something very unexpected has happened, in which case I should already have made a report."

2

It looked this morning, Dr. MacTaggart told himself, as if his new patient might be going to live. It was eight hours since he had last seen Father Bretherton, shattered by his journey, burnt up with fever, his burdened heart struggling with the new calls made upon it by the high altitude. Yet the clear blue eyes met his with instant recognition; and astonished him by their serenity.

Dr. MacTaggart's patients, especially the very ill ones, usually wanted to know urgently and immediately if they were going to get well; and were equally anxious to impress upon their new doctor how far from well they were. This patient's eyes were without either fear or urgency. They asked nothing.

It was puzzling to John MacTaggart to see a man so brutally inconvenienced, as he knew his patient to be, by severe physical symptoms, look so detached from them, and so joined up with life.

"You look much better this morning," Dr. MacTaggart said with conviction, "but I don't want you to talk except in a whisper. I will talk to you. I've got Hardy-Dacre's X-ray report on your lungs, and in a few days we shall take our own plates; but this morning I only want to make a short examination. Up at this altitude, the ear can tell quite a lot that the eye can't. I'll get what I want without your moving."

Father Bretherton surrendered himself easily into the skilled hands of this quiet, determined man, who wasn't in any hurry. Nothing in the over-controlled, deeply responsible face of his new doctor escaped Michael Bretherton. He guessed that this was a man who had stretched his powers to their fullest extent, to meet the needs of others—an Atlas with aching shoulders.

Both men were disciplined, both had devoted themselves to serve mankind; the main difference between them was in the nature of their compassion. John Mac-Taggart's approach to humanity was indirect and cynical. He wanted to relieve pain because he hated pain; and to correct ill-health, because it was a disorder that interfered with life. Michael's approach was direct and full of hope. He wanted to relieve pain, because he loved the sufferer—and to free life, because he believed in life. It was not the illness but the human being behind the illness, upon whom his attention fixed itself.

"Well," John said, with a short sharp sigh, after his brief examination was over, "that's that!" He stuck his stethoscope round his neck, and gazed at his new problem with detached interest. On the whole he decided to tell him approximately the truth. Not all of it, but a good deal more of the truth than he would have told most new patients. "You have got the remains of a splendid constitution," he said at last. "You're under forty; as soon as you are rested out, your organs —except your lungs, of course—will function normally. Fortunately you're not fussy. You'll have to be uncomfortable for a bit. Rest is what you need most. We'll do the best we can for you; but you know already the damage to your lungs is extensive. T.B. cures—and a complete cure is what I hope for you—depend upon four main factors: the patient's hope, his ability to adjust to the limitations of this rather tedious illness—I can't promise you a quick cure—the skill of those who look after you; and luck. Luck enters into every contingency. You are a fool if you forget it—and a greater fool if you count upon it. The other three factors we ought to be able to manage between us."

"Luck," whispered Michael with a twinkle in his eye. "Is that what you call—God?"

"God may be your name for Luck," John reluctantly admitted. "Mind you, I have no objection to religion in my patients. I can imagine that in some cases it could facilitate cure; at its worst it can't do half the harm cocktails or dancing can. T.B. is a long illness, and depends on self help more than any other. For the present, I should be much obliged if you can fit your religion into keeping absolutely still, till those lungs dry up a bit. I'll look in again at six o'clock. Is there anything on your mind that I can take off it?"

Michael's eyebrows drew together anxiously. It was a pity his mind felt so flabby and uncertain, and that he must whisper what he wanted to say. There is something curiously unconvincing in a whisper, however urgent.

"There was a girl," he murmured, "in the train from Basle. She was ill, and very young. Did she—did she come here?"

He still could not decide whether the child's visit was real or a dream.

John replied with prompt distaste, "Yes, a girl arrived with her mother last night from England. These young cases generally barge in with a relation who is half the cause of their illness. This girl is typical, a pretty spoiled brat, who doesn't want her mother but won't do without her, since no-one else will spoil her as much. She happens to be your next-door neighbour."

How in the world had he come to speak of one patient to another? In his unflinchingly rigid code this was an inadmissible disloyalty. The Head of a Sanatorium is a lonely person like the captain of a ship. The responsibility of everything that happens in the Sanatorium is his alone and cannot be shared; and yet now John felt merely astonished, not disturbed by his indiscretion. A strange sense of mutual responsibility bound him to his new patient.

"She is spoilt perhaps," Michael whispered. "But life is not spoiling her! Such an illness at her age is a cruel handicap!"

"I hate T.B.," John said impatiently. "In my opinion there is no excuse for it in the young. Bad heredity—bad environment—neglect—pampering—these aren't risks children should be allowed to run. They are flaws in our civilisation. Perhaps we shall get rid of them in time, since they're avoidable; but unfortunately our best brains are all occupied with murder. None of our great scientists are teaching people how to live; as far as that goes, they don't know themselves, or they wouldn't be so interested in how to kill!

"That girl next door turned up after you'd arrived. She refused to go to her room with nurse till she'd been given tea in the lounge. She mistook me for the waiter, and I brought her the tea she'd ordered myself. I didn't explain—she was too upset by her journey. But now she'll have to accept discipline or I won't keep her. You can't cure fools who have this disease—and a great many fools *do* have it—unless you can cure their folly!"

"But that was—a mistake," Michael whispered urgently. "She—won't like having made one!"

It hadn't occurred to John to do anything about it. But suddenly the anger in the young girl's haughty eyes came back to him, struggling with her weakness; and without the irritation he had felt before. It was almost as if the girl's weakness and arrogance were struggling inside himself.

16

"What can I do?" he asked hesitatingly. "As a matter of fact I was going to put her case in my colleague's hands. I hadn't intended to see her at present unless he called me in."

"But you'll see her now," Michael pleaded; "once, at least! Make friends with her—she'll feel better for it! She mustn't have a bad start!"

"I'll drop in if you like," John agreed a little awkwardly, "but I don't make friends easily—especially not with young girls. However, don't you talk any more. I've been talking to you far too much already. You can *ask* for anything you want, but for God's sake forget *how* to talk—and get that girl out of your mind as well. I'll attend to *her* troubles!"

John had got to the door by then, and was out of it instantly. There was nothing left but the sunshine and the unhindered whiteness of the snow.

Michael had not slept all night, but now his eyes filled with this shining vision softly closed. He could not think any more—words escaped his shaken mind—but he could still see pictures. How young that girl had looked bending over him at dawn in her shell-pink woollen dressing gown—striking through his exhaustion and pain with her urgency. She wanted to be all the things she wasn't. Yet what she was *had* loveliness; how velvety her dark blue eyes were under their beautifully drawn slanting brows soft as a moth's wings! Behind the thorns and briars of her pride, he must believe that she was as good as she was beautiful. And if she wasn't he would still be on her side, as he was always on the side of anyone who had need of him. It was part of his safety, because he was quite sure that God was on their side too; so that to be fighting for the souls of men was to share the strength of God. On which side was his new friend MacTaggart? How different was his face from that arrogant, frightened girl's! A compassionate face, orderly, without greed. Yet why was it so tragic? John was no older than Michael, yet his dark thick hair was tinged with grey, there were deep furrows of pain on each side of his firm, generous lips; his watchful eyes were full of tension. Must a man who is at ease in life, giving daily a valued contribution, look so close-shuttered against the forces of joy?

Michael sighed, and opening his eyes again as if for reassurance towards the imperturbable peaks, thought how full life is of hindered qualities.

No wonder the human world goes all awry when fear and greed break through it like the forces of a hurricane at sea, banging their way against a ship's loose equipment, lashing all her puny safeguards into wild disorder. Yet there was no disorder in the endless blue into which one by one the great peaks soared. The new shadows, between the foothills, were a deep lilac, and the trunks of the pines a shining rose colour. Michael's eyes closed again, and at last sleep took him gently, into a moveless peace.

3

Had the whole Sanatorium idea been a mistake, Caroline asked herself? She had achieved the inconceivable, broken down the walls of her mother's resistance, cajoled English doctors inclined to soft pedal the advantage of Swiss mountains, and hushed her own panic fears of finding herself without the life-long support of a devoted boa constrictor. And what was now her reward?—a bare cold barrack of a room with a linoleum-covered floor, not even warmed by a particle of dust, and what appeared to be a host of uniformed jailers all set on putting Caroline right, and overlooking the fact that Caroline *was* right, by divine instinct, and knew on practically every subject considerably more than they did.

By her dawn visit to the patient next door, Caroline had used up the last of her physical strength, and broken the chief unspoken rule of the institution.

These lacerating victories gave her a faint glow of satisfaction; but how uncertain her heart beats were, how shallow her breathing, how violent the knocking of the intemperate blood against arterial walls!

The new forces that Caroline had let loose upon herself, however, had at least routed her mother. This tyrant, the belligerent, healthy and almost omnipotent controller of Caroline's destiny, had sunk without a trace, in her first engagement with Sister Peckham. She had been asked to leave the room, and had left it.

But was this strange retreat altogether the resource Caroline had planned for herself? After all her mother's control had never been quite complete; Mrs. Draycott had a weakness, which made her vulnerable to Caroline. Her mother wanted to keep Caroline alive, quite as much as she wanted to create the kind of Caroline she kept alive. She even wanted, though she went the wrong way about it, to *please* Caroline while keeping her alive. She loved her only child considerably better than Caroline loved her. Adored, saturated, unchallenged, Caroline held her own in the strangle-hold of family love, and never shared anything that she held.

Perhaps it was a mistake to part from her mother, she now thought, while breaking her heart? Might not the loss of a tyrant whom she knew, and in whom she had created room to exert a way of her own, while being fully supported by the bully she outwitted, expose Caroline to an unknown and less malleable series of obstacles?

On her arrival, Caroline's mother had beaten two young nurses off the field with Caroline's passive connivance. Caroline wanted them beaten off, but she would have preferred to do it for herself, and without showing her mother that she hadn't the courage to tackle them alone.

It was far more convenient, if more exhausting, for her mother to unpack all her things, placing them after heated and endless discussions where Caroline had determined to have them, than to see them put into foreign places settled by a stranger.

Caroline never intended to take what the nurses so tactlessly brought her to eat or drink; but she felt robbed of her sense of achievement by her mother's clamorous backing.

She had wished to have two clean nightgowns to

change into after night sweats (her mother wouldn't let her wear pyjamas), accompanied by a large bath towel, on the nearest radiator; but the nurse whisked them away to an invisible hot cupboard, distant and ungetatable.

Caroline had meant to know what her temperature was; but again, she had had to wait till nurse had gone out of the room with the thermometer and an unseen chart, to force her own thermometer out of her mother. Her temperature was quite gratifyingly high, 102°; but what would she have done, had her mother and her extra thermometer not been handy?

Caroline did not want a small blue light, however soothing, on in the night; but nurse told her it couldn't be turned off; and Caroline found it couldn't. She was interested when nurse pointed out the three coloured buttons within reach of Caroline's hand: white for minor needs, blue for Sister, who wouldn't however wish to answer it for anything short of a major problem, and red for haemorrhage, summoning instantly the nearest doctor.

There were four doctors, Caroline learned: one, the infamously disguised waiter, who was the Head of the Sanatorium, two foreigners, one Swiss and one Austrian; and a French radiologist, a woman, with a medical degree. Caroline did not like foreigners. They were unpredictable, and curiously oblivious to the heroism of under-statement, adopted by the British.

Bells that could only bring nurses or doctors did not appeal to Caroline; she would have preferred having someone on a camp bed in her room, instantly available for whatever occurred. Besides, if there was no one to disturb, how could Caroline bear her own implacable disturbances—the sweats, the exhausted restlessness, the endless trooping of the undistinguishable hours?

What was the use of offering her a mild sleeping pill? They might just as well have given her a bread-crumb!

An awful incident started the long night. At ten o'clock, when victory and a camp bed for her mother had begun to loom upon the horizon—and Nurse Oliver, the baffled staff nurse, could fight no more— there was a brief, challenging knock at the door, and an iceberg floated into the room, bearing down upon the two shipwrecked passengers with ominous finality. It was Sister Peckham.

To describe Sister Peckham as self-contained would have been insufficient. She contained so much besides herself—forces that had dealt successfully with bombed hospitals, streets of flame, panic-stricken helpless wards, a sky full of mechanical destruction. Three times Sister Peckham had saved, principally by being herself, the major contents of a London hospital. One small, pampered girl who wouldn't drink her milk presented no difficulties to her. Sister Peckham simply looked at the girl, and then transferred her cold, sea-bird's eyes upon the mother.

"Your room is ready, Mrs. Draycott," she observed. "Nurse will take you there immediately, and then return to deal with the disorder of this room."

Was it possible that Caroline's mother, her strong, resourceful, ruthless mother, should crumple up like a table napkin, and be swept out of the room?

Caroline found herself alone with the Iceberg.

"Now, drink your milk!" Sister Peckham said decisively, but with indifference.

"I can't—there's skin on it," Caroline wildly protested. "I should be instantly sick!"

Sister Peckham smiled. It was not an unkind, or even a mocking smile; it simply asserted that something very easy was being made unnecessarily difficult.

Without a word, Sister Peckham flicked the whole cap of skin off the top of the milk, with the handle of a toothbrush. "Now drink it," she told Caroline, who in speechless rebellion found herself drinking it.

Nurse Oliver returned, and under the silent gaze of Sister Peckham, the whole room became shorn of all Caroline's favourite amenities. There were no medicines within her reach, her thermometer was confiscated.

"If anything goes wrong, or you need attention of any real kind, you have only to touch these buttons," Sister Peckham said with withering unconcern. "The Night Sister will look in by-and-by to see if you need anything further."

The room was empty. Sister Peckham never seemed to move, she was either there or not there. Her words were sparse—and more like deeds than words, since something always happened on their heels.

After Sister Peckham had gone, preceded by Nurse Oliver—who by a wave of the hand was removed as soon as Caroline's last treasure became inconspicuous —Caroline found herself left alone—with her loneliness. The moment she was alone, she was frightened. Roughly speaking, Caroline believed in God; but she had not had any personal contact with Him. Her prayers were automatic, and she had never known the slightest re-actions from them.

She tried to think about Heaven, at moments when the thought of earth became too sharp for her; but fear never provides anyone with pleasant pictures of the hereafter; so that Caroline thought about eternity as little as possible.

Tonight, she tried to think about the man next door instead. Was he the priest in the train? If he was, what had she better do about it? Caroline wanted to be sure that he would hold his tongue about having given up his sleeper to her. She was not sorry for him; on the contrary, Caroline felt annoyed with him. If he were really as ill as they made out, why had he that round, placid face and clear eyes? That was another thing that was wrong with a Sanatorium—other people were ill in it.

It took Caroline some hours to work herself up to her nocturnal visit; but she felt better after it.

It was curious, Caroline thought, how when you wanted a thing with an uncontrollable pressure inside you, and every conceivable reason springing up in your mind to back you, how often you brought it off! She was, of course, far too exhausted after such an effort to go to sleep. She seemed to hang, holding her body up by her nerves, for long hours, suspended from the ceiling, unassisted by God or man; but at last sleep came to her. It dulled down her tortured senses, and, without even her knowledge, freed her fighting soul. Caroline slept till ruffled by the sunlight, and startled by the sudden appearance of a nurse with a cup of tea, she realised that one of her new jailers had dared to wake her up.

4

Marie Céleste Delarabrie, the radiologist of the Helvetian Sanatorium, made coffee for her three medical colleagues daily at eleven o'clock; and looked as if she had never done anything more exciting. Yet she had outwitted the Police of her own country, Hitler's Gestapo; and, what was more difficult, her own family, who were ardent Pétainists.

With the connivance of her aunt, who was the Mother Superior of a Convent at Grenoble, Marie Céleste vanished during the war for months at a time from her family's supervision. The convent made excellent cover, and no one of her own circle ever dreamed that at eighteen years old Marie Céleste made use of her correct English on secret radios, helped to direct the landings of British planes, and spent days and nights on mountain-sides, hidden in woods, sleeping surrounded by male scarecrows, in security but without comfort.

It was under an assumed name that she had been caught at last, outraged, mocked at, tortured and imprisoned; and at length, after being condemned to death, had made her escape to Switzerland.

As soon as it was possible, after the war was over, Marie Céleste returned to her still unenlightened family, her hair permed, her finger nails manicured, her clothes looking as if they came direct from *Vogue*.

She had not become a nun; and her family thought her greatly improved by her prolonged sojourn at the Convent of the Sacred Heart.

"First it was religion—now it is science," her mother explained to the Family circle. "We must be patient; naturally—at the end—it will be a husband."

It was, however, the Sorbonne and not domesticity upon which Marie Céleste's mind was bent.

Marie Céleste was not pretty; but she could always make herself felt when she wanted to be felt. She considered herself austere in the matter of sex. Yet on rare occasions each of her three chief colleagues, for whom the morning coffee was made, had been her lover without the knowledge of the other two. Certainly she preferred men to women, but far more as comrades than as lovers. Passion had been frozen out of her by horror, or wasted by disgust. She had barely enough left, as she once explained to John MacTaggart, to keep herself tidy.

It was not her fault that the war had hustled Marie Céleste out of her morals and her habits, shipwrecked her dreams, and trained her through a series of maniacal adventures. She would have made an irreproachable mère de famille of the best French type, had she met John in her youth, or when she did meet him, if he had not been already married to her English friend, Elizabeth.

Marie Céleste's infrequent tenderness and her severe exact knowledge she kept for MacTaggart. His professional conscience matched her own; but it was Konrad Rainer, a Jewish refugee, who had been with her in the Résistance, with whom she shared her bitterness, her malice and her unsheathed wit. They had lived so close together, dodging death for themselves and for each other for so long, that they knew almost automatically the bottom of each other's hearts.

"A Canadian," Marie Céleste explained to Konrad, after she had persuaded John to engage him as a colleague, "may seem like a child to a Viennese; but remember this one is a good child!

"With his skilled hands and excellent heart, this John succeeds in doing well what he has to do—but how little that is! I can believe in him, and I advise you to believe in him—as a doctor. It is as a human being that I sometimes find him incredible. A tree knows better how to understand a woman! As for understanding himself, this good fellow walks about in his own interior, as a tourist without a guide, who has never read a word of French history, walks about in the Cathedral of Chartres! Sometimes he is far cleverer than he knows; at others, one would think the Almighty had made him as a joke!"

John MacTaggart was the first of Marie Céleste's morning visitors.

She handed him his cup of coffee made exactly as he liked it, strong, sugarless, without milk or cream.

"But why," she asked, with a twist of her thin red eyebrows, "did you box your good friend Konrad's ears this morning? For what reason did you snatch from him this young girl patient who arrived last night, and to whom you had assigned him? Is it a secret between you and your God? You seem to have a God for these occasions, since it is plain there is no sense in such an act of authoritarian secrecy, unless it is caused by a *mystique*. Such is not the behaviour of a comrade!"

John drank his cup of coffee slowly and without immediately answering. He felt at home in the bare workmanlike room, in which Marie Céleste spent most of her time. There were four chairs of polished steel bars and narrow plastic seats which were mysteriously comfortable; a table stretched halfway across the room under the full light of curtainless windows; walled cupboards where she kept her plates and files, hid

27

their normal uses. The wooden floor was without a rug, and washed daily. Marie Céleste slept on a narrow divan; an alcove disposed of her cooking arrangements —an electric stove, a sink and a refrigerator. Nothing was out of place or superfluous. The sun could pour into the room all day long and not find a speck of dust with which to dance.

The china stove was filled, emptied and cleaned from outside the room, in the passage.

"Well, perhaps I changed my mind because I ran across a *'mystique'*," John said at last. "You are a Catholic—you have had a lot to do with priests—do you believe they've got anything—anything, I mean, that works, and that we haven't?"

Marie Céleste put on more coffee; her every movement was direct and clear-cut like a swallow's; and there was very little difference between her movements and the clearness of her thoughts.

"I do not believe in priests *as* priests," Marie Céleste replied. "I was born a Catholic as I was born French— I might say of both of them, *j'y suis—j'y reste!* What I do believe in, however, has nothing to do with my religion or my country. It is this: sometimes I have found a force beyond what I had a right to expect. While I was tortured, for a little while I depended on my courage; when that went, on my obstinacy which, linked with stupidity, is our family's chief quality; beyond that again, something I thought came in—at the end—as I was about to collapse. Perhaps it was merely that I knew I *was* at the point of collapse, and that when I had passed it, I should find myself beyond torture.

"It was after that, they decided to execute me, and shut me up in the dark till I thought out how to escape. But these fine moments—this force—has nothing to do with your bêtise to Konrad! You should know that he is as sensitive as a raw egg, yet you who are his best friend act in such a way as to injure his dignity—without excuse! Did you fall for this new patient in such a big way at first sight?"

"Nonsense," John said, handing his cup back for more coffee. "I never noticed what she looked like, till Sister Peckham told me she might look like an angel but behaved like a spoiled brat. She'll waste a lot of my time, and most probably peter out at the end of it. Her lung tissue is as thin as paper; she has already thrown away several chances of recovery, and is quite capable of throwing away her last chance. Personally I should say this *is* her last chance. That's partly why I decided to take her on. Konrad is twice as brilliant as I am, but he isn't half as patient. He gets irritable with idiots. It's true that priest hammered at me to take her on as well. Pretty mess he was in after that journey, and Sister Peckham and I were with him till three o'clock this morning. A tricky business—two huge cavities closed in on each other—and the massage I had to do for his heart might have started another haemorrhage! However, I think he'll live. He made rather an impression on me—I've never seen a man so ill who was so curiously considerate of others. He might have been another doctor working on another patient. Yet he knew it was touch and go, as well as we did!"

"And this girl—what has she to do with him?" Marie Céleste asked. "Monks are not chosen as a rule for travelling companions to young girls."

"He didn't know her—she was with her mother," John said irritably. "I suppose he may have caught a glimpse of her in the train, but the fellow was too ill to have noticed the Venus of Milo if she'd punched his ticket. He just takes things in at the pores of his skin.

He took me in if it comes to that. I'd told him not to open his mouth; and then I sat down and talked to him for ages as if he was my mother. Here are the others! May I have some more coffee?"

"No! Two strong cups in the morning is enough," Marie Céleste told him. Under her breath she murmured, "Come and talk to me tonight, even though I, too, am not your mother!"

Dr. Schreiber came in first. He was always in a hurry, resilient and tough as a good cricket ball. He had been born on the mountains, and had hardly been off them for forty years. Besides a ward in the Sanatorium, he had a large private practice in the surrounding villages, which he reached on skis, by sleigh, by toboggan, bicycle or horse-back, according to the season and their accessibility. He slept from midnight till six o'clock seven days a week without stirring, ate one enormous meal once a day when his fifteen hours of work were over, bore with a nagging wife and supported and adored his six children. Dr. Schreiber was a good Catholic; and Marie Céleste was the romance of his life.

The time he spent with her was limited to a brief ten minutes daily in the presence of his colleagues, and once a year when Marie Céleste shared an evening with him, and they dined together in one of the distant villages.

Marie Céleste smiled at Joseph, and when she gave him his coffee her fingers touched his hand. She knew how hard and well he worked, and loved him for it.

"A man can be so good that he sees all that it is necessary to see, without being clever," Marie Céleste said of him, to his colleagues.

Konrad Rainer, who followed Joseph, was a slender fellow, with thick fair hair, above the brow of a thinker; his features were insignificant, but his smile lit them into a charm that was never lost upon women, and seldom lost upon other men. His big blue eyes were vague, and sometimes completely blank, as if the brain behind them no longer wished to communicate what could lead to expression.

He had been hunted for five years, and did not always see what to do next now that the hunt was over. "He could pass anywhere for a Christian," Marie Céleste said of Konrad, "if only he looked a little more ill-tempered!"

Meeting his perplexed and saddened eyes, she gave him a quick nod. "Tout va bien!" she said in her clear staccato French. "It is simply that our good John has a *mystique*! It appears that an angel told him what to do in the night—and he had to do it!

"It is all the fault of this new monk-patient of ours, who met the young lady in the train, and was so ill directly after that he nearly died of it. As far as John is concerned, her face might be made out of an old boot. He took her away from you out of mercy. You know that he has a conscience as lively as a red ant and as clumsy as a camel's!"

Konrad's thick fair eyebrows contracted nervously before he began to smile.

"She talks the most awful nonsense, of course," John MacTaggart said hurriedly, "but there's an element of common sense sometimes behind it. As a matter of fact, the priest did ask me to take a look at the girl. Her case looks pretty doubtful, and I thought you had your share of gloomy ones already."

"You've no need to apologise," Konrad said. "Nineteen is not a nice age to die, and it is true if I have to work against hope, I sometimes lose my nerve."

"That is the difference between Latins and Anglo-Saxons," Marie Céleste said, returning to the abstract, with relieved assurance. "Latins—and Viennese are more Latin than German—fight their best, while there is hope. Anglo-Saxons do not fight even well, till there is no more hope. Defeat is not final for them—it is the first stage to success! The French are too intelligent not to believe in defeat as final."

"Well, I'm glad you sometimes see it's a mistake to be too intelligent!" John told her with a friendly wink. "I'm off!" He plunged towards the door, closely followed by Joseph, to whom Céleste gave the sweetest of her smiles.

"Marie Céleste," Konrad demanded as the door closed behind them, seizing her wrist between his fingers, "why did you tell John I minded?"

"Because he must learn to run his sanatorium with logic," Marie Céleste said firmly, "not like a bull in a china shop! Before—when he and Elizabeth were happy —he considered everybody's feelings; now he is unhappy—and considers only his own. It is not good for Elizabeth for John to have taken on this girl. I feel it in my bones it is not good. But my dear—it might be good for *you*! One must play with the cards one has. It might—don't you see?—help *you* to win Elizabeth. And after all why should she suffer because her husband has some kind of stop in his mind, and refuses to be a husband any more?"

"Why do you want me to succeed with Elizabeth," Konrad asked irritably, shaking her wrist to and fro, "when I am John's friend and your lover? It is an absurdity that you should push me towards her—or a trick!"

"It is neither an absurdity nor a trick," Marie Céleste answered firmly. "It is because John has broken Elizabeth's heart. We don't know why—but I for one know very well that I want it mended."

"You care more for Elizabeth then than for me?" Konrad asked angrily.

"Not at all," Marie Céleste said calmly. "I am as fond of Elizabeth as I am capable of being of any woman. She is a good type—sincere, with courage and with no malice. I wish you well with her—because after all what do you get from me? We can give each other nothing but torn nerves and bitter memories. The dead and the tortured stand between us! Granted that we did not betray them—yet we have survived them—in a sense that is also a betrayal. We cannot look into each other's eyes without seeing their pain. How I dislike seeing pain—especially when I am making love! Now we must go to work. I will give you a ring when I expect this Egyptian sorceress for her X-rays. Not today—she must rest after her journey—but perhaps tomorrow. But remember, Konrad, she is a card for you to play. Do not stake too much on her, and above all do not let her play *you*! It is not for nothing they worshipped cats in Egypt——!"

With a quick movement Konrad swung her round into his arms and kissed her with expert intensity. Marie Céleste returned his kiss with ardour, ducked under his arm and slipped out of the room, into the accustomed sizzling darkness of her X-ray studio; but even as she ran her expert eyes over her giant machines, and saw to it that everything was ready for her first photograph, she went on smiling.

5

$\mathcal{T}$ime did not only pass over Michael Bretherton, it ran through him in an unobstructive way, always moving but never arriving, beyond the bars of night and day.

There was an endlessness in this constricted motion without progress, like the length of time in a child's day. All about Michael people lived quickly, and their swift, separate actions drove through the hours in purposeful and beneficent progress; but his days and nights were condemned to stillness, he must lie as if in an oubliette of God's, accomplishing nothing—the object of the accomplishment of others.

Everything he needed was done for him. He was being nursed as only a very ill man, under Sister Peckham's care, could be nursed. "He must not even have to *say* what he wants," Sister Peckham told Nurse Oliver. "Just see that he gets it, *before* he knows what it is. Speak to him, of course, so that he may know beforehand what you are going to do. In a case like his there must be no effort and no surprises."

Sister Peckham herself became the chief landmark of his days. It was reassuring to hear her low voice giving directions, still more to see her, by his side, a silent unhurrying presence, sharing all his emergencies with economical sureness. Sister Peckham had a certainty of touch and manner that reduced strain. She dealt with all the unspoken menaces of his condition, as if they were subject to rules which she had mastered in her cradle. She knew more about his sudden limitations and expansions of strength than John did. For John's visits, Michael gathered up the fragments of his mind, and called on what powers were left him; but with Sister Peckham, he left all the gathering to her. He was simply what his illness made of him, with behind it, his unconfused compliance.

At night an endless restlessness pursued him, no movement eased it, and yet he longed for movement as a desert traveller longs for water. But in the day time, Michael often slept peacefully hour after hour. It was as if Sister Peckham's presence on the other side of the door took even the responsibility of living off him.

One day he opened his eyes to the deep noon light, and in a sunbeam stealing across his room from the open balcony to the door, he saw a vision of the Virgin Mary. It was as if she were made of light—sunshine poured over her, and shone through her blue eyes and corn-coloured hair. Michael made a quick movement to rise, but in an instant she was by his side, her hands lightly and firmly laid on his shoulders, "No!—no! You must not move," she said. "You must keep perfectly still. I am a nurse—I know!" So she was only a woman after all. Michael closed his eyes, that she might not see his disappointment for the lost vision.

When he opened them again, she was sitting near him, on the edge of her chair, her large blue eyes under their rounded arches bent anxiously upon him. It was a young face, but not as young as he at first had thought it. She must be in her late twenties, but the child had not yet died out of her colour or her eyes. Her cheeks were round and smooth and full of health; her soft curved lips drooped a little, and in her expression there was the hint of a person who has had to use more self control than should be required of human beings.

"She is not ill, but yet she is not happy," Michael thought to himself; and he was surprised to think of anyone who was not ill failing to be happy unless they were not good. He could not think that Elizabeth was not good.

"I know you mustn't talk," she said after a moment's pause, "but Sister Peckham thought I might bring you books. This is a book stand we made on purpose for people who can't move easily; but if your eyes are tired, I could read aloud to you?"

Michael smiled his consent. He would like anything she did, his eyes told her. She did not smile back at him; her face and manner were direct and simple as a child's, but she was a grave child, and still anxious.

Michael was aware that her interest in him was both great and impersonal. It did not confuse him to feel that she wanted something from him, nor did he feel any sense of pressure in her presence. He motioned towards the Bible and prayer book that lay on his bed table, and noticed that on picking them up, she instantly found the right lessons for the day. She read him both lessons, and after the lessons, the psalms. She read well, letting the words express themselves without emphasis. Her voice was low, with changing cadences, like a light, travelling wind.

After she had finished, she leaned forward with controlled eagerness. "You are—quite—English, aren't you?" she asked. Michael's eyes assented.

"I was sure of it," she said with obvious satisfaction, "and you see none of the other patients are—except the girl next door—and she hardly counts because she's so young and has not learned to care for her country. So there's only Sister Peckham—and me. Nurse Oliver is wonderfully nice, but that's a coincidence; and all the rest are either Canadian or American—or else Swiss and—and European; and it's not quite the same thing however nice they are, is it? My father is in the Navy—actually he is an Admiral, Admiral Gervais Ravelston; you may have heard his name perhaps; my name is Elizabeth."

"Elizabeth Ravelston," Michael wrote on the pad that lay near his hand.

"No! No!" she said, the colour rising to her forehead. "Not now, of course. I married John Mac-Taggart."

She was silent after her explanation, as if the words had put an end in some mysterious way to all form of communication between them.

"There is no church here," she began again after a long pause, "except the Catholic, of course, in the village; and they told me you were Church of England, so that was why I knew about the lessons; and I brought you books I thought you might like to read, by Albert Schweitzer, and Nicolas Berdyaev—and if you like French, by Charles Péguy. He's unexpectedly nice, as Catholics often are, about Holy People, as if you had a right to laugh about them—not *at* them—if you know what I mean. I like to think people can be *real* and religious at the same time. The books are on my trolley just outside your door; I thought it might be noisy if I brought it in. I am a sort of Librarian here; I don't nurse anyone now but I look after everybody's diet. I choose each patient's food separately. Sister Peckham tells me, of course, anything I have to avoid. I am allowed a lot of margin about the food, because our doctors believe in variety, and individual tastes being catered for; they think it helps a lot in this particular illness."

37

Elizabeth smiled for the first time, as if in this matter, Michael thought, she had the right to be a little proud. It suddenly occurred to him that Elizabeth was a very rare thing in a woman, proud without vanity. Perhaps that was why he had thought her for that golden instant—to be the Virgin Mary. What Elizabeth controlled was not vanity, though many women knew enough about their vanity to control it. What Elizabeth controlled was pain.

"I will come again and read to you if you like," Elizabeth added, rising from her chair.

Michael wrote, "I shall always like it whenever you can come."

The red light that announced John's visits sprang above the door. He came in quickly, almost passing Elizabeth in the doorway; but neither of them looked at each other. They might not have been in the same room; except that the space between them was suddenly expanded into a way of avoiding each other.

Michael quickly looked away from the unguarded pain he saw in John's eyes. He found himself thinking, "What has she done?" It was a curious question, because why should Michael feel that it must be some deed of Elizabeth's, rather than of John's, which had shattered what must once have been great happiness?

John chose another chair, and sat on the other side of Michael's bed. There were only two little chairs in the big sunny room—and the chair in which Elizabeth had sat now looked purposefully empty.

"I've just been hearing about you, that you put up with too much," John said, in his friendly and yet un-intimate way. "Sister Peckham says that girl next door is always writing notes to you. Ought I to stop them? You don't answer them, I hope?"

Michael smiled. "Don't stop them," he wrote; "she's lonely."

John frowned, and ran his hand through his thick untidy hair. "I don't see why she should be more lonely than anyone else," he said, "unless she's a tyrant —tyrants are always lonely. Nurse Oliver is young— she can talk to her; and there's Nurse Bessy, a Canadian pal of mine—she's an idiot, but very good-natured and obliging. Besides there's another girl-patient on the other side of Caroline. Why has she got to pick on you? I'll tell her I want you kept quiet!"

"I keep quiet," Michael wrote.

The two men smiled at each other; they knew what neither of them would want to say about any woman; and neither would ever press the other to say it.

"What you call quiet!" John said scoffingly. "I come in here, and it might be Oxford Street,—Elizabeth talking away to you like mad—and then this girl next door——!"

"Your wife read aloud to me," Michael wrote, "most beautifully."

There was a silence. John got up, and walked to the open balcony door, staring with unseeing eyes at the intricate shadow-pattern of the pines on the unruffled snow.

"Yes," he said, with a sharp sigh, "I suppose she does read out loud rather well. There's no harm in that. It's talking you have to avoid. As for Caroline—I'm going in now to talk to her like a Dutch uncle—not solely on your account either. She's been creating again—the nurses are all sick of her. She wants her mother back now; a week ago she told me—and I believed her— that her mother had been the curse of her life!"

"Some of us cling to our curses," Michael wrote, "if we haven't anything better to cling to!"

John looked down at the pad, and back into Michael's clear, amused eyes. "I'd rather she clung to curses than to you," he answered. "I've often wondered what clergy do about intemperately attached ladies. I'm at my wits' end with some of my women patients. They must have something to play with! Sometimes I have to drag in Sister Peckham to help me out; but it's rather like condemning men to the Front Line trenches—she throws flames at them."

Michael did not answer. He did not feel that his own way of meeting the problem would be either John's or Sister Peckham's. He respected women so much, that sometimes his respect for them taught them to respect themselves. But even this method was not foolproof. Nor could Michael think of any method that would be foolproof.

He knew that John was just as sorry for Caroline as he was. He was even afraid that John might be unnecessarily sorry for Caroline; since it had occurred to Michael that Caroline was not altogether averse to her own sorrows.

6

Caroline accepted John from the moment that John had abjectly apologised for her mistake; and the agonising itch of appearing at a disadvantage before the new doctor had subsided. She had the same feeling for him as a Pekinese has for a huge deer-hound, whom it can outwit at every turn, though it hardly comes up to the top of one of his paws.

John was beneath Caroline's world; she was not even curious about John's world, except so far as he could come out of it to serve her, in hers. She knew that very large powerful men were often vulnerable to the helpless, especially if the helpless were heroic; well then she would be—as far as it was necessary—heroic, for John. She couldn't fool him about her illness, there she was at his mercy. He knew exactly what was the matter with her lungs; but he couldn't—and shouldn't—know, Caroline decided, what was right or wrong with the rest of her. He would have to take her at her own valuation or not at all.

For this purpose, John's morning visits were no good. These were his chart visits. He merely dashed in with Sister Peckham in full sail behind him, and out again. Caroline was not a human being at these times, but the result of what had happened in the night. John simply said what he wanted done during the day, not because Caroline wished it done, and had managed to make him think it was the best thing for her, but simply because of what Sister Peckham and the Night Sister had concocted between them. It was no use Caroline saying what she felt, no use her crying even if she had wanted to cry, beneath the rough-drying expression of Sister Peckham when confronted with tears; if Caroline smiled bravely while John was giving her an injection, she found that her courage was lost upon them both. She could close her eyes and let anguish pass over her features, and neither of them would stop to ask her what was the matter with her. They knew without asking. Her pulse had already been felt, her temperature taken, her night reported on. They were gone, before Caroline had time to think of an arresting word.

Nurses were shock-proof under Sister Peckham's eyes; they flew into your room on *their* jobs, not yours. Perhaps a haemorrhage might arrest them; but it would have to be a real haemorrhage; and there was nothing obliging about a real haemorrhage. Caroline doubted if it could be brought on at a moment's notice; and if it were brought on, it could not be so easily called off. Once you'd had a haemorrhage quick enough to choke you, you didn't want another.

Caroline had to wait, all through the day, till John's five o'clock rounds. He paid these visits alone; and they were elastic. He really tried to find out what was in his patient's mind then; and with a mind like Caroline's he could be held, charmed, deceived, and in time, Caroline thought, dominated. She had not yet decided on any one personality for John; she treated him to a variety—as if they were becoming frocks that she was trying on in order to see which one suited her best.

There was her Nefertiti personality, for instance, occult, fastidious, disdainful, which held John a long way off, as if he were a slave, and might, while serving her at a distance, never be allowed any nearer. Then there was the eager, helpless child welcoming her beloved physician. This had been once or twice startlingly successful. The direct and honest girl-comrade too, appealed to the Canadian in John. Nor was he altogether resistant to the enchantress with mischief in her eyes and a scalding jest on her tongue. Or there was the brave exhausted patient, barely able to lift her heavy eyelids, lying flat on her pillow, fought to a finish, and yet uncomplaining. Compassion in John was not easy to rouse; but when roused it went deep. Still, something told her it mustn't be roused too often, unless the foundation for rousing it was genuine.

Caroline's repertoire was large, and she thought out day by day extensions. John had a hundred patients to whom to minister in twenty-four hours; whereas Caroline had only one doctor, and the whole of her twenty-four hours might be devoted to understanding, and manipulating, him.

There were other possibilities, of course—the priest next door, for instance, and Konrad Rainer, with his vague and yet appraising eyes. Caroline had seen Konrad Rainer twice in the X-ray department; the second time he had smiled at her; and Caroline, a little reluctantly, found herself smiling back. There was Nurse Oliver too. She had a secret—a sad secret, Caroline suspected; and when you are ill and have nothing else to do, Caroline found that the sad secrets of others could be very entertaining; even if they weren't amusing enough, she could always swap them for still sadder, and more entertaining secrets of her own.

At last she heard John's footsteps, quick and decided. He had stayed longer than he usually did in the priest's room—and meant to stay a shorter time than usual in Caroline's. But this was not what Caroline meant.

43

John came in after his short abrupt knock, and stood at the foot of her bed, hardly listening to her answers to his few perfunctory questions.

"Look here, Caroline," he said, disregarding the rather clever little list of symptoms Caroline had spread before him, "you really must leave the man next door alone! He's too ill to be bothered. I know you don't care a damn about him, and so does he! That makes it all the sillier writing him these constant notes. He can't answer them—half the time he isn't fit to read them. Why do you do it?"

Caroline froze with rage. "Did he tell you that I wrote him notes?" she asked contemptuously. "I suppose priests don't know how to behave like gentlemen —any more than doctors!"

"No, he didn't," John said, wishing he could control his annoyance. "It's my business to find out such things when my patients are seriously ill. They mustn't be molested."

"Molested!" Caroline echoed, strengthened rather than weakened by her rage. "What a word to use— like a policeman—which is what I suppose you think you have a right to be! How *dare* you say I molest him! I was being *kind* to him! If he's as ill as you say he *needs* kindness. I can sit up in bed and he can't. I've asked about his nights. I've told him about mine. I've even said nice things about you to him—which you don't deserve!—so that he could be reassured, and believe you were a good doctor, which I now don't think you are! What do you expect of us—lying here in empty rooms all day long—like bits of the multiplication table that don't match? Aren't we human? Besides I *have* seen him. I met him in the train."

"There couldn't have been very much of him to meet—in the train," John said ominously. "Someone turned him out of his sleeper—he nearly died of it. Was it you?"

"Well, he hasn't quite died, and it wasn't me," Caroline lied confidently, knowing that she was safe. "I saw him sitting in the corridor—and I was sorry for him. If mother had let me, I'd have given him *my* sleeper. By-the-by, I've told mother I want her to come back. I must have somebody to do the things I want done. The nurses are all too busy to be really useful. Besides, I need company that I'm accustomed to, and don't have to make efforts over. Mrs. MacTaggart came to see me twice—I found her most difficult to talk to. I know I told you that I hated my mother—and so I do in a way—but she can't *force* me to do things here—you'd be able to stop her. I expect she'll come quite soon."

John came round the side of the bed, and sat down. He looked very large and very angry; but he was going to stay longer than he had meant.

"Caroline," he said slowly and impressively, "you've been here two weeks and I've seen you twenty-eight times. I've asked you a great many questions; but there's one question I've not yet asked you. Do you *want* to get well?"

Caroline drew a long, defiant breath; at least he had the grace to admit she *was* ill; but she didn't like his question; it was one she had too often asked herself, without an answer.

"Of course I want to get well!" Caroline said with bitterness. "Only I'm tired of trying and being badgered because I can't! You know all my medical history. I was never very strong—still I *did* go to school. My father died of consumption when I was six—I've told you that already. When I was sixteen I broke down. I just *was* ill. I had pneumonia first, and never really got better!"

45

"Yes, I know the facts," John admitted, "but you did get better, you nearly got well. Why did you again and again relapse? What happened to stop your full recovery? Was it something you resented, or which disappointed you?"

"A good deal disappointed me," Caroline said, unexpectedly finding herself speaking the truth. "I don't approve of life—for one thing! Besides, when I was sixteen I was stopped from being a ballerina!"

"Why couldn't you be a ballerina?" John asked. "Didn't you dance well enough?"

"Of course I danced well enough!" Caroline cried, sparkling with rage. "I danced better than any girl in the school—for the matter of that! Mademoiselle Rachet said Collette had more stamina, but that I had more grace!"

Tears came into Caroline's eyes, and choked her voice. "Mother," she said, "Mother stopped it—she wouldn't let me become a professional. Can you wonder that I hate her? I had pneumonia after the War broke out, but we didn't go back to England for the first year, we stayed in Switzerland—then we had to—and—there were restrictions and restrictions. I had got better before—twice; but then I got worse, and mother moved heaven and earth to get me allowed here directly the War was over; and now I am here, and all you do for me is to ask me silly questions like the Gestapo. I suppose you learned it from the Germans you looked after during the War!"

John said nothing at all, and he looked so angry that Caroline was quite frightened. He just sat there, looking angry, but as if his anger didn't concern her. After a while, the anger died out of his eyes, and when he spoke again, he said mildly, "It's not quite all I do for you. I gave you streptomycin injections that are already

46

doing you a lot of good; but I want to do more still if you'll let me. It simply depends on if you *will* let me! Caroline, do you trust me?"

John looked at her carefully, and now wholly without anger; she thought by his expression that he really liked her—liked her as much, perhaps more, than he admired her. This was not what Caroline wanted. She preferred to be admired more than she was liked.

"I suppose I do," she said after a pause, and a little unwillingly, "Yes, John, I suppose I do trust you!"

He was a great deal older than she was, and it was the first time that Caroline had dared to call him by his Christian name; but he didn't seem to mind it.

He went on speaking: "If you do trust me you'll do what I suggest. Words don't mean a thing in this illness; you've just got to *do* the things that will succeed. I know what some of these things are—that's my job— yours is to carry out what I tell you. When you said your mother had done you a lot of harm the other day, I agreed with you. I think she has; but it's not only by stopping your dancing. Perhaps she wasn't wrong about that—a dancer's is a tough life. Perhaps you really hadn't enough stamina to make it. Anyhow, she took medical advice, and acted on it. No-one can blame her for that, however painful you may find it. You can get better still, and find something else to do. You'll have plenty of time here to find out what you'd like to do, and I'll help you all I can to get started. It'll take about two years for you to get well, if you play the game according to the rules we give you—if you don't, you won't get well; but you may not die—you may just be so ill that there's nothing left, but hating your mother, and letting her keep you. Not a very bright look out— is it?"

"How am I to help you?" Caroline asked, uncertainly. She had made up her mind to manage John; and helping him might be the beginning of managing him.

"Don't have your mother here, to start with," John told her. "She'll spoil you into being worse. She does too much for you, and not the right things. Let her stay where she is. I don't want you to be excited and nervous as you get with her. You may be bored up here, but you won't be bothered, and dullness is not a bad thing in this illness. Still, I want you to be amused too—and as you get stronger we'll let you be amused more. Isn't there some kind of bargain we could make together? If you'll stop your mother coming, I'll get more things done for you by nurses perhaps—or by my walking patients. Soon you can have visitors. If you'll stop writing notes to our Padre, I'll promise you shall be the first visitor he's allowed to have. He won't mind—I mean, he'll like seeing you!"

Caroline frowned. "I'll see about mother," she said stiffly. "As for Father Bretherton—you're quite wrong, of course—he *lives* on my letters!"

There was a pause. John seemed to grow larger and larger, and yet at the same time to be getting further and further away.

Finally he said, "Listen, Caroline, when you lie here all day long and have nothing to think about, it's natural you should play in your mind with all sorts of fancies, and it wouldn't be at all natural if these fancies weren't about men. A man lying here would think about women. It's just the way we're made, and it doesn't matter a damn—so long as you know they're fancies! But it just happens this man—our Padre— isn't quite the normal type. He's got a lot on his mind you haven't got on yours—he's much older, for one thing! You're nineteen and he's thirty-nine. A lot of

48

R.A.F. men still write to him about their troubles, and he had ten years of Africa before the War, speaking and living with Zulus and went back afterwards for two more years till he crocked up. That's what he thinks most about, Zulus—Zulus—flyers—and God. And they're enough. He's just as much occupied mentally as he can manage. I know nothing about God—but this man thinks he does. Anyhow, he's what I would call preoccupied with God. If I were you I'd leave him alone! And in general, Caroline, take it by and large, fancies about men are all right just as long as you don't build a thing on them—not a thing!—take men as they come—and don't worry—for in your case they *will* come!"

He had made a mistake. Caroline's eyes, wide with horror, gazed at him as if he had been a snake. She was indeed fascinated with horror. She might have been willing to accept—with care—that the picture she had in her mind about Michael was not wholly real; but that his reaction to her image was not what her imagination chose it to be, was unbearable. It was still worse that John might have guessed the much deeper image her mind played with, of John himself. He might even now be hinting that that too was not real—that she must not count on his adoration.

She closed her eyes, and called the dark to come to her; and she could feel the blackness coming—sick and cold and desperate—she *was* going to be able to faint!

John too realised that Caroline was going to faint. He did not want to ring for a nurse, nor to risk a shock by throwing cold water over her; instead he leaned over Caroline and gently rubbed her wrists, and put the warmth of his large hand over her wildly beating heart. Caroline's eyes opened at the firm warmth of his touch.

She looked straight up at him, her innocent, incalculable eyes sweet as a child's.

John did not mean what happened to happen—his lips touched her forehead.

"John!" she whispered. "John—you kissed me!"

She gave up fainting, but John was anything but pleased. Caroline however *was* pleased; there was no doubt about it.

7

John and Marie Céleste had every right to take off
four hours for the ski run they had planned, to climb the
Lärchen Kogel. Their long day's work was over, yet
neither of them could quite overcome a sense of shame,
since they had left behind them, not only their work, but
a hundred men and women condemned to long inaction;
prisoners, with their five senses rioting against confinement, their young lives blocked, or cut into fragments that might never join. Was it fair to set off so
freely into the sparkling moonlit world, carrying heavy
hickory skis on their shoulders as if they were feathers,
their strong resilient bodies filled with health, every
sense they had alert and satisfied? Yet their compassion
came from strength; and these free hours built up in
them the strength their patients needed.

The ground beneath their feet was hard-packed with
powder-snow; in front of them lay nothing but a narrow
valley, a shadow between two mountains. The path
they were on began to climb steeply, and still more
steeply, till the black sentinel pines on either side of
them came abruptly to a stop.

"It is here that I begin to believe that I am safe from
the Nazis," Marie Céleste told John a little breathlessly.
"Until now every pine tree was a frontier guard. I told
my spine to disregard them—but it never does—till
the trees stop. You sometimes say I am a reckless skier,
but I am not really reckless, for what is a precipice or a

concealed tree trunk to anyone who is safe from being chased or shot? Everything is the same as it was then, this valley as bright with moonlight, the bite of the air, the frozen scent of pine, the same old golden moon riding like a steeple-chaser at the peaks—but now, I know I am free to enjoy all this beauty—just because my brother man is not my enemy any more!"

John sighed. "In Europe," he said, "this is a haunted generation. I have the feeling that we let innocence die here, and that whatever is left alive of it is still threatened. In Canada or America there is the freshness and creative drive of a man who has never been sick. Such a man is always stronger than one of our patients who has recovered. And yet does anyone know as much about health as the man who has once lost it—and *has* recovered?"

"*If* he has recovered," Marie Céleste murmured drily, "and also if—when he sees danger staring him in the face again—he recognises it, for what it is!"

John gave her a quick glance, and then bent to fasten his skis, taking longer over the process than it needed. Did Marie Céleste guess what was going on in his shocked mind? She had an uncanny knowledge of the disturbances of sex; but she could not know what had happened to cause such a disturbance. Why *had* he kissed Caroline? John asked himself savagely. What had drawn him so suddenly into a fantasy that he had not known existed, and which he certainly did not share? He knew very well where his heart was, and what had happened to it. He must not let the Dead walk. His life was in his work, and part of his work lay in protecting girls like Caroline from all undue excitement.

They began the long climb in silence. The deep snow rustled softly away from their ski blades, with a faint hissing sound. The freezing air cut at their eyes and lips, and drew the skin tightly over their cheeks. The branch of a small tree, armoured in ice, far below them, snapped with the sharp sound of a pistol shot, close to their ears.

The silence that followed it was so deep that Marie Céleste fancied she could hear John's heart's beating loudly and punctually as a clock.

They climbed slowly and steadily, every muscle they had in rhythmic action, without pause for their evenly drawn breath.

Marie Céleste kept her eyes fixed on the sabre-shaped hollows John's skis made, zig-zagging with economic precision, to save time and effort. She did not want to see the distance there was yet between the silver wall they were on, and the clear darkness of the sky.

There was a sudden scurry of air from the summit, and the snow under their feet stirred, as if a hand moved under it.

The climb was over. They stood side by side, on the peak of the Lärchen Kogel, above a vast field of un-tenanted snow. New mountains had emerged as they climbed, climbing with them and revealing unknown valleys, stretching like ribbons of beaten silver between mountain walls. The golden disc of the moon shone so close above their heads that the steady planets and uncertain stars were robbed of half their light.

Neither of them knew who moved first. There was a faint hiss of snow, as they crouched low and bent forward, before they plunged into a storm of sound. Rocketing headlong through the incalculable air, they clenched and relaxed as their senses ordered them. Instinct, trained by skill, took possession of them; be-yond the regions of sight or sound, they fled, dipped and climbed to dip again, hardly recognising the earth that shot away from them, till the valley rushed up to meet them, darkened by dangerous trees. Their agile bodies moved like rag dolls, slipping now this way, and now that, to avoid instant obstacles, until they could discipline their speed into their own control. Neither caught sight of the other; yet they drew up, swaying, shaken, close to the hut from which they had started.

"And I," Marie Céleste said, laughing breathlessly, "who thought I should never know joy again! I am so happy I could die of joy—and yet it is a pity to know that I am happy—a minute ago I was happier, for then I was no more myself than the snow the air blew off my ski blades!"

"You would make a good Canadian," John told her. "You are as much at home on mountains as I am."

Marie Céleste made no immediate answer. She did not think she would have made a good Canadian. She was not simple; and vastness did not appeal to her. It was not for pleasure alone that she had given up her evening meal, to get the extra hour their tour needed. Pleasure had been thrown in, but, being by nature strictly practical, Marie Céleste meant to use both her pleasure and John's, in order to achieve her aim. She let him take her skis, as well as his own, on his strong shoulders—a thing she would have let no other man do for her—and walked close by his side through the sudden darkness of the pines. She was silent till they reached the valley floor, and the light poured over them, then she said,

"John, it is very strongly my opinion that you should see straight! Why do you not live with Elizabeth—or part with her? For two years now you have done neither. It is making you old and nervous, for you and your work such a life is bad, for Elizabeth, who is ten years younger, and has no work that she enjoys, it is even worse. Whom are you trying to punish—or is it to shield——? Whatever it is—since you are a human being and not God Almighty—it is a mistake! To see a shadow and think it is a tree—that is a pity, but to see a tree and think it is a shadow can be fatal. It appears to me that you are doing both!"

"Has Elizabeth complained of me?" John asked in a harsh voice. It was not what he had intended to say, nor did it answer Marie Céleste's question; but it seemed to do just as well for Marie Céleste.

"Do not be afraid," she told him. "The whole code of the Anglo-Saxon sits in Elizabeth's bones. She has said less than nothing. She talks to nobody; she splits herself doing what she thinks is her duty. And for how long do you suppose she can keep that up, in perfect health, at twenty-six, under the roof of a man she adores, who won't look at her? I know that we are not supposed to know why you won't look at her; but I will tell you this, my dear friend John, had you lived as I have, you would know that nothing, nothing whatever, is inexcusable in a human being except the inability to find excuses for another human being; and I will tell you also this—which perhaps is of equal importance—if you will not look at Elizabeth—somebody else will! If you do not want her, Konrad does, and he knows how to win any woman whose heart is not at rest with another man."

"Elizabeth is just as free as I am to take a lover," John said with extreme distaste, ignoring the more difficult part of Marie Céleste's remarks.

"What a word to use about a lover—*free!*" Marie Céleste replied scornfully. "Who is free when they are in love—except to carry out their love? That is a lover's only freedom—and it is not one-sided! It takes Two! Besides, you are a man—for you it is utterly different!

You are a particularly self-restrained disciplined man; and yet you must allow me to point out to you—you have done me the honour to be glad, from time to time, of more than my comradeship. What fools we are to spoil joy—by manipulating it! You have shut joy away from Elizabeth. You do not even take her down a mountain any more! The best thing in life is this love a man and woman can share together. For four years you and Elizabeth had it—it lit everyone near you. Many of your patients got well because it gave them hope. Now what have you done with it? You have pushed your head into an iron mask—and drawn another over poor Elizabeth's little face!"

"Be quiet, Marie Céleste," John said sternly. "You do not know what you are talking about. I have told you this much—there has been a tragedy in our lives; you must respect it—and be silent."

For a moment or two Marie Céleste *was* silent. Then she laughed. "And why be silent?" she demanded. "If I see you walk over a precipice when I might stop you by a word—am I to be silent? You say you have had a tragedy. My dear, Konrad and I could perhaps even laugh at what you have made into a tragedy! You said just now—and truly—that men who have been ill know what health means better than the strong. People like Konrad and myself—who lived five years hunted, and lost everything we had, except comradeship—we also know that nothing—not virtue nor vice—nor hunger nor thirst—nor shame nor torture—outlast comradeship! We knew only one law in the Résistance—do what you can for a comrade—kill him if he weakens, for he would rather be dead than weak—but don't let him down. In my opinion then—and it is the opinion of a friend—you have let Elizabeth down."

"You know nothing about it," John told her with

cold exasperation. "Elizabeth and I agreed when—when this thing happened—on the life we are living now. If she wishes to change it, she must say so. I would grant her a divorce if she wished it."

"You agreed on a life that you had neither of you lived—and which it was preposterous to try to live!" Marie Céleste told him. "Can you not *learn* by living?—and change these unreal conditions for something more sensible? Elizabeth does not believe in divorce; and as for Konrad—he has a wife and children living in a country he can never enter. For him divorce or marriage apply as little as a postage stamp without glue. I think he has a serious love for Elizabeth—he would devote his life to her—but he is nervous and unstable. Faithful in little ways he could never be; but neither would he ever be intentionally cruel. You know him nearly as well as I do. Would you be happy to think of Elizabeth in his hands—if she agreed to what he could give her? It would not be—what you could still give her, John!"

Bound by the black pines on either side of them, they walked closely together.

When John answered her finally, it was with tragic gentleness. "Marie Céleste," he said, "I cannot tell you any more than I have told you. You are the best friend a man ever had—you make my life bearable—and I thought you made Elizabeth's bearable for her too. But no-one can give us back the past. Do you not know yourself that some things are irretrievable?"

"What does that word 'irretrievable' mean?" Marie Céleste asked him. "I don't think we have it in French—the exact sense of it—escapes me."

"It means," John told her, "that what we have lost, we cannot get back again. We have a dog, that fetches and carries for us when we shoot birds—whom we call a 'retriever'—but sometimes a shot bird cannot be found; and then we call this wasted shot—this dead bird—irretrievable.''

"*Sans remède*," Marie Céleste murmured to herself, " '*irréparable*'—or perhaps '*irrémédiable*'—but all these words, you will notice, are a little different. They do not involve hopeless searches; they are the simple results of disasters. While one *can* search—while one *is* alive—who is to say that a bird is dead—or even lost? It is quite possible to lose a lover—or to wish him to be lost! A lover's relationship comes and goes with us perhaps more easily than with you; but to lose a comrade is not so easy—nor so necessary! Once a comrade—and you stay a comrade—with or without a love relationship. In the Résistance, husbands and wives often found an end to their marriage. Another man or woman, for that purpose, suited them better—or for the time only, suited them better—but their comrade-ship did not end. When it had once been good—better probably than the casual relationship they had needed most in perpetual danger—they would return to their marriage, and all was readjusted—better than before. You can forgive Elizabeth now—if you will forget how good a man you are—and how much austerity you have to keep up! You are far more respectable than the priest you have upstairs; he would give up anything he had for anybody—and think nothing of it!''

"Why should you suppose I have anything to forgive Elizabeth?" John asked sternly. "I have made no complaint against her—to you—or to anyone else!''

"My dear," Marie Céleste said, her arm touching his, "you are an incarnate complaint against Elizabeth. How can I believe that *you* have done anything wrong! —I mean what you call wrong? Yet that there is something wrong—we all know. Besides, can you not see

58

that Elizabeth would forgive you anything? It is a woman's métier to forgive—she enjoys it. Did she not push you into my arms so that she might have a little to forgive you—but it was not enough!"

The lights from the Sanatorium struck through the black pine stems, and made their moonlit world suddenly unreal to them both. John stopped abruptly.

"If I had any relationship with Elizabeth," he said, "it would have to be a *whole* relationship—that's why we can't be comrades. Don't let's ever talk about it any more."

He turned, past her, into the side doorway; he could hardly wait to stack the skis, and glance into his office to see what calls were waiting for him. Fear possessed him. Had he exposed Elizabeth to fresh dangers rather than protected her? Something new and bitter stirred in his saddened heart. Could Elizabeth, after all that there had been between them, think seriously of another man—such a man as Konrad Rainer? John knew Konrad only less well than Marie Céleste knew him—perhaps in some ways better. He was his doctor, he knew the thin ice of daily living, over which Konrad skated. His evasions and duplicities—his frantic fears forcing him into bouts of drunkenness—his alternate excitability and laziness—that made him, brilliant as he was, so uncertain as a colleague. He was worth saving; but you could not save a person; and then stop. John was his continual support, as he had thought himself to be Elizabeth's. Was it possible that Marie Céleste was right? Or was she, with her half-maternal intermittent passion for Konrad, merely jealous of another woman's influence over him? Had John himself been too absorbed in his work, too cut off from Elizabeth, to notice that this influence had increased—that it had become perhaps more than an influence?

"You're a conceited, besotted fool," John told himself savagely. "Why should Elizabeth prefer what I once was to her—to what Konrad can give her now—alive and warm—fascinating and seductive—and always on the spot?"

He flung himself into the lift, and upstairs to his separate flat. A hundred cruel scenes of intimacy raced through his frightened mind—Elizabeth and Konrad were alone together—anger and fear burned through his awakened heart.

The key clicked in the latch, the door swung open, and music rushed out at him. He was in a world of good and beautiful sounds. He crept noiselessly to the doorway, and stood unnoticed listening to Beethoven's "Früling."

None of the things he had imagined were true; but they were playing together, Konrad's violin soaring, with practised sweetness, above Elizabeth's skilled accompaniment. Neither of them heard him. They were in Beethoven's woods and meadows—in the magic of new-born leaves and flowers—in love perhaps—but not with each other, with music.

John turned and crept away to his own room without a sound.

8

Elizabeth sat by her open balcony door, eating her breakfast; it was a good breakfast, but what she liked most about it was the taste of the icy air.

It was eight o'clock, and the unruffled snow lay virgin white, under an apricot sky. The hidden sun that was fingering the distant peaks, had already caught an adventurous pine tree, standing alone, above the tree limits, and would soon pour down the valley in a sheet of gold.

When Elizabeth had possessed happiness, this had been the hour she and John had enjoyed together most; but since she had learned to live by herself, she had found it the most lonely.

Today, however, it seemed to Elizabeth that she was enjoying it in a new way, as if she were a part of the light, and air, expectant of the sun's great revival.

The apricot light, the fragrant frozen pines, the eager air were no different today than any other day. What was this plus quality that turned them into sudden rapture?

Elizabeth was a sensible young woman. She knew that Konrad Rainer admired her, that he admired her increasingly, and although her heart was broken, she knew that it comforted her to be so much admired. "But it isn't only that," she told herself defensively. "It's something that hasn't anything to do with Konrad —or even John; it's something new—it's as if I were coming alive!"

As she reached this strange but reassuring conclusion, the door opened, and most unexpectedly John came in.

John took his breakfast an hour before hers, and by now should have been in his office looking at charts, and preparing his day's work.

"There you are," he said a little awkwardly. "I hoped I should catch you. One day you'll get pneumonia sitting by that open balcony door before the sun's up."

Elizabeth did not answer immediately, but she thought, "I feel perfectly free to get anything—even pneumonia—because you're not in love with me any more."

"I have my fur jacket on," she said at last mildly. "Won't you sit down?" Elizabeth had been brought up to be polite, and when anything unexpected happened, or she was at all at a loss, she became a shade more polite than usual.

"Open at the neck!" John said savagely. "And those gauze stockings!"

He didn't sit down, he towered above her and looked with unwonted disgust at her extremely well shaped legs.

"What I wanted to say was this—why don't you go home for a bit?—to your father and mother in England? It's really not necessary for you to stay on here all the time. It seems to me you need a change—why not take it?"

"How very funny!" Elizabeth said with a nervous laugh. "I was just thinking I didn't!—this morning— for the first time! It seemed as if I'd suddenly got more used to things, and then there's Father Bretherton, I like reading to him—it's so—so quieting. Besides, he's English."

"How you do go on about being English!" John said crossly. "It's a small, powerless island off the coast of a splintered continent, full of pig-headed, mediaeval people, who were once safe because they were rich, and who are now neither rich nor safe—and yet just as arrogant as if they were both. Lazy too—and they don't know it because most of them take a lot of exercise. Since you're so fond of them, however, you'd be much better off living among them. Why don't you?"

"But—but, John," Elizabeth cried, her frail sense of happiness crumbling within her, "I—I thought I was useful here. You couldn't, I think, get another dietitian to housekeep for you in the middle of the winter—not easily—as trained as I am. Or don't the patients like their food any more?"

"They've no complaints," John said impatiently. "I wasn't thinking of the Sanatorium, I was thinking of you."

"But I'm all right!" exclaimed Elizabeth.

There was an awkward pause, because they both knew exactly how "all right" Elizabeth was.

Elizabeth broke it. "There was something," she began in a hesitating voice, "that I did think I should like to speak to you about, only you're usually not interested in it, and I didn't want to bother you. It's—it's religion. "

"Religion!" John exclaimed incredulously. "What on earth are you talking about, Elizabeth? What's religion got to do with either of us? I didn't know you had any!"

Elizabeth's soft eyebrows met in perplexity. It is not very easy to explain that you want something that the person to whom you are talking doesn't believe exists. Elizabeth did not think in words, she thought with her blood, and if possible she put her thought not into words but into immediate action.

"I was always Church of England," she said defensively. "I gave it up when we married because you laughed at it, and I never went regularly except to please Father; but I never quite liked laughing at it. I just gave it up. It's different now. I have the feeling that I want *more* religion not less, because of what happened—and if possible more of Father Bretherton's kind!"

John stared at her. "Women," he said at last, "are more determinedly parasitic than any living thing. If they can't hang on to a man, they want to hang on to God! Granted Michael *has* religion—or what he thinks it is—in a favourable sense, and I will admit as much—what in God's name has it to do with you?"

"Even *you* say 'in God's name'," Elizabeth pointed out. "Religion is a sort of background to everything whether you believe it or not. It might have quite a lot to do with me—it might help me."

"According to what you've just been saying you are getting on very well without help," John drily reminded her, "but I really must say, Elizabeth, without wanting to be nasty, that I don't see why you should *be* helped, beyond being given the means of leading a useful life. I've just been suggesting that you should live it, in circumstances and with the people who seem to suit you best. The War's over, your parents have lost their other child, and with your father's influence it would not be difficult to find you a job."

There was a pause, in which Elizabeth tried to get rid of some of the things that had hurt her, in John's remarks, and failed completely.

"They're not my contemporaries," she said at last, "and they have each other. I was with them for eight months after the War was over. You see, as far as being attached goes, I *am* attached to you, and Marie Céleste and Konrad Rainer. You *are* my contemporaries, and we work well together. I do think that counts —unless you aren't satisfied with my work, of course——?" Her voice shook, and knowing that John hated audible emotion she stopped speaking.

"Oh, that's all right, of course," John said uneasily. "You're over-conscientious, if anything, and no one has ever said you weren't efficient. I'm not going to force my suggestions upon you. You know your own mind presumably, and can follow it if you choose; but if I were you I should drop this business about religion. It's a great mistake to hoodwink yourself. You did very well without it when you were happy. It seems to me both cowardly and self-deceiving to start it all up again just because you're unhappy."

"Why do you *want* me to be unhappy, John?" Elizabeth asked in a low voice.

There were moments when John wished that primitive emotions could take primitive forms—or else die out in men who were forced to be civilised. He wanted to swear, to hit Elizabeth, to use in some violent way, his bitterly roused emotions. Instead he reminded himself that he was not only a gentleman, but a doctor, and Elizabeth a woman. She was also a woman whom he profoundly loved; but this he tried to forget before he answered her.

"That's nonsense," he told her. "Be as happy as you can—and as religious as you must! But may I ask, what particular form this religion of yours is going to take?"

"I don't know—yet," Elizabeth said after a long pause. "I don't even know if I'm going to get it. I only know I want it—and there is something I want to do about it." She stopped, as if reluctant to tell

E   65

him what it was that she wanted to do. He had time to think, with exasperated tenderness, how instantly Elizabeth always wanted to control thought by deeds. She did not give her mental processes time even to be a thought; and never left them free without her hands upon the reins of action.

"How much better is Michael?" she asked, without lifting her eyes to his.

John seemed to hover over her like a cliff, and Elizabeth thought desperately that there were no hand holes or crevices by which she could negotiate the precipitous height. If only John wasn't so miraculously good, without being kind!

"I'm going to let him have a pillow for an hour or two; he'll like having his head raised," John told her proudly. "He's made incredible progress. He can talk a little now, but not much or at all continuously. I hope to get him out on his balcony in a couple of months. He's a wonderful patient and a good fellow. No hurry— no set-backs—no nerves. I'm glad you like him. But if it's a question of getting on to religion with him—I think you'd much better keep off it for a bit. Or have you already begun?"

"Oh *no*," Elizabeth said. "He's never said a word about religion to me—he's not like that. I just read him his lessons and his psalms, and I found him some books that I thought he'd like. We haven't talked at all—except a little about Zulus. He's very fond of Zulus."

"Oh well—Zulus!" John said more tolerantly. "He's lived with them for ten years. I don't see why he shouldn't talk about them as long as he doesn't get excited. I've seen his African photographs. Now I must be off," he added, "and so must you: we're both late."

"But there's just that one thing first," Elizabeth urged, fixing John suddenly with her clear eyes. "If he is well enough—when he *is* well enough, I want to make my confession to him. He's a priest. I know I promised never to tell anyone—but Michael isn't just a man—it's telling God through him—it's knowing, if I *can* know it, that I'm free!"

"But you can't *be* free," John told her inexorably. "Neither of us can, Elizabeth. We must make up our minds to live shackled. We can do it! We *are* doing it. I don't believe we should even *try* to escape the consequences of what has happened."

Elizabeth dropped her eyes, and for a long time she neither moved nor spoke.

"Well," John said at last, moving away from her, "I don't want to be hard on you, Elizabeth. Marie Céleste seems to think I am a brute to you—and I've no doubt Konrad thinks the same; but this idea of yours about God—just doesn't appeal to me. As I see it you should learn to stand alone, and take your punishment. That's what we *all* have to do all the time. Ethics I *do* believe in; and while we're talking about them, I should advise you to notice—if you haven't—that Konrad is in love with you, and like most Viennese he makes love damned well—and damned often—to different women. Do what you like about it, but don't get fooled! Nor—about God either if you can help it! I don't forbid your speaking to Michael. I'll let you off your word. I'd much rather you didn't, of course, but your soul's your own. Take it to him to get washed if you believe in his particular brand of washing powder. I don't! But what I believe doesn't matter. I *do* believe in him as a man; and while you're about it —you might perhaps ask yourself if *you* believe in him as a man—or as a red herring? It seems to me rather

67

important *which* he is to you—for him, as well as for you!"

John had reached the door by now, and got out of it without having to see Elizabeth's bent head. He knew she wouldn't say any more. There was one thing about Elizabeth that John had always liked. When she had once said what she had to say—she didn't go on about it.

9

Caroline had a nearly sleepless night; but she enjoyed every moment of it.

Out of the long, dark, restless hours, she was building a new life.

She was accustomed to day-dreams, playing, by turn, the parts of a queen, a film star or a champion skater. (Caroline just knew how to skate.) She would sail through a succession of not too unlikely incidents with unvarying success. She took lovers, won prizes, quelled revolutions, and held world-wide audiences enthralled by her beauty. But hitherto her bricks had been made without the binding quality of straw. Now Caroline had something to build on. She had John's kiss.

It was true that John was stubborn, and his morals backed by a Presbyterian conscience. He would not yield lightly to a wilderness of Caroline's. Yet constant proximity wisely handled might, Caroline felt, lead rather than drive John, into getting rid of Elizabeth. Perhaps Elizabeth too could be made to see the advantage of being got rid of. There is nothing like working at both ends of a problem at the same time. There would be a divorce with no scandal attached to either party, just an undefended technically correct suit; and then a year for Caroline to achieve the kind of health that she believed sufficient for married life. She would always be delicate enough for John to be anxious about her, but not too delicate to rule the Sanatorium. She would rule it gently and let it run on devotion, but she would rule it as Elizabeth had never attempted to rule it. What Caroline liked would be there, and what she didn't like would be somewhere else. Everything, even the Swiss climate, would serve Caroline. She would dismiss Sister Peckham instantly. She might keep Konrad Rainer; but that would depend upon his being able to develop a hopeless passion for her. Caroline would always be true to John. John was indeed the kind of man to whom a woman had to be true —otherwise she would have been ruthlessly kicked out. But a few hopeless lovers can surely be allowed the strictest of heroines.

Some of the worst cases in the Sanatorium might die of hopeless love for Caroline. She would sit at their bedsides, watching them die, while John—not knowing, of course, why they were dying—fought hard to save them. Caroline would keep their secret to the last; but after they were dead she might perhaps mention it to enhance her value.

Caroline was quite sorry when the dawn came. She suddenly became aware of the darker edges of the balcony door, and the wash-stand. There wasn't anything else till the mountains drew away from the sky, and broke up the darkness.

Caroline began to consider her make-up. What should she look like for John's brief morning visit? Very pale, with scarlet lips, and a touch of mauve under her eyes? She would probably have shadows there anyway, after her sleepless night, but these would not be becoming shadows. Nature is not good at make-up. Caroline would have to help nature out. Her manner, she decided, should be tenderly reproachful. She would unite herself to John by her tenderness; but Caroline would reproach him as well, because John would certainly think he had gone too far, and Caroline had the sense to realise that John was full of ideas about his duty, which she could only get rid of by appearing to share.

Caroline gave Nurse Oliver a terrible half hour dressing her for breakfast. She insisted on trying on all her bed jackets, and three foundation creams—an orange one made her look too daring, and perhaps bilious as well. A lipstick of cyclamen didn't suit her, and when Nurse Oliver said in a tone of desperation, "Well, I'm sorry, but I can't do any more for you. I *must* go to the girl next door!" Caroline fell back on the scarlet lipstick, and her natural pallor.

Her best bed jacket, made out of white angora and trimmed with swansdown, increased her likeness to a snowdrop. No blonde could have shown so effective a contrast as Caroline's dark hair, smouldering against the dazzling whiteness of her pillow. At the last moment she had insisted upon a fresh pillow slip.

Caroline toyed with her breakfast. Her heart beat thick and fast, and she was thankful when the tray was taken from her, and she was left in peace.

Very large, biscuit-thin snowflakes pushed themselves to and fro in the grey air. They seemed to move backwards as well as forwards, like a distracted hive of silent bees. There was very little light and no wind. The mountains were invisible, and there was nothing to look at but the snowflakes. However, Caroline could hear everything. Two nurses were in Michael's room, making his bed, and giving him a blanket-bath. Caroline could hear the nurses' voices instead of his; she thought that they always seemed to want to talk to Michael, and stayed longer in his room than they needed to stay. Even Sister Peckham lingered when she brought

Michael his post; and the worst of it was he always had a post.

The next door girl was able to wash herself and was actually humming while doing so; that just showed, Caroline thought spitefully, what an easy sort of night *she'd* had!

Sister Peckham's unflinching tread came down the corridor to her office. The doctors wouldn't be long now. What Caroline thought was her heart, rose into her throat and fluttered like a bird.

She heard John's deep, abrupt voice; his crisp footstep passed her door. He was going to Michael first. A slower, lighter footstep followed John's. The red light for doctors sprang out above her door, and Konrad Rainer knocked and walked in. He stood at the foot of Caroline's bed smiling at her. His eyes did not look straight into Caroline's with intensity, as John's always did, as if eyes were meant solely to observe and store up facts. Konrad looked at her as an artist looks at an object which seems to him the promise of a work of art, something to which he can give what he has, if it reacts to his senses, in the right way.

"You——" Caroline whispered. "But you're not my doctor!"

"For this morning I seem to be," Konrad said with easy serenity, "but I don't suppose there's anything for me to do. MacTaggart has an emergency operation, and asked me to look in."

Caroline had had so much to think about which was now pushed out of her mind, by what had happened, that she found it difficult to hide her chagrin. Yet what she felt was not altogether disappointment. She was conscious of something fresh, a challenge in the man before her, which she could take up or if she chose— pass by; yet if she passed it by, she might be sorry to

72

have lost it. It was as if Konrad's indolent yet speaking eyes said to her, "I have been impressed by you, and I should like to make an impression on you; but don't worry about it because there are plenty of other impressions open to me, if you prefer to let this one drop."

Caroline did not ask Konrad to sit down, but against her will her eyes wandered to the chair on which John usually sat.

"You haven't got Sister Peckham with you," she said a little severely. "She usually comes in the mornings with Dr. MacTaggart."

"Should you like to ring for her?" Konrad asked. His smile reached his eyes, as they met Caroline's—and Caroline found herself smiling back at him.

"I don't mind," Caroline said, "whether she comes or not."

"Then let's *not* ring for her!" Konrad said, taking John's chair as if it had been offered to him. "She disapproves of you, I expect, because you're easy to look at—and of me, because I *like* women to be easy to look at. Sister Peckham thinks that the only way to be safe from a thing is to dislike it. I think the exact opposite. The only things that I find dangerous are the things I dislike."

Caroline digested this thought in silence. She had already come to the conclusion that if there were to be any advances, they should come from him; and if there were to be obstructions to these advances, they should come from her.

Cats awe dogs by not plunging towards them, or away from them. They keep still. Caroline decided to behave with the same spectacular passivity.

"I'm not going to bore you," Konrad said lightly, "by asking doctor's questions. I've seen your chart and I know you've had a bad night; but of course I

73

don't know why. People know their own minds, and it's usually their minds that keep them awake. When it's just their bodies, we can handle it."

"I suppose I'm ill," Caroline said drily, "or I wouldn't be here."

"You're not my patient, as you've already observed," Konrad replied, "but I should like to know if you could tell me, what in the first instance upset you into being ill? Epidemics, blows, germs and contagions—I believe in all of them in the most orthodox fashion; but I must confess with the long organic illnesses I think that there must have been, just at the start, some general consent of the Management—something that, as we say, 'disagreed with you'."

"I don't know what you mean," Caroline said hurriedly and with some annoyance, for she had a vague feeling that she *did* know what Konrad meant. Hadn't she often, in the dull, feeble hours of her long illness, wondered if somehow or other she might not have avoided it altogether? She couldn't now—the illness had got the better of her—but as Konrad said "at the start"? Had she had it in her power *not* to start it? Was she sure she wanted to be a ballet dancer unless she knew she could be the best ballet dancer in the world? Couldn't she have broken her mother down into letting her try? Or if she couldn't have been a ballet dancer after all—couldn't she have been something less flattering, but more usual—more usual than being an invalid at Death's Door? But was what she really wanted most to avoid being usual?

"You *are* ill, of course," Konrad said reassuringly. "Don't think I doubt it. I've seen your X-rays, and I know what a weight this lung illness is—it takes so long—and it clears up so slowly, though I'm glad to think in your case it *is* clearing up. But I've always had the idea that we could get well quicker if we asked ourselves what would have been *worse* for us than being ill—and then found another way out of it; because I believe with most people—I wouldn't say with all, but with most of us—there is another way out."

Caroline stared at him defiantly. To begin with, this kind of talk was not what a doctor's short morning visits, with nurses and charts, were meant for. Konrad needn't have sat down on John's chair, as if time didn't exist, just talking like an ordinary person, after Caroline had had an appalling night and no breakfast. It wasn't fair! Tears rose slowly to her eyes and she thought of fainting; but the balcony door was wide open, and the circulating snowflakes, between their diaphanous flurries, let in plenty of air.

"I've told John all that I want to tell anybody about my life," Caroline said at last with a shaking voice. "I don't want to talk any more—I'm tired."

"I expect John spoils you," Konrad said, getting up, but still looking at her with laughing, conniving eyes, as if there would always be a joke between them. "Big, strong, positive fellows are easily fooled. You and I would understand each other much better if you'd give it a try—and it would be much more fun! But of course it's up to you whether you want fun or not. You may prefer being bottled up with boredom in this immaculately empty room!"

Caroline shuddered. There was something in Konrad which John did not possess, something alive and dangerous that she suddenly wanted as a plaything, though she knew she would be much better without it.

She closed her eyes to shut out his image, but it had not gone when she opened them. He still stood at the bottom of the bed, looking at her as he had looked when he first came in.

"You do look like Nefertiti!" he said softly, "the Egyptian queen—three thousand years young! I think I shall always call you Nefertiti!"

Caroline was pleased. She liked looking like an Empress—even an Egyptian one. "It's first thing in the morning that I'm so tired," she murmured. "In the afternoon—after tea—I'm better."

"Then I shall come next time," he said, "in the afternoon."

He was gone as quickly and lightly as a snowflake falls.

There had been, she thought a little uncomfortably, something unsubstantial about this whole interview—unsubstantial and at the same time disconcerting. For why, after Caroline had arranged in her mind to let all advances come from Konrad, should she have suggested that she felt better in the afternoons?

10

Sister Peckham had the rare faculty of being able to stand perfectly still indefinitely, although prepared for instant action. She took surprises by the throat as terriers seize rats; emergencies fawned at her feet.

Nevertheless in less active fields she had her moments of indecision. When Father Bretherton said to her, "I want to hear Mrs. MacTaggart's confession tomorrow morning. Can you arrange things for me, after the doctor's have gone?" she found her sympathies fighting with an obscure resentment. Confessions might be all very well for Catholics, or for criminals on death beds, but she did not like to think of her chief's wife, for whom she had an austere affection, making one, in a patient's room. Besides, she did not consider Father Bretherton was well enough to hear confessions.

There was the hospital also to consider. If such an act were to take place, it must be hushed up, otherwise it would cause a great deal of regrettable gossip, especially in Elizabeth's circumstances. Many of the Swiss patients and all the Swiss nurses were bitterly Protestant. It hardly mattered, Sister Peckham said to herself, what Nurse Bessie believed, since she was only a probationer; but she had a long tongue and must be kept out of things. Nurse Oliver was a strict Presbyterian, but not one to make trouble over a patient's wishes. Sister Peckham would have to enlist their services while keeping them in ignorance of what was actually taking place. The doctors were of course different. They would have to know in order to ensure their keeping out of the way. It was a pity, because they were irreverent enough already and Sister Peckham shrank from the thought of their joking about confession which—whether she approved of it or not—was a religious subject.

Michael, however, did not seem to notice any hesitation in her, for he said, as if the main question were already settled, "I should be very grateful if you could get my surplice ironed for me, it got crushed in packing. My stole is all right because it is such heavy silk, and was packed very carefully."

"I could do that, of course," Sister Peckham admitted, deciding instantly that she would iron his surplice herself as soon as she was off duty, and couldn't be overlooked.

"But does Dr. MacTaggart think you should make such an effort? He has said nothing to me about it. You've hardly sat up yet for more than a few minutes at a time."

"Yes, he has agreed," Michael told her. "It's just a question of settling an hour to suit your convenience, and of our not being disturbed."

Sister Peckham looked a little grim; she knew that it would be about as easy to check up all the myriad activities of a hospital routine, and sweep the corridor free from any chance wayfarer, as to divert the traffic of Oxford Street in a rush hour.

Still her mind found itself functioning in agreement with Michael's. No-one must come or go, she decided, past Michael's door while Elizabeth was there. She herself would take charge of Michael for the whole morning; and no explanations should be given to anybody.

She would smuggle an armchair into Michael's room over-night, and borrow a prie-dieu to put under his crucifix before which Elizabeth could kneel.

"Perhaps we shall need about an hour," Michael told her, "for Mrs. MacTaggart might like to stay and talk to me a little, after she has made her confession."

Sister Peckham gave an etherialised sniff. It was, she thought, like being asked to hold her thumb on a severed artery, for a similar period. Still, she had on one occasion done this, and she supposed she could do it again.

"In case anyone thinks she's there longer than usual," Sister Peckham told herself, "I'll have that trolley of books of hers standing outside his door." Aloud she said, "I don't think there'll be any difficulty. I shall sit in my office with the door open, and no-one can pass it without my stopping them. As soon as Mrs. MacTaggart leaves you, I shall bring you some milk and get you back to bed. I am rather surprised Dr. MacTaggart has not discussed the matter with me first, but the best of doctors never knows how much strength a patient has when it comes to making efforts. They *can* make them, of course, but they have to pay for them afterwards—and so have their nurses!"

Michael smiled at her. "I think," he said, "you'll find it will do me good to be used a little instead of having to use so many other people!"

Sister Peckham sniffed again; she didn't say that she couldn't possibly see what use a confession would be to a sensible young woman accustomed to do her duty, such as Elizabeth; she would, however, have said it to anyone whom she respected less than she respected Michael.

The next day the sun shone over freshly fallen snow, just as it had done, two months before, when Michael had waked up to his new world, and thought he was in Paradise and that Elizabeth was the Virgin Mary. The snow spread out in endless regions, like the sea, blue shadows made a path of azure under the pine trees, softly curved drifts and sudden hollows interrupted any sense of flatness, and flowed, like the smooth lift of waves, towards the shining peaks.

Elizabeth came in exactly at the moment arranged for her by Sister Peckham.

She had never made a confession before, but Michael had explained the procedure to her, and he looked, she thought reassuringly, the same, even in his surplice. She had learned the form of words he had given to her, by heart, and knew that she must kneel down when he put on his stole, and could get up when he had taken it off. At first she could hardly hear her own voice above the hard and rapid beating of her heart; but when she came to the end of the accepted form, her voice steadied itself. It was, she thought, like taking a ski-jump—you were air-borne—once you had taken the plunge.

There was a protective quietness in the little room, as if silence itself were helping Elizabeth's words to escape from long captivity. Elizabeth was no more conscious of Michael as a person than if he had not been there; but she was conscious of a great compassion meeting the greatness of her need.

"I always hated him," Elizabeth began. "He was the very worst type of Gestapo—sadistic and a killer. John did not think he could live at first, and he fought us when we tried to dress his wounds. He was appallingly injured and burned. But he was too strong to die, and week after week he went on living in torment, and making torment for all who tried to help him.

"He was in my ward; and from the first he taunted and insulted me. He knew I was English, and he had guessed that I was going to have a child, though no-one else but John knew it. He used to curse me and my child.

"It was to be our first after four years: we had almost given up hope. John asked me to stop nursing, but I wouldn't. We were very over-crowded and under-staffed. Later I wanted to go to England. I did not want my baby to be born surrounded by Germans and under their influence. It was quite natural for John to refuse my wish because of the bombing; but I began to want to go terribly. My brother was a Spitfire pilot, and my father wanted me to be with my mother. There were only the two of us children and we were a very united family. They all three liked John, but my father thought it made a difference his being a Canadian.

"Perhaps I ought to have told John the things Andreas von Brandt said to me—but I couldn't; besides, it might have been worse for the other nurses than for me. I was so full of hate, when I came off duty, that sometimes I was afraid to speak.

"I think my baby died before it was born. John was with me; the Lausanne clinic was a very good one, but it was a late, difficult breach birth, and the child was born dead. They let me see him. He was a very perfect little boy.

"When I came back, I felt quite well again, so I took back my ward. The hate was still there in my heart stronger than ever. Still, I think I would have done my duty to Andreas von Brandt, if I had not got the telegram while I was dressing his wounds. He laughed when he saw my face. It was to say that my brother Mark was killed. The telegram came at eight o'clock in the evening. I was on night duty, and alone in the ward. Andreas von Brandt was still critically ill. John had told me to watch his pulse and his temperature, and to give him a blood transfusion if I thought he needed it. I had already prepared it, to give him. Towards morning I knew that he needed the blood plasma. So did he. His eyes met mine. He smiled and said: 'Now's your chance! Are you going to kill me?' And I said: 'Yes, I am.' He could have called for help quite easily; but he didn't. He went on watching me. I cleared everything away as if I had given it to him, and at five o'clock he died.

"I did not mean to tell anyone. All the other patients were asleep. His death was not surprising. But John was not satisfied. He had not expected Andreas von Brandt to die. When we were alone, he asked me, 'Elizabeth, *why* did he die?' So I told him that I had killed him. I couldn't lie to John.

"This hospital is really his, he thought it all out. All the new ideas and conveniences were his, and our splendid cures. It was as if he never took his mind out of the hospital. Although during the War the Swiss controlled our Sanatorium it was only nominally run by Dr. Schreiber to save appearances and satisfy the Germans. John really acted as its chief just the same. He had had T.B. when he was a boy, so he was a non-combatant anyhow—and a Canadian. They trusted him, and let him go on working, and they took me for granted too, because I was his wife. That was what John couldn't forgive—that I had broken his trust as well as my own. There wasn't any difference really, but I had acted as if there were a difference. I had acted away from his whole heart.

"I began marriage the right way—I——" Elizabeth stopped dead. The silence deepened round them until it seemed as if nothing could ever be heard in it.

"What did you think *was* the right way?" Michael asked her at last.

"To be everything he wanted, I suppose," Elizabeth said slowly. "It was so wonderful to be what he thought me! Perhaps it was too hard, for John was always too good for me. So when I went the wrong way—it was suddenly into pieces—like that! We decided after a while to work together—and to live apart. For the first eight months I went to my people. No-one thought that very strange because of Mark's death. Then I came back here. I had learned to be a dietitian instead of a nurse, by then, because John said I could not be a nurse any more."

"What made you repent?" Michael asked her gently. "Because I think you have gone very far into penitence."

"I don't know when I began to be really sorry," Elizabeth said hesitatingly. "I felt frozen at first. It is very odd when you have had a baby—and it isn't there any more—nothing in the future fits into it; and besides, sometimes you think it is there still. I thought a lot about my baby that first year. Then I began to think more about John. I had to do so many things to help him—but without bothering him of course. I asked Marie Céleste to be his mistress. She laughed at me at first—and said things didn't work like that—but I think in the end—though I have never asked her— she made them work like it. I made friends with Konrad too—but not in the same way. We were all four tremendous friends—but we told them nothing.

"Perhaps when I first began to read out loud to you, I felt different—I mean, sorrier I'd done it—not only *because* I'd done it and spoiled John's life and mine by doing it—that had begun quite soon, and didn't particularly help. I don't think I had seen before what being sorry meant. I had suddenly to bring Andreas von Brandt into it—I could think about him again.

John had said to me, when I first told him that I hated Brandt: 'All patients are the same. The only difference is some need you more than others.' I began to think then that this man *had* needed me. He was terribly wounded—if he moved he bled. I was always very careful of him and gentle in my touch—perhaps this made him angrier, to have to need me, and so made him more horrible to me. I had only thought of him, while he was alive, as a Nazi—but he was my patient."

"He was your brother," Michael said firmly.

"Oh no!" Elizabeth protested. "Think of the War going on all the time and Mark in it; think of what this man *did* and wanted to do! He *was* my enemy!"

"I don't think we can afford enemies," Michael told her. "We have to face it sooner or later—that unless we meet every responsibility we have for a man as our brother, we are murdering him, and every living creature *is* our brother."

Elizabeth felt as if a knife had pierced her heart. She would have liked to say with Juliet: "O happy dagger! This is thy sheath! There rest—and let me die!" for she felt that while she suffered, she was not dealing that other blow that stood between her, and her lost Paradise.

" 'A broken and a contrite heart'," Michael reminded her gently, " 'God doth not despise.' Your heart has been broken, Elizabeth, and I think that it is contrite."

"I shouldn't do it again," Elizabeth admitted. "I think I am sorry now—not only because of the pain—John's pain and mine—but because I killed Andreas von Brandt. John still despises me, but there is something new in me that feels less broken because of it. I can't tell you why—or what it is—but somehow I feel more alive! Only John doesn't feel I ought to be alive—nor to forgive myself. I think perhaps the difference is that I believe in God more now. I can believe He may forgive me!"

"The door is always opened to you if you knock," Michael said. "Forgiveness is part of Him—you are always forgiven if you forgive others! You will know for certain that you have been forgiven this crime—when you have quite forgiven John."

"John!" exclaimed Elizabeth in astonishment. "Why! —I have *nothing* to forgive John! He has always been right!"

"It is sometimes hard to forgive people who are in the right," Michael suggested mildly. "I think it was John that you were hating. Hate is so often our insufficient way of showing love. You see when you married you were—or he thought you were—part of his rightness. You had to *be* right for John! I expect he thought you were perfect.

"But you see we are all imperfect human beings; we can't always be in the right—not even John. If you had not had to be so right you could have shared your anger against the Nazi officer with John, you might even have given up the ward, or when you wanted so very much to take your unborn child to England, you might have insisted on taking it. I do not say this would have been the best thing to do, because these over-powering wishes against the wishes of someone else whom we think we love, are very seldom right. The only safe way of controlling a wish, is by loving more than wishing. You need not—for instance—when your baby died, have gone back into the ward you hated, in order to face this cruel, taunting Nazi; instead of killing him, you might even have let a less experienced nurse look after him."

Elizabeth's wits beat round her brain to find an answer. She felt instinctively and with passion that

Michael was cruelly wrong. And yet could she deny that she had felt a deepening resentment against John, a resentment that had begun before the knowledge that she was to have a child?

"You can continue your confession now," Michael said at last.

Elizabeth stared down at the little book in her hands. She found she hadn't anything of her own to say any more—but the words she had learned by heart were still there. She recaptured them slowly from the page; and said them, one by one.

Then Michael spoke. She had not thought his voice was so resonant. She heard every word of the Absolution as if she were hearing it for the first time. It was as if a foreign language had suddenly become plain to her.

By and by Michael said, "Elizabeth, I have taken off my stole, and I want to talk with you a little. Will you get up and sit beside me?"

Elizabeth moved then, and looked at Michael. To her surprise, he looked as if nothing had happened. Yet she had really murdered Andreas von Brandt, and Michael now knew that she was a murderess.

"Now you have told me all this," Michael said in his usual friendly voice, "we can talk more easily about the trouble between you and John. I am free to tell you now, that though I think you were quite right to take the full responsibility for this great sin upon your shoulders, yet actually I think John shares it—just as you share his pain. Fortunately—for we should not make very good judges—we are none of us in a position to judge each other. Each of us sees with his own eyes, and he can seldom tell what the other one sees—or why he sees it. John thought far too much about his Sanatorium, and the great trust everyone had in him.

It wasn't really his—any more than it was yours. He let himself be absorbed away from you, when you needed him most. The child-to-be was his business as well as yours. I am sure, though you have not told me so, that during this difficult period of the War and of your pregnancy, you felt yourself very much alone.

"You would not have wanted to have your child born in England with your parents, rather than in Switzerland with John, if you had not felt estranged from John—and for this he had probably given you good cause.

"John was not enough with you, in this new life, the responsibility for which you shared equally. To marry is to share, and if we will not share—to the uttermost farthing of our emotions and our principles—we lose what we once possessed in each other. When we first love and look at a blade of grass—we see it double."

"Yes!" Elizabeth agreed. "Yes! Between us, for those first years, it was just like that. All my life—and everything in it—was enriched by John. How did you know that?"

"Well—all love is the same," Michael told her, "until we vitiate it by our selfishness. Love creates and contains everything. Do you remember the poem of Shelley's you once read to me—where he says: 'For to divide is not to take away'? Only a man who had loved very deeply would have dared to say a thing like that. Most of us divide in order to take away—because we are such poor lovers! John took away something from you when he grew too absorbed in the Sanatorium, and then you took away something from John, when you wanted to take his baby away from him, into immediate danger. What a punishment! That is where your difficulty began. Now you will learn to begin to put something back. You know now that God

87

is with you—so you can safely become more and more alive!"

"You look very tired," Elizabeth said with quick compunction. "I shall leave you at once, or Sister Peckham will be very angry. I *will* try to put things back! But Michael—before I go—can you tell me if I *do*, if I *can* put things back—will John ever forgive me? After all, I can't make him!"

Michael's eyes fixed hers with a shining intensity. "Elizabeth," he said, "you must!"

11

The snowfall was over. The low grey sky brooded heavily above the little valley muffled to its eyelids under its new, soft blanket. Not a peak was visible. The Sanatorium stood behind its screen of white-capped black pines, without stir or sound, lifeless as a phantom.

This was the hour of silence. No footfall must be heard, no careless voice raised between two and four o'clock in the afternoon. Woe betide the nurse who let a door slip out of her hand, or a cup tinkle! Even the doctors moved warily about the hospital as if they were mere mortals, and had footfalls like anybody else's.

Patients slept, or since it was also the hour of rising temperatures, their restlessness fought against their exhaustion, till they gave up sleep and took to reading. If they had anxieties besides their illness, this was the moment in their long day when these monsters came out of their dens, and insisted on due notice; it was also the hour when Caroline's dreams took their most masterful and alluring shapes. But to which shape this afternoon should she devote her sculptor's hand? Should she absorb herself once more in John's presence or that of this engaging interloper who had taken his place on his morning visit?

If she could choose, Caroline asked herself, who was to come again before next nightfall, which should it be? She knew very well that for the long run, only in John's firm and reassuring presence could she find the strength she needed to live. She craved for John's voice, his steady eyes, his unchanging concentration. She knew that her life would burn itself to nothingness without him.

But there was another lighter self in Caroline, one that mocked and wanted to be mischievous, a poltergeist that could only be happy mislaying the treasures of others, or rapping sensitive and unsuspecting persons over the knuckles.

This self of Caroline's yearned for an irresponsible and ruthless playfellow; and had found one in Konrad Rainer. What happens when two such capricious soul-hunters have each other for a quarry had not occurred to Caroline.

Since she could not influence the decision of who was to be her visitor, Caroline sank deeper into her dreams of what she should do with her playfellow once she had captured him.

At four o'clock Nurse Bessie brought in her tea, and Caroline changed into a dawn-pink jacket. She could afford pink now, for she had her own evening colour to match it, and her dark blue eyes were brightened by fever. After tea, time stood still. The grey world had turned black, and Caroline in her little world of emptiness and light had forgotten its existence.

There were three books Caroline could read while her impatience mounted. Shakespeare was on her reading board to impress John, because he really read Shakespeare when he had time to read anything; a detective story was hidden under Caroline's pillows; and a more serious novel, that had something to do with tracking down a panther, lay closest to her hand. Caroline took up each in turn, and found nothing to soothe her excited nerves in any of them. The doctor's red light might spring on at any moment between five and seven. After that, there was only supper, Sister Peckham's final visit; and the endless night. At half past six Caroline rang the white bell for Nurse Bessie. She had to ask her where the doctors were, although she felt it a confession of weakness. Nurse Bessie was, however, so low in the hierarchy of Sanatorium authorities that it hardly mattered if she thought Caroline weak or not.

"I suppose," Caroline said, "they must be somewhere about, though they're fearfully late! Is there an avalanche or ski accident or anything to account for their being so late?"

"Dr. MacTaggart is still with his operation case," Nurse Bessie told her, "and Dr. Rainer has been and gone. He only looked in at the Padre on this floor."

"Do you mean to say that I'm not to see a doctor tonight at all?" Caroline demanded furiously.

"Well—it looks like it, doesn't it?" Nurse Bessie said with cheerful indifference. "Of course Sister'll look in before she goes off!"

"I never heard of such a thing in my life!" Caroline cried indignantly. "I've always seen a doctor every evening for two months since I came! Why—I don't even sit up except to have my bed made! I must be *just* as ill as that man next door—whether he's a priest or not!"

"You know what doctors are," Nurse Bessie replied indulgently. "They do *have* favourites—say what you will! I've known some doctors that like men patients better than women—and the chief's one of them. He takes trouble to make the stupidest man—even the one that throws his food about in the second block—interested in something. Of course it's quite the other way round with Dr. Rainer; he takes far the longest time with women patients, especially the young ones; but

he hasn't had a chance to meet our Padre till today—
and he's heard that everyone in the hospital adores
him. You can't get the porter out of Father Bretherton's
room, when he brings him his paper!"

"Why do people like him so much?" Caroline demanded. "I should have thought he was the least
interesting of men!"

Nurse Bessie lightly balanced herself against the
bottom of the bed, a tiresome habit in nurses, which
Caroline usually corrected.

"It's funny," Nurse Bessie admitted, "I can't see
what there is to see in him myself, but I do like going
in there! He smiles at you like a good baby and whatever you want seems to be what *he* wants. He doesn't
put it on either, he doesn't seem to put *anything* on!
It makes you feel quite at home with him somehow."

Caroline frowned. Nurse Bessie's remarks sounded
to her a poor explanation of charm. The trouble with
Nurse Bessie was, that she was common, she was
quite ready to tell you things, but what she had to tell
was never what Caroline wanted to hear. Still Caroline
thought it did no harm to impress her, on the low level
at which she lived.

"I am going to be his first *real* visitor," Caroline
told Nurse Bessie importantly. "He wishes it, and Dr.
MacTaggart has agreed. Of course, nurses talking to
him doesn't count. If you're going to see Sister, you
might just tell her that I'm feeling extremely ill tonight."

Nurse Bessie made a face, not a rude or unkind face,
but one of mingled consternation and amusement.
Fancy telling Sister a thing like that! She saw in
advance the freezing look Sister would give her, before
she asked: "What are her symptoms?" and if you
couldn't produce suitable symptoms, then you'd find

there was something the matter with *you* rather than with the patient.

Still, Nurse Bessie did just mention to Sister, before she went off duty, that Miss Draycott's temperature was a degree higher than usual.

Sister Peckham charted the fact in silence; but a few minutes later, she stood by Caroline's side.

Caroline was crying bitterly. It was just about the most dangerous thing Caroline could do, and Caroline was doing it with extreme thoroughness; she shook herself with sobs.

"Please tell me what is the matter?" Sister asked in her most non-conducting tones.

"I—I don't know!" Caroline gasped. "I'm just—just ill!"

"You were ill a few hours ago when I saw you last—without crying," Sister Peckham said. "Other patients too are ill, but they don't cry. You must surely have some reason for it?"

"I'm terribly unhappy!" Caroline sobbed.

Sister Peckham stood silently beside her, with a complete absence of either annoyance or sympathy.

At last Caroline's sobs died down. "I wish you'd go away!" she said crossly.

"I will go away soon," Sister Peckham agreed, "but I am going to make a suggestion first. If I bring you some cold water to bathe your eyes, you'll look quite nice again. That pink dressing jacket suits you—and then perhaps you would like to see a visitor. No-one tiring, of course—and not for long—but Dr. Delarabrie, the radiologist, often visits patients. I notice she cheers people up. It's usually the French and Swiss she sees most of, naturally, because of the language. German she won't speak, though she can—but our Americans like her. She speaks English as well as anybody."

Caroline hesitated. She saw Marie Céleste once a week for her X-ray. She thought her cold and crisp, rather like a fresh lettuce; on the edge of being interesting, but too old to matter. Marie Céleste must be at least thirty. She had untidy short red curls, a wide mouth, and eyes that seemed to take you in without letting anything out. Caroline would certainly not get much sympathy from Marie Céleste; but she might get some information.

Caroline knew from Nurse Bessie that Marie Céleste was an intimate friend of Elizabeth's, and also of Konrad's. An old flame, Nurse Bessie had said; an old flame burnt out, Caroline decided, might provide her with exactly what she wanted. So she said at last, to the motionless peak towering above her, in icy serenity, "Yes, please, if she would care to come and see me, Sister. I've been alone all day—I should like to see a puff adder if it would talk to me!"

"Puff adders are noiseless, so I have been told," Sister said, "though of course poisonous. Rattlesnakes make an effective sound, but not as some people believe by way of warning. It's simply the snake's method of bringing up its poison. As soon as you have bathed your eyes, I will telephone Dr. Delarabrie."

Sister Peckham's bathing was both soothing and successful. She left Caroline with wet pads on her eyelids, returning in five minutes to present her with her powder compact and a hand mirror.

"As soon as you have drunk this milk, Dr. Delarabrie will come up," Sister Peckham told her.

Caroline had not meant to drink her evening milk, but with Sister Peckham's eye upon her, she drank it, and indeed found it unexpectedly palatable; for although Caroline did not know it, Sister Peckham had laced it with brandy.

Marie Céleste had just come from a cocktail party. She was dressed in sherry-coloured taffeta, and her red-gold hair was tidier than usual. Her heavy-lidded green eyes danced at Caroline.

"I wish you'd been at the party," she told her. "Swiss and Americans mixed! The Swiss, never very *mouvementés*, drank themselves stiller than ever; the Americans, always quick, became faster and faster; but all of them drank; and after they had drunk—what they said to each other became—for them—amusing! I myself hardly touch alcohol, for I find things amusing enough without it. My father used to tell me: 'Never say you *don't* drink alcohol to Americans: it's a slap in the face! Just keep your glass three quarters full, and take what seems a sip occasionally. You can pour the remainder away before you go—into a flower pot.' But I hear you've had a dull enough day without having to listen to people talk, whose minds are half-seas over."

"It didn't begin by being very dull," Caroline confessed, "but this afternoon was long. I can't think what happened to the doctors. I have always seen Dr. MacTaggart however busy he was, for a few minutes after tea—and I'm certainly *not* any better than usual!"

"With this illness—in a day—one doesn't change much," Marie Céleste agreed, "though I find that patients are often not as ill—or even as well—as they feel. It was probably his rib-section boy that kept Dr. MacTaggart absorbed. A big operation—the arch had to go as well! These majors are a great shock to any system, even though the patient knows nothing whatever about it—hardest of all for the young. Older people have already survived many shocks, and reconciled themselves to losses; that makes the nerves tough."

"Does it really?" Caroline asked with interest. She knew that Marie Céleste had once been a heroine of the French Résistance; but this was a long time ago, and being a heroine had made very little difference to her appearance. It was her dress that really interested Caroline. It had been made by a very great artist; every time she moved, Caroline noticed afresh that it followed the fine and definite lines of Marie Céleste's slim figure. Marie Céleste might easily have passed for a boy; but in this dress she was very certainly not a boy. Perhaps after all she knew, and knew in a different way, more about Caroline's fictitious lovers, than Caroline herself.

"You see," Caroline said, "the only people I see, who *can* talk—because I don't count nurses: nobody could ever really *want* to talk to Sister Peckham, unless they were *more* interested in clean sheets than anything —*are* the doctors. So if I don't see them, it *is* dull. Though I daresay in a way you know them much better than I do. You can go out ski-ing with them— and to dances—and I have just to lie here stupidly and be looked at! Besides, they're *paid* to look after me, and they're *not* paid for looking after you—so I can't know whether they like me or not—and you can!"

"What you say is very just," agreed Marie Céleste with a kindly smile, "and I have often thought it very boring indeed, for the young, to learn to lie still all day long; for to move is life. But you are storing up strength to move with—you will move in time! And I will tell you this—I do not think a doctor's being paid concerns them very much; they think like artists with absorption of their work itself. Scientists and artists— perhaps also saints—are in a way the same; for what they think of most is something other than material advantage. Of this they may think too, but the best of them not so much. John is the son of a lumber king in Canada—a very rich man—but he lives most simply, and would not mind if he lived simpler still. When he wants a thing it is for the Sanatorium—for some sick person who cannot afford it—or perhaps for Elizabeth who is just as simple as he is. To such a man each patient is as it were a fresh romance. As for me, to Dr. MacTaggart I am only a colleague. If I do my work well he values me."

"But you know Konrad Rainer not only as a colleague," Caroline observed. "You saved his life, didn't you, from the Germans?"

Marie Céleste's slanting eyebrows rose a little—so did her slender shoulders. It was as though she pushed a weight off them, that was always there.

"In those days," she said lightly, "there was so much danger that we had no time to notice whose life was saved by whom. One only noticed if anyone lost a life that might have been saved. I must admit that was distinctly noticeable."

Marie Céleste's rather large mouth gave a little twist. Suddenly Caroline realised that Marie Céleste knew much more than she did. There were layers beyond layers of living behind those cold green eyes. Nor did these layers only concern herself. The world Marie Celeste lived in, and had so often nearly died for, gleamed for a moment before Caroline's eyes—fugitive, disinterested and real—then as suddenly she was talking to a woman, who took photographs every week or so, of her lungs. Caroline was once more the centre of her universe, and the world outside her—like the peaks and the stars—invisible.

"How terrible," Caroline remarked, "that war-time existence must have been; and I was almost a baby and knew nothing of it!"

Marie Céleste smiled politely. She did not say that, to her, Caroline was a baby still.

"In those days," Caroline continued, not yet having found out what she wanted to know, "when you were both in such constant danger, I mean—you must have got to know each other awfully well."

"For acquaintance there was also very little time," Marie Céleste answered. "How much physical strength a comrade had—if he was too thirsty, too lazy, too sleepy—perhaps if he talked too much—for the job required—that was of course most on our minds. Also, there was our mission—if at the moment we had a mission. Some things we noticed specially about each other, of course—reliability—accuracy—speed—and also which of the five senses we had that were most needed. A person who knocked things over—or who was unpunctual—was an added burden. I often think I should have liked Sister Peckham with us because she keeps so still! Konrad moved like a wild animal—you could never hear him till you saw him. That was often useful, and he had a wonderfully keen sense of hearing; this makes him very good now listening to the sounds from shaky lungs—for he still has it. John too would have been good to work with. He is reliable, he has a time sense, and would always be—somehow or other—where he was most needed. As for Elizabeth, she would have made an excellent all round comrade—only she asks too little. She asks nothing. She would fall to pieces without asking anything. That I find exaggerated."

"You seem to like Elizabeth very much," Caroline said, watching her guest narrowly.

"I do—indeed," Marie Céleste replied a trifle drily.

There was a short pause.

"Then don't you think," Caroline ventured, "that it would be much better if she and John divorced? They don't seem happy at all together. It seems rather a waste they shouldn't have partners they might make happy—and be happy with as well?"

The light of Caroline's reading lamp showed up Marie Céleste's clear profile. It seemed to have become suddenly even more definite and older. "Who can tell?" she murmured. "Is divorce a prescription for happiness? There are other reasons for unhappiness besides marriage to the wrong person—if he is the wrong person. There is more than one skin to an onion!"

Marie Céleste smiled, a smile that seemed to Caroline extraordinarily suggestive, and yet which suggested nothing at all simple. It was impossible to say what Marie Céleste's smile suggested—beyond its subtlety.

"Now I must go," she said, "or else Sister Peckham will say that I am giving you a bad night. I hope that you will sleep very well indeed, and wake to a day that will be very much less dull!"

Caroline did not want Marie Céleste to go just when their conversation had reached so interesting a point, but she had not time to say so, before Marie Céleste, with an exquisite swirl of the sherry-coloured taffeta, had reached the door, and with a wave of her narrow, hard little hand, had vanished.

12

*M*arie Céleste watched John covertly as he packed his rucksack. Perhaps he had seen through her trick, but if he had, it suited his necessities so well that he welcomed it. Old Peter Taugwalder and his son Ernst were delighted to ring John up and suggest a chamois-hunt on the Rettenstein. They really *had* sighted a chamois above the tree line, the day before. The snow was as fresh and firm as a girl's cheek; and with luck the weather would hold another forty-eight hours.

The worst was over. John had seen the boy's parents and made all those necessary, insignificant arrangements which release the living from the dead.

Defeat and misery, Marie Céleste had expected to see in John's face, for all doctors feel defeat at the death of a patient, and some feel misery. But why did John look guilty?

The operation had been conservative and beautifully performed. Marie Céleste was present in the theatre, and had seldom seen more inspired craftsmanship. Nor had one expedient been overlooked in the long uphill fight for the boy's life afterwards. John had massaged the boy's heart with tireless patience, till it stopped.

"*Der kleiner Bub ist schön fort,*" Karl had told Marie Céleste as she came in from a late run to the village. It was as if his little spirit had passed her going out, as she came in. That was all that there was to it—the little boy was out; but it was not all that John was making of it.

Suddenly John raised his head and stared at her with blank amazement. It was Elizabeth whistling like a blackbird. The high, ringing, under-water notes stopped abruptly. Elizabeth stood in the open doorway, her eyes shining and her cheeks aglow.

"Peter told me," she said breathlessly. "I'm going too."

For two years Elizabeth had neither whistled nor shone; but, Marie Céleste thought a little grimly, she had not chosen a good moment to begin.

John bent his head to finish strapping his rucksack.

"Nonsense, Elizabeth," he said with cutting finality. "It's quite out of the question for you to come with us."

"But why, John?" this new Elizabeth insisted. "What question *is* it out of? I'm dressed and ready! All my jobs are done."

"Any question!" John said ruthlessly. "This is a chamois-hunt—only suitable for men—not a ski tour. We shall go great distances and at a great pace. You have never hunted on skis, or off them. The hut is ice cold—and the idea of your staying there by yourself is simply ridiculous."

"I shall only go with you *as* a cook," Elizabeth explained breathlessly. "There's heaps to do in a hut if it's fine. While you're away hunting, I shall get firewood in the pines below, and ski by myself on the easy slopes. Ernst has trained me—you haven't seen me ski for ages! I've just been talking with Peter and Ernst in the hall. They say the Rettenstein would be a piece of cake for me—and I've an awfully nice *new* frying pan in my rucksack and a Tommy cooker."

John gave Marie Céleste a look of instant dismissal. The brittle framework of civility between man and wife shook visibly, but he did not want publicly to deflate Elizabeth, even before the eyes of their most intimate friend.

"What is a man's tour?" Marie Céleste provokingly demanded. "Something biologically more advanced—or just something men like to keep to themselves because it's more fun?"

John threw his rucksack across his shoulders, and without a glance at either of the women clattered out of the room. Calling to the guides as he passed them that he would meet them at the station, John fastened on his skis, and drove himself headlong into the icy darkness.

The road from the Sanatorium dipped steeply in a series of zigzags between the pine woods, towards the valley.

The trees flew past him, their dark clutch opening, and closing above his head and giving him sudden glimpses of the severe edged constellations, blazing their implacable trail across the sky. John knew the road and its hairpin bends by heart, but if he was to meet anything tonight, he would probably kill himself ski-ing against it. No matter if he did; the drunkenness of speed had entered into him, and helped to dull the keen edge of his mind. Now he could come to terms with death, and accept it as part of the landscape, without feeling that he had let the boy be snatched from him by a gangster.

The thing that had happened weighed on John like a crime—but it was not a crime—it was a cruel accident for which fate, John told himself defiantly, was wholly responsible. When John was quite certain that the boy was dead, he had gone straight upstairs to Michael.

"Michael, he's dead!" he had told him. "My boy's dead, the one I operated on yesterday morning!" He knew he oughtn't to have spoken to any patient about the death of another, but he had felt like a child taking his broken toy to his mother; and Michael had looked at him, just as his mother used to look at him long ago, as if his broken toy was a sad, but not a final, dilemma. Michael hadn't said anything, but he had suffered with John, as if by sharing the boy's death, he could lessen John's agony at the boy dying; and John had strangely felt his agony lessened.

It was the sense of responsibility that still remained gnawing at his very vitals. He had not *let* the boy die, but was there something in the back of his mind that had been interfering with the purity of his concentration?—a piece of spiritual sabotage so small as to be invisible even now—a piece of grit caught in the delicate machinery of a surgeon's automatic skill? Had his *whole* mind been clean before he had acted? He reminded himself—pitching head forward into a pool of moonlight—that he had not seen Caroline alone since he kissed her. Had he been right to leave her without a word? And had the sense that he was shirking a duty clogged the full freedom of his working mind? This was surely nonsense. Cannot any expert craftsman work as well with a bad conscience as with a good one? Yet in what sense did Shakespeare mean that conscience makes cowards of us all? He must have meant something because great poets never say things without meaning them.

Shakespeare was also—apparently—a great sinner. Had that by any chance made him see more clearly? Could you know what takes place in the whole man from a violated conscience, unless you had violated your own conscience?

The road ceased to drop and John's pace forcibly slowed. He stood for a moment in the sudden taut silence, that took the place of his noisy passage. Far off he could hear through the icy stillness Elizabeth's clear voice talking to the guides. So she had come after all, in spite of his disapproval! He felt now that perhaps there would be no great harm done in her having come, since the guides wanted it. Elizabeth always got on well with uneducated people. She acted as if there was no inherent value in privilege. Her dignity was for others rather than for herself.

What John had once liked most about Elizabeth was the way in which she met obligation—any obligation— as if it were on the same level as herself, never as if she had to stoop to meet it; until she failed to meet the greatest obligation of all, and cut the ground of living from under both their feet.

He was at the station at last; he had done the three miles in under fifteen minutes. He took the tickets and after a moment's hesitation included one for Elizabeth. She was his wife, and it would look odd to the station-master as well as the guides if he didn't take her ticket. When he saw Elizabeth, standing under one of the station lights a few minutes later, she looked as young as Caroline, though she was actually seven years older.

The diminutive mountain train puffed its slow casual way from village to village, whistling its long uncertain whistle, and stopping jerkily before and after every tunnel, until at last they reached the empty, silvery slopes of the Rettenstein, and found themselves spilled out on the crisp snow, under the stars. There was no village, only a few far off farms edged themselves into the black masses of the pine forest, twinkling like dropped stars.

The Taugwalders knew their mountain, and led them by the quickest way through the pines, on to the towering snow fields above them. None of them spoke as

104

they climbed, except for an occasional swear word if an invisible patch of *Harsch* trapped them, or a ski struck against a snow-covered stone, so that the rhythm of their climb was broken. The men led by turns, but one of the guides was always above, and one below, Elizabeth.

Occasionally the leader paused, and they all paused with him, to slow the heavy knocking of their hearts. They could see now the dim world about them. Deep troughs of shadow alternated with shining slopes; but the peak itself, towards which they climbed, remained invisible.

The cold moved silently against them, stinging their lips and eyes.

John's shadow shot gigantically upwards through the moonlight, till the sky swallowed it. "He is always taller and higher than anyone else!" Elizabeth thought half proudly and half resentfully. "I know that it was awful of me to come, and I shouldn't have whistled; but he can't get that dead boy out of his head unless something else gets into it. Being angry with me *must* be better for him than the dead boy; besides, he's more used to it. But it's funny that I don't feel more upset when *he's* so upset. Usually I can't bear it and crumble into bits!"

A falling star skirted the mountain, and shot downwards through space, as if a child had flung it out of a careless hand. Their four lonely shadows hardly seemed to belong to the earth, but to be hanging on the curve of a dark ball silvered with moonlight—a ball that moved as easily as a dancer. "If we listened hard enough," Elizabeth thought to herself, "there would be music," and she thought of Holst's "Planets" sinking into space, with their shining notes reverberating from distance to distance.

They came on the hut suddenly an hour later, on an eyelid of mountain, deeply bedded in snow, and hung with long blue icicles thicker than a man's thigh.

They had to use their axes to cut themselves into the hut, but once inside they found a neatly stacked wood pile, and a stone fireplace. Four bunks had been built into the walls, two on each side, stuffed with hay mattresses.

In half an hour comfort was blazing all round them, and Elizabeth, happily crouching over the fire, was preparing the supper she had planned. To take the raw materials of food and make them into a work of art was Elizabeth's greatest joy. She liked to come into direct contact with appetite, and satisfy it. Above all she liked to satisfy John's appetite. Whatever John might still be feeling about her company, she saw with secret delight that he thoroughly enjoyed her meal.

Everyone had enough, and yet could have eaten twice as much. "That," Elizabeth thought to herself, "is the secret of a good meal!"

They discussed the mountain, the habits of chamois, and the chances of the snow. There was thirty degrees of frost, and the temperature was still falling. Whatever was frozen now would stay frozen for at least the next twenty-four hours.

The guides took out their tobacco pouches, and their long hoped-for pipes, and when they had prepared them, they looked eagerly at Elizabeth.

Elizabeth knew what they wanted. She sat with her arms clasped round her knees, and watching the firelight went over in her mind the words and tunes of the *Lieder* that were a part of their lives.

But dare she sing them? Would not John be upset to hear her voice again? Must she take steps away from him, just when she felt, welling up within her, the strength to reach him?

106

Yet what she had was surely hers to give, whether John would take it or not? For so long her sin had been a wall that stood between them—impossible to climb. The sin was still there. It was irrevocable; but now there was no wall—she was forever free. Elizabeth raised her head, and her voice, clear and light as a young boy's, filled the hut with music.

She sang their own district song that both men loved; and then they chose their favourites in turn, first Peter, and then Ernst, joining in the singing. Although John had a good voice and knew the words, he did not sing with them. He sat quite still with his head turned away from Elizabeth; yet she thought there was no rigidity in his body, his blood ran as theirs ran, into the homely, nostalgic tunes. It was not John, but Elizabeth herself who said, "There, that's enough. You'll have too short a night!"

They took up their old ritual of mountain habits, each going out by turn into the silver world, returning to his hay mattress, and the dark.

The moon had plunged behind the peak, but the stars still divided up the darkness. The Milky Way stretched like the white skein of a bride's veil, across the sky. The hay rustled, good nights were offered and returned, the firelight flickered and died down into red ash; but before the slow invasion of the cold reached them, they were all four fast asleep.

John was the last awake. He had stiffened himself against the beauty of Elizabeth's voice, but the peasant songs, creeping into his heart unaware, had eased him of its heaviness. He could hear Elizabeth's breathing close beneath him; it was as light and easy as a child's. The thought of her so near him, and asleep, made him think of Desdemona, his favourite of all Shakespeare's heroines, the one—he used to think—most like

Elizabeth. Elizabeth had the same gay gallantry of spirit that made Desdemona launch herself into Othello's adventures with him; pitying his sufferings, but incapable of pitying herself, could she but have shared them.

Material drawbacks did not exist for Elizabeth any more than they had existed for Desdemona. Once sure of John's heart and her own, she had given up everything she possessed to follow him, and was willing to accept any risk. She too would have stood up against a beloved father's will (in fact, Elizabeth had), and she would have used her wits to match the glittering, civilised white world of Venice, in much the same simple yet subtle manner. Elizabeth would have been ready to take that wild windy voyage to Cyprus alone, to join her dark lover; and been just as innocently tactless in reminding him of Cassio's claims to forgiveness. Othello would have hurt, but not frightened, John's Elizabeth; nor silenced her while there was any sense in speaking; and she would have forced herself back from the clutch of her murderer—as Desdemona did— to shield John from the consequences of his guilt, with the same gallant lie.

There was only one difference between them, John reminded himself. Desdemona had been innocent; and Elizabeth was guilty.

13

A light, familiar touch roused John at dawn. He knew without seeing whose hand had touched him. Three rucksacks neatly packed containing Thermos flasks full of hot coffee and packets of sandwiches stood waiting by their ice axes.

It was still dark when the hunters stumbled out into the dawn. The icy air sucked their breath away from them, as they slowly and painfully climbed upwards. The stars lost their brilliance and shrank back into the hollows of the retreating night. Huge shapes blocked the sky that could no longer hide them. Light without colour took the place of the dark. The peak above them shot up—an ice-white spear—probing the socket of the sky. Shadowy snow fields below them broke, like grey-backed Atlantic waves, against the black line of the pine woods.

The three men reached the rocks below the summit just as the last stars went out.

The whole mountain side cleared itself before them; they could see the edge of the great glacier with its knife-like crevasses blue with ice, crossed by perilous snow bridges. The sun was close behind the peak, and a ray of light caught a small tree venturing above the forest line, turning it into flame.

Nothing moved. There seemed no region of the mountain side that had not been empty for a thousand years. Far, far beneath them the unstirred village lay like a child's toy on the flat valley floor.

The men drank their coffee and ate their sandwiches, taking John's *Gneiss* glasses in turn, to stare out over the limitless expanse.

"A man hunting a chamois must think like a chamois," old Peter told them in his low guttural voice. "These are winter-hunted, famished beasts; they have eaten all the dried leaves and dead grasses they could find in the woods. Now they must venture out onto the snow fields, hunger driven, seeking lichen on the rocks, or what their sharp hooves can kick up beneath the melting snows. They will follow any hope now, this last month of winter, but they will also be aware of any danger. A chamois has a nose that helps him like a good wife."

"Their senses act," Ernst agreed, "more keenly than ours, but it is we who have the guns. Besides, a chamois thinks of his enemy only when panic rouses him, but we can think of him all the time without panic, and can make our plans. To spot the beasts is the main thing. Will the *gnädiger* Herr lend me those glasses again?"

John passed them to him. They spoke in low tones, for every sound was audible for miles; and against the still, unchanging background of the snows, any movement however slight would be visible. A chamois' acute, unhindered senses re-act to every stimulus; most dangerous of all, the air, tainted by the smell of men, travels faster to him than light.

Were those dots like match ends, John asked himself, the stripped branches of a wild cherry, or had the match ends moved? Old Peter took the glasses from him, and pointed a huge wool-covered finger triumphantly downwards. The little group of dots against the snow stood out like a pointillist picture: "Beasts!" he said succinctly. "We keep down wind all the time," he ordered excitedly, "and whatever happens! I will make for the big rock at the top of the North gully—beyond the glacier. There I will sit till the beasts pass me. Ernst will drop straight down the other side of this ridge and work round through the woods up towards them. Ernst, if you get near enough without their hearing you—the shot is yours! If not, drive them upwards towards the gully. You, Herr Doktor, wait, till you see me stationed; then follow under the ridge straight North. Keep the big drops—there are only three of them—well to your left, and stay high, so that the beasts don't see you, till Ernst drives them upwards. Plunge on to them after the top of the gully is past. Go fast and anchor firmly after your jump; turn, before you shoot; and as for me, what you lose I take—and if I lose, the chamois gets the sport, since he escapes! Do not forget that he cannot go as fast as you can, running on skis, but he can jump better than you! Think twice, Herr Doktor, before you follow his jump!"

The old hunter crossed himself, reminding God of their need of Him, bent double and slid away from them, travelling at right angles to the moving dots, with the whole width of the uncrossed glacier between them. Peter had been on the glacier the week before, but though he had studied the chief crevasses well, he went slowly across it, knowing that there might be surprises. Ernst disappeared soundlessly and left John alone, in a pool of golden light.

The sun rounded the peak and burned down on him, warming him from head to foot.

The colourless sky above changed into a deep cloudless vault of gentian blue.

John wondered what Elizabeth was doing alone in the little hut, or on the sunny slopes between it and the pine forest. He could not keep his mind off Elizabeth. In the last few days she had changed, and changed completely. She had lost her apathy, the strain had gone from her eyes and lips. It was as if a burden had literally fallen off her back. She sang with a free heart, and twice yesterday John had heard her laugh. What had caused this sudden transformation? Does a woman regain beauty and gaiety without a lover? Marie Céleste must be right. Konrad was responsible. John had not been mistaken—when he stumbled away in agony from their shared music. They were not making love as his jealous heart had stabbed him into fancying—a much more entire thing had happened—love was re-making them. They were unaware of this swift process, but John could not be. He went over in his mind every incident connecting them for the last week; and all incidents connected them. He saw himself giving Elizabeth up to a vice-ridden man, unnerved and haunted by his past, incapable of rectitude or common sense.

Facts are unalterable, John told himself bitterly. Words cannot change them, dreams break against them. Elizabeth had cut herself off from normal living by an act. Now—if she accepted this lower level of life in Konrad's arms—she would sink yet further. What could he do to save her? Long ago, he had promised her her freedom, and taken his own. He had believed that in a life of hard work and friendly contacts Elizabeth might find, as he himself had found, enough to live on; and eventually regain peace.

John had suffered terribly in Elizabeth's sufferings. There was no deprivation forced upon her by their changed life that he had not felt forced equally upon himself. It had wrung his heart to watch her growing old and sad under his eyes. But it had never occurred to him to change their decision, nor even to gain the relief of discussing it with their dearest friends.

Perhaps in the back of his mind John had felt unsure of their looking at Elizabeth's act as he himself looked at it. People who have been hunted by the German Gestapo for over five years, with torture and death hanging over them by a hair, lose their sense of values. Konrad and Marie Céleste believed in nothing and trusted no-one. They did not even trust themselves. Morally, John had often thought, both of them were wastrels. But they had never betrayed a comrade or lost their nerve in danger. As doctors they were reliable; but even as doctors, in their human relationships with patients or nurses, they were unaccountable. They might be equally unaccountable about Elizabeth. They had good manners—they would not force an unpleasant fact upon John; but it was conceivable that they would think it a very good thing for Elizabeth to take a lover. They did not know Elizabeth as John knew her; nor that when she once saw plainly what she was doing, she would say, and mean it, as Desdemona had said and meant it, "I would not do such a thing for all the world."

John took up his glasses and watched Peter crossing the glacier. The old hunter moved with slow persistence, as a caterpillar moves forward on the leaf it is eating. From moment to moment nothing visible happens to the caterpillar or the leaf, but suddenly there is no more leaf, and the caterpillar has slid himself on to the next one. Old Peter was now across the glacier; inching himself onward towards the big rock above the North gully, he became part of it. Nothing moved any more. The dots were out of sight. The whole world was wrapped in a deep golden stillness.

It was time that John himself was off. He hitched the straps of his rucksack, and found that he had come to a decision. Elizabeth by her ridiculous and childish confession had freed John to talk with Michael. There *was* someone now who shared their secret, someone whom John could trust to take no light view of murder, and who would certainly not encourage Elizabeth to break any other moral law.

He did not know how he had arrived at this decision, but he knew that he was relieved by having arrived at it.

The snow was alive and sparkling with blue lights, his ski blades cut through the glittering surface with the easy swiftness of a knife. Every breath he drew filled his body with new relish.

As he rose out of a hollow, the dots appeared again; they were moving faster, as if they had begun to suspect some challenge to their speed. Perhaps the snow-fields promised them nothing and they intended to leave the mountain altogether. He must take to the ridge again and move quickly to be exactly above them, if they turned.

It was a long, wearisome trek, the sun ached into his shoulders. John could seldom allow himself the relaxation of a run; when he moved downward, it was only to negotiate a hollow or to avoid too steep a drop.

Suddenly the dots paused; some sound had reached them, differing from the accustomed hiss and thud of soft snow falling from a tree. Their leader guessed that something alien and alive was violating their sanctuary.

He leapt onto a rock, and sniffed the tell-tale air suspiciously, while the herd waited.

Now was John's moment. The run was clear beneath him. Crouching low, he swung off into space. There was no seeing anything now beyond immediate dips and climbs. The leader sprang from his rock, and bounded away, the herd following him. John took his jump then, slewed himself sharply round, and found the youngest and leanest of the band within his range. Scrambling uneasily over the mid-day softened surface of the snow, panic and inexperience slowed the chamois to his doom; but inexplicably John held his fire. He could still feel beneath his surgeon's fingers the struggling muscle he was trying to free—stop; and life stop with it. This young chamois, trying to take what should have been his last leap, seemed part of the dead boy's ineffectual struggle. John, turning his head away from the floundering beast, knew that he could not kill, what he had tried to save.

The leader swerved wide of the North gully, and the herd passed rapidly out of sight; but not out of sound, for a minute later John heard old Peter's shot.

14

All day long John kept his muscles at a stretch and his mind empty. John and Ernst had gone off by themselves for their second day's hunting, to a higher peak behind the Rettenstein; while old Peter, satisfied with his prowess of the day before, helped Elizabeth cut wood for the hut's next visitors. It was a vigorous golden day and the chamois kept themselves persistently invisible. Nothing happened, the snow held firm. The Kitzhörn was a hard mountain to ski over, with more disagreeable surprises than the Rettenstein; once or twice they tasted danger, and escaped it only by a fraction. It was curiously kind and comforting to return at night to the warmth of the hut, and an astonishing last meal from Elizabeth.

It was not until they had turned towards their own familiar valley into the woods that John felt his accustomed drag of anxiety about the hospital. Was anyone worse? Had anything happened? There was a desperate tubercular laryngitis case that the streptomycin injections hadn't yet quite got hold of—a young railway guard from Bern with a wife and two children; he must save him. And there was Father Bretherton—he was using his voice too much—better put him back onto silence for a week or two. John felt about the Sanatorium as a pregnant woman feels about her unborn child. He knew when it was at rest; and when it was restless, he was restless with it.

There seemed nothing wrong as he looked up at the big building surrounded by its pines.

Patients were on their balconies or carrying out the slight exertions and easy efforts permitted to them. The sunny air rang with voices and laughter.

Freedom and occupation, John thought to himself, were his chief allies in his fight against T.B. How to fit these habits of mind into the pattern of a man's weakened organ was his major problem.

Somehow today he did not want to stop and speak to those happy outdoor patients. A sense of quickening urgency drove him into the house. Before Marie Céleste met him in the hall, he knew that something was wrong.

"Alors! c'est toi, Jean," she said in a quick undertone. "I must speak to you alone, before there is time for you to change!"

John caught Elizabeth's quick look of participation change to acceptance of exclusion. He had a sudden curious feeling that he wanted her not to be excluded this time; but he followed Marie Céleste into her office without asking Elizabeth to join them.

"Tiens!" Marie Céleste said with dry relief. "Something absurd has happened! Not terrible! As you see, the Sanatorium is not burned down and no patient has died. But that little bitch of yours, Caroline, declares that Konrad has raped her! There has been a fine to-do about it! Sister Peckham believes her. Nurse Oliver would like to murder her—and possibly Konrad into the bargain. Caroline wants to kill herself, but unfortunately does not quite know how. There has been no common sense whatever about the whole affair."

This then was what was lurking in the back of John's mind. He had not given one thought to Caroline for the past three days; but he had known something was wrong for which he felt himself directly responsible.

He rocked back on his heels and glanced at Marie Céleste as if she were to blame for the whole affair. "You are certain," he demanded, "that nothing really happened—or are you trying to cover up for Konrad?"

Marie Céleste's eyebrows and shoulders rose together.

"About rape," she assured him, "I am something of an expert. One does not get raped unless one wants to—without some alteration in one's clothes. I saw Caroline ten minutes after the incident was supposed to have taken place. Her very pretty nightgown and bed jacket were not even disarranged.

"Also, about Konrad I know something. He would be incapable of using force to a woman—he is far too vain—he wants to be admired for himself. Besides, for a Viennese, what attraction has a skinny scarecrow? Caroline would arouse no feelings in him but pity and a little mockery. He is also very much afraid of infection. No! Anything that happened to Caroline, happened because she *was* Caroline and for no other reason."

"It's her lung condition that matters," John muttered, taking up the telephone. "She sounds quiet enough for the moment," he added a moment later, hanging up the receiver. "I'll take a shower and change, and see each of them in turn. Have you been able to keep the thing out of the hospital?"

"As quiet as a place can be kept when a girl is shrieking the house down," Marie Céleste answered sharply. "Lungs—she must have wonderful lungs, that one—to put up such a barrage of sound! Naturally I offered to make an examination, but that was taken as a fresh assault. She sent up a temperature of 106° last night and had a collapse at dawn today. The imagined rape took place on Saturday. The priest next door was dragged in this morning by Sister Peckham, who thought her dying. I was however convinced that Caroline would outlast us all. I gave her a shot of morphia to keep her quiet, and by now she is none the worse, I fancy—perhaps a little exhausted. The priest next door is also no doubt exhausted. Sister Peckham—truculent virgin as she is—has never slept a wink since. Nurse Oliver changes guard with her at intervals—she too may be exhausted. Konrad was, as you know, at one time her lover. He is drinking himself into a stupor; and I too am exhausted from using so much self control in order not to slap Caroline! One good hysteric can exhaust a regiment! Now go! Take your shower—and begin to function! Some time tonight when it is all over come and tell me about it. At present I have had enough of it. I prefer my photographs to your Caroline! They do not make a noise and they tell me the truth!"

When John confronted Sister Peckham a quarter of an hour later, he was horrified at her appearance. She had green shadows in her colourless gaunt face, her eyes had receded into the back of her head, and her very lips were white. "If she doesn't take care she'll develop jaundice," John said to himself. He listened in silence to her version of Caroline's story.

"Here is her chart," Sister Peckham wound up with acid indignation. "Saturday afternoon is when this incident took place, on his second visit alone to her. As you know, I deplore this practice. A nurse should always accompany the doctor on the prolonged visits to women patients. I think you must agree with me that a temperature of 106° is a little severe for *nothing* to have happened! I had to ice-pack her for fear of

119

brain fever. This morning there was a complete collapse, and as she asked for Father Bretherton, I thought it better to have him taken in to her. I don't think it did him any harm, and she was quieter after it. Dr. Delarabrie administered morphia. She doesn't believe a word of it. In fact, she suggested making a—a test, but this I couldn't tolerate in the patient's condition. I hope it won't be necessary! The very idea of a young girl being handled in such a way is deeply repugnant to me! Besides, I *did* see him coming out of her room with a red mark down one side of his face. I don't want to harp upon it—but doctors don't slap themselves."

"Still, Sister," John said, "a slap doesn't prove a rape. It only proves that Caroline lost her temper with him. We must, I think, have some kind of *evidence* as to exactly what took place. I'm sure you have handled everything splendidly and kept it as quiet as possible. I'm very much obliged to you and Nurse Oliver for taking it in turns not to leave Caroline alone: a very wise precaution under the circumstances. As to doctors seeing their patients alone, it is impossible to give your patients confidence in you with a nurse always at your elbow, and with T.B. confidence in your doctor is half the battle. You must admit, we've been running this hospital for nearly eight years, and nothing of this sort has ever happened before!"

"Happened!" Sister Peckham said coldly. "I might admit nothing has *happened*, but undue excitement *has* taken place! Girls sitting up in bed gnawing at their fingernails, and sending up their temperatures because they think another girl has had a longer visit from one or the other of you! That I *have* observed! And I think it very doubtful if, with so little to do, any sex contacts at all should be tolerated. Doctors are men, and patients are women, and T.B. patients very often *young* women

120

into the bargain. Still, I know it's not for me to indicate policy to my chief!"

John smiled and patted her shoulder. He was shocked that she flinched from his friendly touch. "Now, Sister," he said, "you are the best woman in the world, but you must know as well as I do that it isn't only women who are in danger from such opportunities! What of our men patients nursed by attractive young women? Don't *their* hearts and imaginations run away with them without the nurses being to blame? And if they do—it isn't nearly as bad for them as you think! I'd far rather a patient thought along sex lines than that he or she sat thinking of their own diseases—and so would you!"

Sister Peckham pursed her lips and shook her head. Yet she was sorry that she had moved away from John's friendly hand. On a desert island, in her extreme and not unpleasing youth, she would have known herself safe with John; but not knowing how to express her confidence in him, she merely said with increased stiffness, "Well, all I can say is, sir, if after this you keep Dr. Rainer on your staff, I shall feel obliged to resign!"

15

Michael was peacefully finishing his tea, and wondering where Elizabeth was ski-ing, and what it would be like to be with her on the golden mountain slopes, when Caroline's piercing shrieks shocked him out of his quiet visions.

Sister Peckham's efficient handling soon subdued Caroline's screams into low, agonising moans, but they were no less terrifying to Michael. He bore them for as long as he could, before ringing his bell for an explanation.

Nurse Oliver promptly answered it. Her gentle, sad little face was hardened into a Medusa's stony mask.

"There is nothing whatever for you to be alarmed about," she said sternly. "A patient has had a nerve storm. We regret that you have been disturbed; but she's quieting down now, and there's not likely to be any more of it."

"But, Nurse Oliver," Michael pleaded, "I know those screams were Caroline's! Caroline is my friend. It sounds as if she is in very serious trouble. Can you not let me help in any way—or at least tell me what the trouble is?"

Nurse Oliver frowned, but she became more human.

"Sister Peckham is with her," she said, "and she told me to tell you that it would be quite all right soon, and that you were not to worry. She'll come in herself to see you later, when I'm on duty in her place. We shall take turns sitting with Caroline till Dr. MacTaggart gets back. If you ask me, she's upset *herself*! But there, I don't want to talk about it. Besides, Sister Peckham told me not to! Is there anything I can get for you?"

Michael shook his head. Nurse Oliver could not put his wondering, compassionate heart back into his breast again. He could only wait as if he were a sentry on guard, to prevent danger from reaching Caroline from any invisible direction; but without knowledge of what went on behind the door of Caroline's frantic spirit.

It was not until dawn that Sister Peckham felt free to come to him. She stood by his bedside for a moment without speaking, trying to smile reassuringly at him; and trying at the same time to draw reassurance from him.

"Caroline," she said at last, answering the question in his eyes, for he had not spoken, "has been very much upset. It is a little difficult to be certain what has caused it: no doubt she will tell you her story. She wants urgently to see you now, and I must warn you, she is very ill indeed, and I was afraid of the consequences should I refuse to let her see you. It is against common sense and all hospital rules, to ask you to get up like this, but Caroline's is an exceptional case—it is a *moral* need the poor child has, rather than a physical one; and I felt you were the only person who could help her. So if you agree, I will wheel you into her room in the carrying chair, and stay just outside the door for a few minutes, within call if you need me, and then come in, and bring you back."

"I have been waiting to go to her," Michael said quietly.

He found Caroline almost unrecognisable. Her pin-pointed eyes stared fixedly at him as if they could no longer see what they were looking at. Her face was that of an old woman, and Michael had to admit it—of a very wicked old woman. When they were alone, he asked with deep compassion, "What is it, Caroline—what is troubling you?"

Caroline looked for what seemed an age into his clear eyes, climbing out of the pit of her panic by his tranquillity.

"If I tell you," she said at last, "it's safe, isn't it? You'll never tell anyone what I've said—no matter what it is I tell you—or what they ask you?"

"Whatever you tell me I shall never repeat," Michael promised.

Some of the fierce tension in Caroline's wild eyes slackened.

"All right," she whispered, "it was lies—all lies about Konrad. He never touched me! I just made it up to spite him! Because he wouldn't kiss me! I hate him! How dared he *not* kiss me, when he'd been making love to me with his eyes? Besides I—I asked him—I said he *might*! That's why I slapped him! I'll never forgive him—never! I didn't have to ask John."

There was a long silence. Caroline's quick, shallow breathing was the only sound in the room. She sank further back into her pillows, and her eyes ceased to stare at Michael's questioning eyes; they turned away instead, and fixed themselves on her small weak hands playing continuously with the counterpane.

"Well," she said at last grudgingly, "I suppose—if anything happens to me now—I shall be all right! Don't you have to say something like that to comfort me?"

"No," Michael said consideringly, "I don't have to say anything, Caroline. You see, I can't! You've told me the truth, and that is a good thing to have done; but you haven't done anything about clearing away your lies. You must put things straight first; then I will be glad to give you the comfort of absolution. I have waited all night long. There has not been a moment when I was not anxious to come to you."

Caroline closed her eyes, and considered his remarks in silence. They both confused and irritated her. If Michael was really sorry for her—and she knew that he was sorry—why did he not take her burden away from her at once, and let her die, if she had got to die, in peace with God? She had sent for him to give her absolution, because she could not face death without it.

"I am afraid," she whispered at last. "Why won't you give me peace?"

"But, Caroline," Michael said with inexorable gentleness, "peace is what *you* make yourself. I can't give it to you—I can only tell you how to make it. You must tell John the truth."

"Never!" Caroline whispered, slow tears slipping from her long lashes, down her hollowed cheeks. "Never! Never!"

Didn't Michael have the sense to know that she was dying to punish John? Her dying would be wasted on John, unless she could wring his heart with the remorse she intended him to feel. If she had to die, she must die as an angel, not as a naughty little liar. It was really intensely stupid of Michael not to grasp that what she wanted was to punish John.

Michael sat miserably silent, longing to take from her the burden she would not relinquish. Slowly Caroline lifted her long wet lashes, and gave him a long, appraising look.

"Then if you won't help me—you'd better go away!" she told him severely.

"I will go away," Michael agreed, "but I can always come back, Caroline—whenever you want me. You

125

need not always say no! You can see for yourself—you can't cheat God. Don't die, Caroline, until you've stopped trying to cheat Him!"

A faint, a very faint smile touched Caroline's lips. Michael had grasped one fact then, however stupid he was, the question of dying was still within her hands.

The tears went on sliding down Caroline's cheeks without her volition or control, softening the hardness of her angry heart. Michael had not released her from her trap; but against her will, or perhaps only against part of it, she had felt his deep compassion, and seen that there was a way to release herself. Only, Caroline reminded herself fiercely, she wasn't going to take it.

The blue light showed Sister Peckham's gaunt and implacable figure rising up behind Michael's chair; and Michael felt himself being swept out of the clean emptiness of Caroline's room, into the more brilliant emptiness of the long corridor.

He felt weakened and crushed, as if there was no strength left in him any more; and the worst of it was, he had lost his strength without having given any of it to Caroline. He was a stupid fellow, he told himself, unable to convince or relieve someone who most needed relief and conviction.

Perhaps he had done Caroline active harm; but Sister Peckham said she didn't think he had.

"She's much quieter now," she told Michael with satisfaction. "I shall give her a second injection and she will be certain to go to sleep after it, and I shouldn't wonder if she isn't a great deal better when she wakes up."

16

Michael, waking unrefreshed from an exhausting sleep, found John standing by his side, with the strength and glow of the mountains transfiguring him. John was burnt a deep golden brown, and his eyes shone with health and vigour. Michael, looking up at him, felt as a Patrol lost in the desert might feel, when a Relief Column has found it.

"I hear they've been taking you to do my work," John said genially. "Hauling you out of bed at dawn too! I'm sorry we had to fall down on you like that in my hospital. Serves me right, though, for going off into the blue, after that boy died. There's no let-up in my job, and I shouldn't have taken those three days off, though they were priceless to me. Not that I think you're much worse for it, Padre!"

"It's not me—it's Caroline," Michael said, ashamed of his shaking voice. "I'm all right, but I couldn't help her! I tried—but I failed. I'm glad you're back."

"I'm worse off than you," John admitted. "Probably Caroline wouldn't have come this cropper at all—if I'd looked after her properly. I'll go in and see her in a minute."

He moved restlessly about the room, picked up a photograph of a Zulu chief, who was one of Michael's best friends, and put it down again; took up a chair, and thought better of it; and finally came back to where he had started by the bedside.

John was not at ease, Michael thought. What was it that Caroline had said yesterday, which had troubled Michael off and on ever since?—"I didn't have to ask John!"

"The trouble is," John went on at last, "we're in a bit of a tight place, all of us. We don't quite know what started Caroline off. She says she's been raped by Konrad; but it's not at all likely. There doesn't seem to be any evidence, or any means of getting it till she's calmed down. I might put her under an anaesthetic, of course, and find out for myself; but not just at present —her heart's too weak. We know Caroline was peeved enough to hit him, because Sister Peckham saw the mark down one side of his face when he left her room, and Caroline started screaming directly after. But there's lots of things a girl can get peeved with a man about besides rape. Did Caroline say anything to you that would give me a lead before I see her?"

Michael saw that John was only pretending to take what had happened to Caroline lightly; this he was doing partly to lift Michael's anxious depression, and partly perhaps to brace his own nerves for the ordeal before him. If John had not been able to trust himself with Caroline, he would not be in a good position to trust anyone else. Not that Michael felt anything to weaken his own confidence in John's behaviour to Caroline. He had had some experience of neurotic girls, and he was convinced that very few men could not be put into difficult, if not impossible, situations, by Caroline. What distressed Michael was that John would be certain to exaggerate any weakness he had discovered in himself, and minimize any weakness that he had found in Caroline.

It was as if John only saw a very small part of what had happened to Caroline. To John, Caroline, even if he

128

discovered her lies, would only be a naughty little thing; she would not be a human soul who had deliberately determined to cheat God, so that she might keep to the last her false image of herself intact.

"I thought she was very ill," Michael said at last, "much more ill, I mean, than if nothing had happened to her. In fact, I am sure that a great deal *has* happened to her; but don't you think these things can happen in the imagination as well as in reality? I have always had a feeling that Caroline has had very little to do with reality."

"Damn all," John agreed, his hands moving on the rail of the chair he was handling, "if you ask me! I should say her mother treated her like a doll in a doll's house—from her birth. Caroline's never had her own teeth in anything all her young life. When will parents learn that education is teaching children how to live in a tough world—with a lot of half-baked brutes that haven't begun to be human beings? It's not what the poor kids get out of books, it's what they learn from their parents to put into anything they handle, that they have to reckon with later on! However, I'll go and put the fear of Hell into Caroline now. The line I shall take is—that she tells me the truth or gets kicked out of here. I may have to kick her out anyhow; but I certainly won't keep her unless she tells the truth or submits to having it found out. It's not fair on Rainer letting it be held up too long either. These kind of things get out, however much you try to hush them up. You don't by any chance *know* the truth already, do you, Padre? It would save me a lot of trouble if you did?"

Michael gave a short, impatient sigh. "I don't know that I want to save you trouble, John," he said. "You seem to me sometimes to need it. You cannot take these short cuts with human beings! They are more than unconscious bodies upon an operating table. Caroline has great confidence in you. If I were to repeat what she told me it wouldn't help you as much as you think; it didn't help me, but her confidence in you could help you."

"Religion and science," John said with a wicked grin, "ought to work together, oughtn't they, according to your ideas?"

Michael was silent for a minute, then he said, "I think they do; but they only work if we use them both together. Otherwise we're as unreal as Caroline."

John slightly shrugged his shoulders. Religion was nonsense to him. Nevertheless, it was quite possible, he thought, that Caroline had told Michael something vital to her recovery, just because she and Michael shared the same nonsense.

He hesitated for a minute, then he drew forward the chair he had been playing with and sat down. "How am I to do my bit," he asked, suddenly serious, "if you won't do yours? If there's anything whatever in this rumpus, I must sack Rainer; and if there isn't I must get rid of Caroline. All I'm asking you to tell me is, do you *know* if there's anything in it? The girl's life may depend on how I tackle this business—and a man's reputation certainly does!"

Michael shook his head gently. "I can't tell you anything whatever that I know," he said quietly. "I can only tell you that I believe your best card with Caroline —indeed your only one—is that she has this confidence in you."

"If she has, she oughtn't to have!" John said abruptly. Then he added with a displeased look at Michael, "Don't you think anything of a person's own self-respect? What has confidence in another human being got to do with how to behave?"

Michael felt his physical strength ebbing fast away from him; cold sweat broke out on his forehead, and his thoughts ran loosely and vaguely in his head. Yet he was quite sure John was talking about himself now, not about Caroline. What was it that he had meant to say to John? He had to switch his exhausted mind too quickly to catch up with it; yet he made the effort.

"You don't need to arrange all this beforehand," he said slowly, "as if nothing would help you! Go—and see her for yourself. I've done what I could."

Michael met the slightly doubtful, slightly anxious look John cast at him, with his accustomed serenity. He did not lose consciousness until the door had closed after his visitor.

17

*I*t is hard for a man accustomed to his own generosity to realise that he is acutely jealous. John believed that he gave everyone round him freedom to live, his orders were impersonal and based on common sense; but as he never gave himself freedom, he did not always know what freedom implied for others.

Behind all this talk about Caroline, John had been conscious of the bitterness of having to share any of his knowledge of Elizabeth with another man. He did not believe that Michael could possibly know anything about Elizabeth unknown to himself; but he deeply resented Elizabeth's wishing to impart any knowledge of herself to any one but him.

Now it seemed that Caroline too, who would live or not live largely on the confidence she felt in John, was making part of this confidence over to Michael, who scientifically could be of no use to her whatever.

Michael had had the sense to admit that he had failed to help Caroline; but he had also had the audacity to remind John, of what John already knew, that Caroline's life might depend on her confidence in John's wisdom. "Of course she's got to trust me!" John told himself savagely. "But I messed the thing up by kissing her—probably the little fool told him that too! Confessions generally give other people away, rather than the one confessing. The main thing now is to get at what exactly took place with Rainer. If Caroline's lied, I shall

132

pack her off. I can't have criminal libel running loose in my hospital, and so I shall tell her!"

John knocked sharply on Caroline's door, and strode into her room, packed with these severe intentions.

She lay on her bed, a little lower than he liked to see his patients lying, hardly lifting the coverlets with her pencil-thin little body; and when he looked at Caroline, he forgot all about the neurotic who wanted shaking, and saw instead a young girl who was very ill.

He reached her bed in a stride, and knelt by it. "Caroline!" he said under his breath. She lifted her heavy eyelids and looked at him with the dreadful gravity of a child in pain.

"You!" she whispered. "Oh, John—you!"

"It's all right, Caroline!" John said quickly. "I'm here, and I'm going to stay here, and you're going to get better. I oughtn't to have gone away—I'm sorry!"

"Not without telling me," she whispered. "I didn't know! I didn't know anything!—when you were coming back—or if you were ever coming back to me—after you'd kissed me."

"No—I know! I was a brute! But, Caroline," John said earnestly, "I'm your friend as well as your doctor. I'm nearly old enough to be your father too; but of course I'm *not* your father—and I knew that what had happened wasn't fair to you! I couldn't be any help to you, if you thought of me as a lover. Besides, I love my wife. I shall always love her. It's damned unremunerative for a girl to fall in love with a married man!

"Everything's been so mixed up, Caroline! I can't explain. The boy I operated on—the day before I left—died. And I thought it was because I'd kissed you! I just had to run away—and find out!"

Caroline moved her hand as if it was a heavy weight, although it looked as light as a leaf, and laid it on John's.

"You do care a little then?" she whispered, "that's the great thing!"

John made a sound between a laugh and a groan. "Oh, I care all right," he admitted. "I cared so much I missed shooting my chamois. He was almost under my nose—a perfectly easy shot—but when I got him in my sights, and saw that he was a lean little beast—young and hungry—I just let him go! I was such a sentimental fool too that I was glad the chamois old Peter shot, a minute after, wasn't the little beggar—I'd taken care to miss!"

John put his fingers round Caroline's wrist, and felt her flying pulse steadying under them. "I'll get her through after all!" John thought triumphantly; and then he suddenly remembered Konrad Rainer and frowned.

Was this another trick of Caroline's to catch his pity and twist it into a fresh link between them? Had she forgotten Konrad, or was she only making John forget her cruel libel?

Caroline's eyes closed. She felt secure enough not to have to keep them open any longer. John would not desert her now whatever happened.

She wondered if she dared risk repeating her lies to John, and if she would fail to convince him if she made the effort? She felt too tired to bother; besides, she did not need lies any more.

She was dimly aware that John had moved and rung for Sister Peckham; they went too far away for Caroline to hear what they were saying; but she still felt untroubled for she knew that John was arranging things for her benefit; and that if he went away he would come back again.

"It was just a brainstorm," John told Sister Peckham decisively. "Lucky she escaped meningitis. She's gravely ill with T.B. and any organ is at the mercy of her illness.

I'll go and have a talk with Rainer just to put matters straight. He needn't see her again; he certainly won't want to see her after such an accusation. I imagine, though he may have been a bit indiscreet, he had very little, if anything, to do with this attack."

Sister Peckham had her own opinion of organs and their influences; but she was not going to contradict her Chief. She merely said: "Do you want her still to have a special always with her, as she has been having up till now? She constantly threatened suicide!"

John hesitated. "I think that's all part of her nonsense," he said finally. "I'm not the least afraid of her trying to take her own life, even if she had the strength to try—which she hasn't. Besides, she's not frightened any more, if she ever was! I should keep her under pretty constant supervision though, simply because she's seriously ill."

Sister Peckham's lips closed tightly. It was obvious that she wanted to say something, and wasn't going to say it. John was not sure that he wanted to hear it; but he decided that he still less wanted her to keep it back.

"Well, Sister, you've got your own ideas of course," he said finally. "I should like to hear them."

"If she's not to see Dr. Rainer again," Sister Peckham answered with icy composure, "I am, of course, relieved of any further responsibility; and I will withdraw my resignation. I can only repeat that I am not at all satisfied that Dr. Rainer should attend any of our younger patients, without a nurse's presence. I don't know what *did* occur with Miss Draycott, but brain storms, even in a T.B. case like hers, don't come on without something that starts them off!"

"Yes—but you see I happen to know what started this one off and it had nothing to do with Rainer," John said decisively. "You know me pretty well, Sister, by now, and I think you can take my word for it that I'd sack Rainer sharp enough if I wasn't satisfied that he hadn't touched her!"

Sister Peckham shook her head. "I saw the girl directly after it happened," she said firmly. "She was screaming from shock, and I know what real shock is when I see it. No actress could deceive me. She had a rigor that lasted an hour afterwards."

"I don't think you could be deceived," John agreed, "but there are such things as self-induced shocks! A delayed shock—self-induced—is what in my opinion Caroline was suffering from. I even know what induced it. Rainer had nothing to do with it."

"Did he really know," Sister Peckham asked herself, as John's confident figure swung away from her, down the long corridor, "or had he merely made up his mind as to what he preferred to believe?"

Nurse Oliver, who had really been very good about it all, and not opened her lips to anyone, now joined Sister Peckham for the crumbs of certainty, that it was her due to share.

"We can't be sure, of course," Sister Peckham told her cautiously. "The Chief wasn't here when it happened, but apparently he's made up his mind—on what he sees now—that Dr. Rainer had nothing to do with it. It's not for us to question his decisions. I can only say that if he had been here, he might have thought differently. I've told him all I knew, and all I saw— and you saw very much the same, and heard her accusations for hours afterwards!"

Nurse Oliver blinked; much as she admired her superior officer, she knew that she hadn't seen the same things, or drawn the same conclusions from what she had seen. Her eyes were different. Nurse Oliver had looked too often into Konrad Rainer's eyes, and with too much tenderness, to suspect him of violence. It had taken her a long while, and infinite grief, to realise that Konrad no longer wanted her tenderness, and had never had any use for constant women, with their imaginations ruthlessly riveted to altars; he was merely, she knew now, a man to whom a love-affair was the best form of amusement a man and woman could discover. To please, as much as he was pleased, would be essential to Konrad's self-respect.

Nurse Oliver hesitated. Then she said, more to herself perhaps than to Sister Peckham, "I don't think he cares very much for skinny girls."

18

Konrad Rainer's two best friends sat on each side of his bed; and he had to lie with his eyes shut so that they might not see how much he hated them.

His eyelids were glued together; his head throbbed as if a dozen brass bands were shut up inside it. He could not get the taste in his mouth out of his mind, nor the memory of how brutally sick he had been the night before, with Marie Céleste standing over him, and doing for him all the things he was incapable of doing for himself.

He had been dead to the world for twenty-four hours, and now he had waked, with the worst hang-over he could ever remember.

Without opening his eyes, Konrad knew that Marie Céleste had put his room in order, as clean and fresh as if no such physically degraded wreck as he had been a few hours previously, had ever fouled it.

He could not forgive her for knowing what it had looked like, or for putting it right. Still less could he forgive John MacTaggart for having never given the same kind of trouble to any woman.

Every nerve in Konrad's body was raw with irritation and resentment. The only spark of comfort he felt was that apparently they both thought he was still unconscious, so that he could continue to keep his eyes shut.

"If you have once been washed away by the sea," Marie Céleste was saying defensively, "any wave can frighten you, even a ripple! It is so easy to be brave, John, when you have always been safe. If Konrad loses this job—where does he go? What has he got behind him? No country—no relations—no past on which to build a future. A refugee is as helpless as a new born child—but not so appealing! Besides, a new born child has no memories!"

"He is not in danger from anyone here," John replied stiffly, "nor is his job. I have already satisfied myself that Caroline didn't know what she was talking about! She's been appallingly ill—a near go to meningitis—I daresay she's quite forgotten what she made up about Konrad by now."

Konrad dragged open his sticky eyelids. "Not on your life, she hasn't," he murmured, "not Caroline!"

"Oh, you're awake at last, are you?" John said rather grumpily. "Well, you might as well tell us then what you think started her off. You were in charge of her! Only Sister Peckham and Nurse Oliver know anything about her rape story, and both of them will hold their tongues, but they must know what they are holding their tongues about!"

"It's no business of theirs!" Konrad said fiercely. "God-awful, self-righteous, Anglo-Saxon virgins! I don't want even to *think* of them! I'd rather have an emetic!"

"That you stand in *no* need of!" Marie Céleste crisply reminded him. "Don't think of the British nurses if they affright you!—but think a little of *us*, for a change! You have got yourself into a mess, and all we want, John and I, is to get you out of it!"

"Mein Gott!" Konrad observed with a groan, closing his eyes again. "I want to think of *you* still less! I resign, John! I resign immediately from this immaculate hospital, where you observe the ten Commandments, as if they were the latest orders from America, upon the observance of which all future nourishment depends! I have already told my version of Caroline's drama to Marie Céleste. Are you the Gestapo, that I must tell it over again, to you?"

"I think you might at least give me a report on my patient's condition," John said severely, "or else tell me why I find her considerably worse than when I left her in your hands."

Konrad opened one bloodshot eye and fixed it upon John. "You are a damned fool, my dear fellow," he said with great distinctness. "If you can't see that the two things go together! Wasn't there an English poem about a girl, who died because a man who had never been her lover left her without saying goodbye to her? Such poems do not occur in other languages! Nor do girls die so easily in real life. I found Caroline after your departure in very low spirits, so I cheered her up. We got on very nicely, and suddenly, not very appropriately I thought, she asked me to kiss her—rather as you might offer a lump of sugar to a successfully performing dog! I instantly declined. I am a man with no particular morals, but I have never believed in kisses without a follow up. Also, I have my doctor's code and Caroline was my patient. I kept my code in this instance, and got slapped for my pains. As to last night, being denied both woman and song, I took to the third ingredient of life's main values—I drank myself off the scene. I still cannot think why Marie Céleste should have thought it necessary to startle and harrow me back into circulation again. I was very well off as I was!"

There was a prolonged pause. Then John said in a tone of sardonic gloom, "If anyone resigns from this Sanatorium it will be me. You *didn't* kiss Caroline—but I *did!*"

Marie Céleste went off into prolonged peals of laughter.

"The fuss you two men make about a kiss," she gasped. "My dear friends, I would be delighted to give either of you a kiss, if I did not know that I should annoy both—should I kiss the other one! Poor little Caroline, for the first time I feel some sympathy with her! She finds herself gloomily kissed by a remorseful John, and wilfully eluded by a licentious Konrad! What is left for her, but to have a brain storm?"

"I kissed her because I was damned sorry for her," John admitted, "on the forehead, as if she were a child. But I've never done such a thing to a patient before, and there's no possible excuse for it."

"On the contrary," Marie Céleste contradicted him briskly, "I find all manner of excuses for both of you! It is Caroline for whom I find no excuses! A clever girl never has to ask for a kiss, and only a very foolish one invites a kiss that involves remorse. There is, of course, no sense whatever in either of you resigning; but I'd not say there would be no sense in sending Caroline somewhere else. You have a hundred patients, ninety-nine of whom you have treated with praiseworthy skill and circumspect regularity. Can you not afford your-selves a slight error of judgment—over the hundredth? I find myself agreeing with Nietzsche: 'Nothing is so dishonest as remorse!' here you are grieving over some-thing neither of you have done. Ask yourselves instead —is there nothing you have done, or wanted to do, which you might well grieve over instead?"

John got up impatiently. "All right," he said, "per-haps we have taken all this too seriously. As soon as I get Caroline round this corner physically, I'll get her to clear Konrad, for Sister Peckham and Nurse Oliver.

She must do that for all our sakes, or leave the hospital. Will that be O.K. for you, Konrad?"

Konrad grinned. His irritation had died down; even his physical symptoms had lessened their grip upon him. He found that he could after all love both his friends again. He could overlook in Marie Céleste her cynical logic, and even the value she set on the practical application of her affection.

John was, after all, a fine fellow, whose wisdom and self-control could be infused into good comradeship.

He saw that they both looked at him with deep affection and without reproach.

"Let Marie Céleste give you one of her famous pick-me-ups and a couple of aspirins," John told him, "and you'll soon feel fine!"

He held the door open for Marie Céleste to accompany him, but she shook her head and remained behind.

"There he goes," she said after the door had shut, smiling at Konrad, "the good John! And he does not know—and will never suspect—that it is Elizabeth and not Caroline that has put you off your stride!"

"What has changed her?" Konrad demanded sharply. "You know very well, *I* haven't! If I had managed to change her, she would have stayed and made music with me. What an opportunity! Then perhaps I would have been a little less entertaining to Caroline. And I certainly wouldn't have got drunk."

"I don't know what has changed her," Marie Céleste said thoughtfully, "and I'm quite sure *she* doesn't! John has made no contribution to the recovery of her good spirits. Indeed, he made every effort to prevent her joining his trip and was as near insulting to her as it is in his nature to be. She went of her own accord, and came back with the same unaccountable change in her.

If it is not you—it is certainly not John who has knocked her chains off her! I think all this talk of resigning on your part great nonsense, as regards Caroline; but, Konrad, it has occurred to me that you might be happier somewhere else than here! Up till now I had believed that you might make a good affair with Elizabeth, if John remained obdurate. Why should you not profit by it, if her own husband refuses to live with her? But now I am less sure! This feeling Elizabeth has for John—seems independent of John himself. Perhaps no other man will ever succeed with her. If you stay here and fail, you will be angry and discouraged, and if you are discouraged you will drink yourself to pieces. There seem moments in life when nothing is such a success as to be where success is no longer possible. This is when it is a temptation to fall into the gutter, and make a home of it!"

"But you would still be here, Marie Céleste," Konrad said tenderly. "I think if you are near me I shall not need the gutter very often. Sometimes I might need it; but then you would come and tidy me up, and laugh at me, and I should get out of it again and find some other way of making my peace with myself.

"If I stay here, Elizabeth will give me music, if she does not give me love, and after all I am pleased when I remember that I am still rather a good doctor, and holding down a decent job."

$\mathcal{S}$unday morning at the Sanatorium was different from week-day mornings. There was no post, breakfast was later to suit the Catholic patients who were able to go to Mass. The doctors dropped their afternoon visits. Nurses had longer hours off duty. The patients wrote more letters, took slightly longer walks, and felt time hang more heavily on their hands. Those who ran temperatures found that they rose higher on Sundays than on week-days.

A week, since John's return, had made a great change in Caroline. She sat upright in bed against a nest of pillows. She wore a daffodil yellow woollen jacket; and could stand the colour. She slept longer at night, and ate more in the day. John spent more time with her every day. He was genial and confidential to her, telling her of the short golden Canadian summers of his childhood, describing a winter spent with trappers in the North, and the animals that he and the trappers understood and hunted together. When he left her, Caroline weaved climate, scenery and animals into a pattern of the imagination, under enormous blue skies, where she could be wafted by skilled hands from beauty to beauty, adored, and ministered to, by John, and a retinue of silent servants. She did not mind their being Indians if they were silent. She decided to spend her future life wintering in the Alps and her summers in Canada. Aeroplanes, she thought, not boats, would best solve the fatigues of travel.

John had not spoken to her of either Elizabeth or Konrad; and for the time being Caroline respected his silence. She did not find that she needed the existence of either Konrad or Elizabeth. Her renewed fellowship with John, backed by her dreams, blotted them out of her mind.

John came in suddenly, and alone, on Sunday morning. He was unsmiling, and after a few minutes spent in physical examination, he sat down and said abruptly, "Well, Caroline, you know without my telling you that you are a great deal better. You are where you were approximately when I left for my short hunting trip ten days ago. The prospects of your recovery then were good but I told you long ago that they depended largely on yourself—and they do so still. People don't recover from T.B. in safely walled-in sections, or through the administration of correct drugs alone; they recover if they have the nerve and patience to co-operate with their doctors. They have to practise common sense all the time, and in all their human relationships. I've let you alone about what happened while I was away till now, but I've got to go into it this morning. Are you prepared to apologise to Konrad Rainer for that ridiculous and wicked lie that you told about him? You won't have to see him to apologise—a note will do. Nothing more will happen, since no-one else need know that you ever told it. You will be free as air—and so will he. But you must apologise; and Sister Peckham and Nurse Oliver must see your written apology."

Caroline was silent for a long time. She was very much shocked; but she realised that she could do nothing to shake John by just being shocked.

At last she said in a low voice, "John, I wouldn't for the world hurt you—or your hospital. That's why I've said nothing all this time! Only Michael knows—

I had to turn to him in my trouble—I myself could hardly believe it true—it was so sudden—so hideous—such a nightmare! I screamed and screamed—I nearly died of horror! Sister Peckham understood—she was very good to me. I told her *I* wouldn't tell you, if *she* didn't—but it was true! If they have told you it *wasn't* true—that's only because they want it hushed up! They want to protect Dr. Rainer, and no doubt the reputation of the Sanatorium. You know Nurse Oliver is in love with him. And Dr. Delarabrie is his mistress. I hate to speak of such things, but you force me to. They will certainly lie themselves blind to deny what he did. You must believe me! Now you are here I am not afraid any more, that is why I *could* get better—but it was true!"

John said firmly, "Look at me, Caroline!"

Caroline raised her eyes to his. They were very beautiful eyes, velvety, dark as sapphires, fringed with long lashes, dramatically intelligent, but singularly, John thought, unscrupulous eyes.

"You will have to face up to this," John told her sternly. "I happen to know Rainer very well. What you tell me is unthinkable. He may have flirted with you—that's your affair and his. I have nothing against flirtations except that sometimes someone gets hurt by taking them too seriously; but you're my patient and Rainer is my colleague: he couldn't have used violence towards you. It would have been an appalling crime and Rainer is no criminal. If you persist in saying that he did, you must be examined for a physical proof of your statement. Unless you were *not* a virgin when you came here, such a proof would be convincing. If what you say is true, he would have to leave the hospital immediately, and I should make it practically impossible for him to find another job—even if for your sake, to avoid publicity—we avoided prosecuting him. If what

146

you say is false—as I believe it to be—you would of course be guilty of a criminal libel against *him*, and you would certainly have to leave the Sanatorium. In your case too, since you are ill, Rainer would be unlikely to prosecute, but people would certainly know that you were not leaving here for nothing."

Caroline hesitated. "Of course I was a virgin," she said at last stiffly. "You could not make such an examination against my will, John. You could only force me to leave the Sanatorium, if I wouldn't have it! But if you send me away—I shall die! You know that as well as I do—and now—now—that we're friends again —I don't want to die!"

John ignored her interruption. "As I see it," he went on firmly, "you were feeling very ill and excited. Rainer *did* flirt with you—and perhaps not in the exact way you wanted. You became resentful and this brain storm was the result. Such things can happen when people are ill—they may even exaggerate what they thought might take place, into a delusion that it *has* taken place. Therefore, if you do what I tell you, the whole thing need not be taken too seriously; but for Rainer's sake you must clear him completely."

Caroline's eyes filled with tears, but they did not fall, though her lips quivered. The violets pinned on her yellow jacket rose and fell with unsteady swiftness.

"John!" she whispered.

John ignored her appeal. He drew a notebook out of his pocket and wrote rapidly, tearing the page out and handing it to Caroline when he had finished.

"There," he said briskly. "Sign this—and everything will be cleared up!"

Caroline read through her tears: " I wish to apologise to Dr. Rainer. The accusation that I made against him was false. He made no assault upon me of any kind."

John handed her his fountain pen. Caroline took it between trembling fingers, and signed: "Caroline Blanche Draycott" with surprising clearness.

John got up and stood with his back to her. Caroline had no idea before that a back could show as much disapproval as a face. John's back looked very square and utterly unrelenting.

"John," she whispered, "John—you must be kind to me—now I've told you the truth!"

John turned round and took the paper. He looked as if he had swallowed something very nasty indeed, and was trying to get the taste of it out of his mouth.

"I suppose I must," he said reluctantly, and sat down again. "It didn't," he said, controlling the anger behind his voice with difficulty, "occur to you, Caroline, what a damnable thing—how harmful, I mean—such a story might be to Rainer? He has had a pretty tough time anyhow, and he hasn't any backing except ours here in this hospital; all his people are dead or irretrievably lost. He hasn't an atom of margin to live on—his work is his life. If you shook our confidence in him, you would be signing his death warrant."

Caroline felt herself very unjustly treated. She had made an immense concession; and she had had to decide between lowering her moral value in John's eyes or losing him for ever. She had—out, as it seemed to her, of a strange magnanimity—decided to keep John at the expense of her vanity; but she hadn't expected him to rub in her loss.

"I didn't know," she whispered. "How could I? I was dazed with unhappiness when you left me—without a word! And then he behaved—like he *did* behave—he certainly insulted me! If people pretend to be in love with you, shouldn't they kiss you if you wish it?"

"I don't know much about pretending to be in love,"

John said shortly. "No doubt it has its dangers—and perhaps its code. All I know is that to tell a lie about a man if you're a girl—or even to tell the truth about a girl if it is disadvantageous to her, and you are a man—isn't decent. Decent people respect their own and other people's privacies, Caroline—and they avoid lies."

"And am I not then a decent person?" Caroline asked him.

John hesitated. "You're hardly more than a child," he said at last, "and ill. I'm not your judge, Caroline, but I'm your friend, and I owe you the truth. What you *did* wasn't decent. It was despicable to take away Rainer's reputation because you were annoyed with him. Also you dragged in an ill man next door, and put him in a hell of a spot. The Padre naturally—when you told him the truth—wanted to save Rainer; but owing to his professional etiquette he had to keep his mouth shut. I tried to get him to tell me, but he wouldn't. I had to take a chance, and act on my own hunch. Fortunately it's come out right, and you've owned up. So there isn't from my point of view anything more to worry about."

"You're still my friend?" Caroline urged. Her tears fell now, but her face did not distort or twist with crying, her eyes remained beautiful. She fixed them upon John in liquid pleading.

John was a truthful man, and he looked at Caroline for a long time before he said grudgingly, "Just—Caroline!"

20

It was a great relief to John to find himself in Michael's room, after his session with Caroline. It was as if he had come into an open space after a prison cell.

When John came into his other patients' rooms, he was immediately aware of the attack of supplication. Each patient wanted something from him—pity, hope, admiration, or relief from pain. They might hide their needs from other people, but John must share the burdens of their physical weakness; he could not be ignorant of their inner breakdown of courage; or fail to be harrowed by their impossible expectations. But Michael offered John obedience without demands. When he met Michael's clear eyes, the world that was on John's shoulders shifted a little, as if Michael took some of the weight of it on to his own.

"Ah," Michael exclaimed smiling, "I can guess you have just seen Caroline, and you have got what you wanted from her. Now tell me how you did it!"

"You are asking science to give away a secret that religion kept!" John replied genially. He felt suddenly pleased with himself. He had triumphed where Michael had failed; and he had triumphed not only out of Michael's failure, but out of his own; for John had accepted full responsibility for Caroline's break-down. This freeing Rainer from Caroline's accusation had freed John as well.

He decided to talk the whole thing out with Michael,

and if the talk led to it, even to confide the deeper problem that beset him of the change in Elizabeth.

"Apparently, from what Caroline tells me," John began, "she told you the truth, while preventing you from passing it on. A nasty trick; but she thought she was dying, and was trying to make the best of both worlds. If she died she went clear of her lie to the judgment seat; and if she lived she could switch back to her lie again while keeping your mouth shut. Well —she did switch back with me at first. She told me a most convincing whopper: I could quite see how Sister Peckham fell for it. I had to bring Caroline up pretty short against physical proof before she admitted it was an invention; but she gave in finally, and signed a complete retraction. The incredible part of it is that I don't believe even now she sees what she was prepared to do to Rainer—to the hospital—or, as far as that goes, to herself."

"If she had seen it," Michael said with conviction, "she could not have done it. It is our failure to understand that explains—though it does not justify—every wrong we do to others."

John felt vaguely irritated by Michael's comment. The difference between truth and platitude is hard to define, perhaps it is intensity that makes the difference; there was a personal conviction founded on experience in Michael's words—it was not the experience of others handed on without personal conviction. John decided to ignore what Michael had said and return to his success.

"I wish you could tell me," he went on, "why I was able to get this retraction out of Caroline, when you couldn't. After all, if I had my authority as a doctor, you had yours as a priest. You had all the securities and sanctities of your creed to back you. It puzzles me

151

that though Caroline was too frightened to lie to you, she wasn't frightened enough to let Rainer off!"

Michael was silent. He listened to the vague sounds of the outer world as if they might help him make up his mind what to say next. A *Föhn* wind blew, and the earth, softened by its persistent warmth, loosened its coverlid of snow, and melted the heavy garlands off the trees. It was not yet avalanche time but it was avalanche weather—the tautness of the mountain silence had been shaken. The secret life of the earth was unclenching itself towards spring. The little sounds of it were like friendly voices.

John did not want to tell Michael that, since he had won Caroline's consent by force, from Michael's point of view his triumph was empty. The truth Caroline told Michael had come by consent, and therefore had a deeper significance. It was much that she should have told it; but hers was an untaught, unused soul, incapable of further flight. Not even to obtain the absolution she craved had Caroline been capable of accepting a blow to her vanity. She could confess to God—but not to man. She would not be less vain now that John had forced her to give way; but she might easily become more dangerous.

There is a Russian proverb: "God sees the truth, but waits." And Michael thought of this, as he listened to the faint sounds from the shifting snow, and met John's observant and slightly hostile eyes.

"I do not know," he said at last, "what takes place in the Sacrament of Confession between the soul and God. Perhaps Caroline moved a little towards the truth, and then moved away from it again later, when she felt her need was less. I only administer sacraments: I don't know what happens in them."

"But you must have some idea," John persisted, "as

to what is likely to happen and is peculiar to this rite you administer. Just as I cannot tell the exact reaction of a patient to a remedial drug; yet I anticipate a good result, or I should not try it."

"I have only this idea," Michael said slowly, "that a sacrament contains the grace of God. There may be obstacles in the soul that prevent the grace of God from functioning; or it may function in a way we do not understand, and without a time limit. I was disappointed—indeed I was alarmed—for Rainer, that I had failed to convince Caroline; but you see that was simply my lack of faith. *You have* convinced her, and she has told the truth. So all that was necessary, as regards Rainer, has been accomplished."

"I only succeeded," John explained magnanimously, "because I played from strength. There are times when force is the only solution. Caroline saw that she had to retract or go. Well—she preferred to retract. I didn't expect to improve Caroline by forcing her, I only intended to clear Rainer."

Michael, too, did not think that John had improved Caroline, nor even that he saw how important it was that Caroline should be improved.

"I always realised," Michael said after a pause, "that Caroline had great confidence in you. But, John—don't forget that people in whom we have too much confidence have to pay for it sooner or later!"

John frowned. A faint sense of uneasiness replaced his triumph.

"I don't propose to let her confidence down," he said drily. "The morality I believe in has to stand on its own feet without reward or punishment, other than the consequences of its own acts. It does not ask for grace, or absolution, or eternal life, or any other celestial pat on the shoulder; and that is where we differ. I do not deny that religion can act on those who believe in it, as first aid; but mine is the surgeon's knife required for more serious accidents. Caroline only came round to practical decency when she was obliged to. We were fortunate that she came round in time, and that nothing irretrievable had happened. She hadn't actually driven Rainer to commit suicide, for instance. What sort of good can confession do, after a crime has been committed? Would you have been prepared to absolve Caroline then?"

"Absolution does not depend on what crime is committed," Michael said slowly, "but it depends on the state of the soul that has committed the crime. Crime is just like any other illness: a wise physician judges his patient, not only by his symptoms, but by the amount of health left in the patient with which he can co-operate. We too have to make hard decisions, and it is upon the state of our patient's soul that we rely, to decide whether it is a fit moment for absolution or not. Naturally, if penitents have no desire to redress their wrongs, they have not reached the operative moment. It is when the heart is broken and contrite that it is most open to God—grief has destroyed the barrier of its wilfulness."

"These imaginary—or, if you prefer, actual but invisible—states of the mind are not what I am most interested in," John explained with good-humoured tolerance. "Patients morally or physically can put up a lot of emotion at any time—given the incentive: however, the actual influence of their manufactured emotions upon their conduct subsequently, is usually extremely small! What I am getting at is—what good can you do when a thing is irretrievable? Can you put back the clock? Take Elizabeth's case for instance. I suppose we can talk of it now that you know what it is? She has taken a life. What do you propose to do to help her that I haven't already tried? She's my wife, and I naturally want to come in on any help there is for her. Are you prepared to give me your opinion?"

The word "Elizabeth" altered the character of the room. Michael was aware that there was instantly a barrier between himself and John. They differed over Caroline, but they had spoken of the same Caroline. If they spoke of Elizabeth, they would not be speaking of the same Elizabeth.

To Michael, Elizabeth was a defrauded angel. Never had he known a woman so innocent, so kind, so clean-hearted and courageous as Elizabeth.

To John, Elizabeth was a heart-breaking swindle. He too had believed in her as an angel but by her he had been defrauded. Nothing in John's eyes could excuse or change Elizabeth's plunge into depravity—nothing except madness; and regretfully John had had to resign his belief in Elizabeth's madness. As a doctor he knew that madness does not spring from a void and return into one. Elizabeth had no past history and no present symptom of mental disease.

"I must tell you," John said after a long pause unbroken by Michael, "that I thought at one time that Elizabeth was not wholly responsible for her act, but that I have had to give up this idea. She had had a difficult first confinement, her baby was born dead, her only brother was killed directly after. There were other adverse circumstances that I was unaware of at the time. Still, women have had exceptionally difficult times over their physical emergencies before and not committed murders. I have regretfully accepted the fact that Elizabeth was sane, because except for that one act, her behaviour ever since has been consistently normal. She fully agreed to the only course open to us. We had our work together here—and we decided to continue it—but we lived under the same roof merely as colleagues. She took the first eight months in England with her parents—that made it easier—and of course she gave up nursing.

"This way of living has been difficult for us both, but possible. Now suddenly—and without explanation from Elizabeth—it seems to have become impossible. Elizabeth has completely changed. She appears to think that she can get over an act as if it *were* over—even this—this thing that took place! But to me it is an unchangeable fact. Elizabeth took a life: she can't put it back again."

"No, of course she cannot," Michael agreed. "Life is not under our control. Even when we preserve it, or destroy it, it has never been ours to preserve or destroy. It belongs to Someone else. But when you say an act is irretrievable, I don't quite know what you mean. In what way irretrievable? To whom? Through what space or time? I cannot speak of what Elizabeth told me or did not tell me in confession; but I am free to talk as if your opinion were a fact, and to discuss it with you on those terms. If Elizabeth acted as you say she did, I understand that, as a nurse, she did not so much 'take' life as let it escape; but we accept that she did not do this from mercy—or indeed, from any good motive—but as you have suggested—inexcusably, since she was sane. I agree that the consequences of such an act are irretrievable to the life that has been taken; but the further consequences which you have imposed upon yourself and Elizabeth do not seem to me in any sense irretrievable. Religion does not admit the impossibility of pardon. We are even told in that deeply significant parable of the unjust steward that the only safeguard from complete deterioration is to forgive each other everything. We are indeed advised in the same parable

156

that if we are unable to forgive, it would be safer for us to give up religion altogether and join the 'children of this world', who—*in their generation*—are wiser than the children of Light. In the Lord's prayer too we are again told of forgiveness as an interlocking necessity. Why does science deny to Elizabeth this merciful release?"

"Elizabeth," John said stubbornly, "broke our marriage, when she betrayed the principle upon which our love was based. A doctor and a nurse work together to save life, not to destroy it. What difference does it make whether a patient is a Gestapo thug or a saint of Paradise? Our responsibility is the same. I took—and Elizabeth took with me—full responsibility during the War for an international hospital. She did not only betray her own principles by killing Von Brandt; she betrayed mine. I was responsible for the hospital, and for everyone in it!"

"What does marriage mean to you?" Michael asked abruptly. "If Elizabeth did an heroic act, would you feel you were equally heroic? You speak as if her soul were not her own!"

"It was her own—and mine too," John said with passionate earnestness. "Ours was, I suppose, a singularly perfect marriage. I lived in a sort of sunshine of her approval. I referred in my mind everything I did to her. It would not have been possible for me to act against her or so I thought, and it was unthinkable that she should act against me. I had been lonely before I met her, and tied up in myself. My father is a very rich man. I was his only child, and both parents were determined that I should live the same kind of spartan hard-working existence they had shared in their early life, before he made his fortune. I daresay it was good for me—to go up to the North and live among the

157

trappers; but it cut me off from the natural life of my contemporaries. My medical studies did nothing to break down the barriers. When I met Elizabeth I was shy to the bone—and hostile to the human side of my profession. I have always thought Dante must have felt like I did, about Beatrice—even if they only saw each other in the street twice, he was surrounded by what she gave him—a new heaven and a new earth! Well— that was what I lost—when this atrocious thing happened!"

John got up and walked to the open balcony door. The sky was low and thick with clouds. It hung heavily over the little valley. The mountains rose up like walls to meet the sky. The pale, sallow light shifted uneasily over their slopes, and lost itself in clouds. There were no peaks visible.

Michael ached with the pity he could not show. His compassionate admiration for John was so great that the thought of his sorrows bewildered him. Why must so good a man suffer so much, he asked himself, although he knew the answer. Only so good a man *could* suffer so much. Yet John's sufferings had not yet reached the point where his world could get broken up again, and freed as love had freed it. The sense of his own rightness fettered him, as Samson—blind with all his strength —was fettered by the Philistines, after he had been betrayed by Delilah. "But he is his own Philistines," Michael told himself. "The pillars he must bring down are the pillars of his own building; and Elizabeth is not —and never has been, as he thinks—Delilah!"

21

A nurse came to the door, carefully concealing the urgency of her summons by the unconcerned air with which she said: "May I speak to you for a moment, sir?"

John looked up; Elizabeth—the history of his heart and hers—vanished in a split second.

"Right, nurse," he answered in a tone of cheerful duplicity that matched her own. "I'll be back soon!" he added over his shoulder to Michael; but Michael knew as the door closed behind him, that the John who had been discussing Elizabeth with him would not return.

Perhaps it was as well that the conversation should be over without either of them having arrived at their goal. Michael saw now why John had failed Elizabeth. John's skill was his life, and the person who called for it must always be his immediate object.

Elizabeth had made a new heaven and a new earth for John; while John—apart from her share in his work —had not given Elizabeth an inch to stand on. Even the little faith Elizabeth had possessed in anything beyond himself, John had taken away from her by his impatient scepticism; so that when he took himself away from her, in his outraged integrity, Elizabeth had found herself with nothing at all.

Now at last she was beginning to find something; she had found Michael, and she was learning through Michael how to find God.

Very slowly and carefully, for his body felt like an over-filled glass that might easily topple over and break to pieces, Michael crossed the room and knelt before the prie-dieu that Sister Peckham had found for him. He was allowed now to kneel for five minutes at a time, and though he knew that prayer was limitless and free in every posture, he found that kneeling brought with it a certain quickening of his spiritual attention.

The flurry and panic of his sympathies died down, and he could listen to the deep quietness that took their place; even the quick beating of his heart steadied. Something outside of time, and independent of space, was finding a way of helping him to meet Elizabeth's need. But it was not an easy way. Elizabeth was in his charge only to release her towards a new life with John. He must not hold her, even in his heart.

Michael knew that Elizabeth was in great danger. In her sudden escape from the sense of guilt, for which Michael was responsible, she might find an urgent relief in loving, and—if John refused to accept her love— Konrad with his irresponsible and passionate eagerness was there to take his place. Konrad would not judge or oppress Elizabeth; he would merely take this new blossoming of her heart towards life as an advantage for himself. He would initiate her into a life of dangerous deceptions and quick reactions to pleasure, a life that never in the end would content Elizabeth. Satisfied by Elizabeth's love, Konrad would probably release himself from habits that would be repulsive to her. He had eager and beautiful tastes, half their life together would be music; but he had neither discipline nor standards beyond his tastes. Elizabeth, who had both, would soon find herself tied to a man undermined and damaged by easy vices. She would have to step down from her innocence and sincerity, into the mirage of inconstancy and corruption which stood between Konrad and real living.

What was her alternative? Not Michael—never Michael! Elizabeth must learn the hard way, without lovers. She would be still more irrevocably lost than John had lost her, if she found instead of God— Michael.

Michael got up from his knees. He had knelt long enough now, knelt—until he saw himself as he was— fallible, shaken, vulnerable—a man in love who wanted to deceive himself in order to win the heart of the woman he loved; but who could not deceive himself, because he was a servant of God.

Michael was not surprised that he loved Elizabeth, and certainly not ashamed of loving her, because although it had long been his intention not to love any woman, he had no great value for his intentions as such; they were only valuable to him if they carried out a purpose that was discernibly God's.

Michael was aware of his senses and had suffered from defrauding them; but they were subsidiary to a deeper longing. He did not expect too much of himself, and of others he expected nothing.

He saw now that if he judged John for giving Elizabeth only his blind enchanted love, he would fail completely to help either of them.

Nor was there any need, he told himself, to blame John, for he had seen in John's face, when he turned to meet emergency, the splendid completeness of his aim. "I very nearly harmed John just now," Michael thought with quick compunction, "till I saw that look in his face, and remembered what a great doctor he is, and that I owe my very life to the greatness that is in him! I can see now that he simply thought that Elizabeth was exactly the same as he was, and shared his every feeling.

But she couldn't be the same, because she was both another individual and a woman, and an unspoilt woman's foremost aim is motherhood. When Elizabeth knew that she was to be a mother, she began saying 'My soul doth magnify the Lord' instead of 'My soul doth magnify John.' No doubt John felt it a shocking difference: any man would! He was sorry for her, when the child died, but he expected her to be the Elizabeth who had never had a child; and she was not. She was an impoverished, broken-hearted, resentful Elizabeth! I am outside these things myself, for until now I have never loved a woman, but now I begin to understand how much farther on in life people are who break down in love, than those—who like myself—have never possessed it.

"John and Elizabeth are both very great souls on their way to completion, and all the greater that they have lost each other; but could they come back to each other strengthened by having lived alone, and by the awfulness of having once lost each other, they would become still greater. If I work only for this, although I am a much smaller, less complete soul than either of them, I may be allowed to be of service to them!"

Michael was greatly comforted by this thought, and though he was aware of the immensity of the discipline he would have to exact from his body, and use in his every action, he no longer felt dismayed. "I shall be 'in love'," he told himself, "and up till now love has only been in me—and what a small cup I am to hold so great a draught!"

He reached his bed in safety and lay down again, curiously refreshed by his new knowledge. When he looked at his watch he saw that he had knelt ten minutes instead of five. It was a fault of discipline, but he felt stronger rather than weaker for it.

When he had first reached the hospital, Michael had expected to die. He was prepared for death, and dying had seemed to him a simple though painful process, with beyond it—and even perhaps in it—the joy of a complete relationship with God.

The slow intervention of returning life had been an uncertain, and a far more complicated affair. Every week he had felt some small new signs of life, alternating with startling returns into feverish discomfort and the old restless exhaustion of mind and body. But now he knew that something was stirring and moving in him, like the slow sap of an alpine spring, under its heavy weight of snow.

He slept longer, eating was an easier task, he breathed without the knowledge that he was drawing breath. He no longer had to make a careful effort to speak. Everything he ceased to feel physically was an advantage to him, and gave him back part of his old freedom. He had time to listen to the thoughts that came to him. They were no longer a jumble of distracting images, but coherent thoughts that gave him back the worlds he had lived in with their separate disciplines.

Michael could rest now. He could, in imagination, hear the chapel bells of his monastery summoning him to join his brothers in the quiet ritual of their daily prayers. He did not have to be a splinter any more in a far off land broken off from their continuous strength. He could even take his present world back to them, so that the new claims he must meet need be neither burdens nor temptations, but opportunities shared with a common strength.

Suddenly the thought of Caroline filled Michael's mind with the urgency of a summons; it was curious that the summons should come from Caroline rather than from Elizabeth—just now—when he was first aware of being in love with Elizabeth; but perhaps Caroline needed him more, so he prayed deeply for Caroline.

It was six o'clock, and quite dark outside. There was no sound, but the little puffs of the *Föhn* wind stirring the pines beneath his window; then he heard his balcony door creak, and looking up he saw that Caroline was standing in the open doorway.

22

Caroline trembled all over; it was impossible to guess how long she had been standing on the open balcony. Snow glittered in her dark hair; and all she had on was a peach-coloured crêpe de chine nightgown, under a knitted pink coat.

"I meant to kill myself," she gasped. "I tried three times, and each time you called 'Caroline! Caroline! Caroline!'—so I came!"

Michael said quickly, as if he had been expecting her, "Wrap yourself up in my eiderdown and drink this hot milk nurse has just brought in. Now sit down in my armchair, and tell me why you wanted to kill yourself!"

Caroline obeyed him mechanically. She pressed her ice-cold hands round the warm glass, and drank the hot milk in long gulps, between fits of shivering. Michael saw that she wanted to control her teeth chattering; but she could not control them, nor the long shivers that ran over her from head to foot.

At last she said, with pauses for her shaken breaths, "John was horrible to me! He forced me to write dreadful things! He took Konrad's part—he wouldn't believe me! I'm too unhappy to live. I thought he was my friend!"

Michael's eyes rested on her with a compassion so deep that it reached behind the words she said, and warmed her heart.

"Why did you call me back?" she demanded reproachfully. "I would have thrown myself down into the snow! No-one would have heard me—it wouldn't have been hard—only cold, and I couldn't be any colder than I am now—and *not* be dead! It's much more horrible to be *alive* and cold!"

Michael took his hot water bottle and put it on her knees. "You can be warm and happy again, and then you'll like to be alive," he told her. "I'm sure you're mistaken about John, he really is your friend, but you see he's Konrad's friend as well. He had to save Konrad."

"But he didn't *believe* me!" Caroline cried, her eyes desperate with pain. "I know what I told him wasn't *exactly* true, but it was quite as true as what he made me write—that wasn't true either, because if Konrad hadn't looked at me in that way, I wouldn't have told him he could kiss me—and then nothing would have happened! I didn't make *that* part of it up! If you see a person *wants* a thing—and you say he may have it and he doesn't take it—of course you're annoyed, aren't you? After all, I'm not so *terribly* strong, and I only slapped him! It's what John thinks of me I can't bear —I'd rather die!"

Michael's clear, kind eyes never left Caroline's, but he felt anything but clear in his mind as to what he should do with her. Physically the only sensible thing would be to ring for Sister Peckham, and get Caroline put to bed surrounded by hot water bottles; but spiritually this act of common sense might be fatal.

Perhaps to let her sit there pouring out her heart wouldn't do her as much harm as once more forcing her to act—or be acted upon—against her will. The brandy he had poured into her glass was beginning to take effect. The blue lines round her lips and nostrils vanished; she was shivering less often.

"John wouldn't think any the better of you for killing yourself," he said at last. "It would make him think you were less to be trusted and more hysterical than he thinks you now. After all, he is trusting you a good deal, isn't he? He believes you have the courage to acknowledge a great mistake. All of us do wrong things we haven't understood; and when we understand them, it takes great courage to undo them. I know John is very pleased that you wrote the truth about Konrad—for it *was* the truth, wasn't it? You can't think how relieved we all are—Konrad, Marie Céleste, John and I— because you have written it! Even Sister Peckham must be rather pleased not to have to think quite so badly of one of her own doctors!"

"There you're quite wrong, Michael!" Caroline said with returning animation. "Sister Peckham wanted to believe Konrad had raped me—she quite liked me for it; now she'll hate me for ever for *not* being raped! As for Nurse Oliver—she never believed it—but she hates me so much now, that they've had to give me a Swiss nurse to take her place. It's horrible having everyone hate or despise you. I can't think why you called me back or even how you knew. I was *just* going to jump when I heard your voice!"

"I didn't exactly call you," Michael said slowly. He knew that he had been in the Presence he believed in; and had been made a messenger; but he could not explain this to Caroline. He said instead, after a pause, "I suppose we can share acute moments with each other sometimes. All that happened was that you were in great trouble, and so your need reached me."

"In that case," Caroline said with some asperity, "you might have helped me to climb the balcony rail! I had to get over it first before jumping—and I'm not very good at climbing. That was what I really wanted!

167

—not to be called back! I wish I knew an easier way of killing myself though. When Queen Cleopatra wanted asps, she could get them! Besides, they didn't hurt. I don't know anything that I could get hold of that would be 'as sweet as balm, as soft as air, as gentle. . .' I think she was going to say 'as gentle as Anthony!' when she died; but John wasn't gentle at all, he said— oh Michael he said—I was barely 'decent'!"

That was her trouble, Michael thought, Caroline had always pictured herself as a queen; and when queens fall, they fall a long way.

"I just couldn't go on lying looking at the ceiling, and being alone," Caroline continued, "and remembering what John had said. At the time he was there, I could *just* bear it, because I had to make up my mind, and act. I knew I didn't want to leave him, but now I feel he has left me, because he doesn't approve of me; and I don't think John ever stays with people he doesn't approve of! He doesn't even stay with himself, if he doesn't approve of himself—he runs away to shoot chamois!"

"Yes, I see what you mean," Michael agreed, "but he comes back again after he's shot them! I think he will come back to you, Caroline. And as for feeling lonely— that's what we all have to feel. We are born alone— and we die alone. There are always, in every life, periods of complete loneliness."

"What do you do with yourself when you feel lonely?" Caroline asked him. "There were those two whole months when John wouldn't let you speak, and even now you've only just begun."

Michael hesitated. His religion was what he did with his loneliness—there had been no gap in it; but he could not explain this to Caroline in any way that she could share; so he said after a pause, "There are such a lot of interruptions—aren't there?—in a Sanatorium: meals—nurses—doctors! Even being ill is in itself an occupation. Now I am really better, as I hope you are; and soon we shall be allowed out on our balconies, and perhaps even in the Solarium with the other patients."

"I shan't be well enough for that this winter," Caroline told him. "It's only the end of January now, and Mother won't come out till June—unless I send for her. Before I came here I was never without Mother. We didn't always get on—in fact, I found her very tiresome. She's fearfully fussy and energetic, and we had awful rows—still, I generally got what I wanted done. John made me be alone. I thought he would cure me if I did without Mother, and I do *want* to be cured. I'm only nineteen—and if I had him, I think I could get better!"

Her voice failed her. Her body lay loosely in the armchair, as if she could not control even the bones that held her together.

"I don't think John will fail you," Michael said reassuringly. "I doubt if there is a better doctor in the world—the whole of him is in his faculty of curing! Besides, he *is* your friend; you can talk to him and tell him about your loneliness. He may know better than I know how to deal with it. I don't have enough of it to know how to help you."

They were both silent. Caroline still shivered every now and then, but she was growing warmer and she had begun to feel sleepy.

Michael ventured to say at last, "I think you should go back to bed now, Caroline. I was wondering how you could get there. You must not go out into that cold again. After all your door is next to mine; you ought to be able to slip into your room without anyone seeing

169

you—if you can reach the door. Or shall I ring for help?—we could make up some kind of explanation."

"Certainly not!" said Caroline, raising herself. "No-one must know I have been here. Of course I can get to the door by myself. I walk to the bathroom every day now. But before I go, there's something I want to ask you. You wouldn't give me absolution when I told you the truth—that time I thought I was dying—do you remember? Well, now I've signed that horrible thing John gave me to sign, couldn't you do it?"

"Not immediately," Michael said consideringly. "It would have to be part of real contrition. Besides, there is one thing we have to remember, Caroline. Absolution isn't mine to give—God gives it to you through me—if you can take it; and you can't take it unless you are quite sure you hate what you have done—not the consequences, but the thing itself. Otherwise what happens is that you still belong to what you have done; and you might do it again—or something like it."

"I don't see much use in absolution then," Caroline said crossly. "Aren't sins ever over?"

"They are over when you love enough," Michael said gently. "Whatever we do that's wrong comes from not loving."

"Well, I'm quite sure I love John enough," Caroline said decisively, "or I shouldn't have signed that thing! I'd just have gone on saying I'd been raped, and that I wouldn't be examined. I'd have left this horrible, *damned* hospital still saying it! After all, it was what I wanted to do."

"To find absolution," Michael told her, "you would have to love truth—not only John."

"But you see I did what you wanted when I confessed to you," Caroline reminded him. "I let Konrad off!"

"That was a great step in the right direction,"

Michael acknowledged, "and it freed Konrad; but the only way of being absolved from a lie is to hate it—then you are freeing yourself. Caring for people as you do for John is quite a good way of helping you to do what they want—but it doesn't free you."

"No, it doesn't," Caroline admitted, "I quite see that. It didn't free me at all caring for John so much that I signed that thing! It made me do exactly what I *didn't* want."

Michael dropped the subject of John. He asked instead, after a pause, "You don't want to kill yourself any more now, do you?"

"Not just at the moment," Caroline agreed. "I'm too tired; but of course I might any time again, later on. Why do you ask?"

"Because I think it would be such a pity! Once you've taken your life, no-one can give it back to you again; and you could always do something better with it than taking it. I was going to ask you if you ever had such a feeling again to come and talk to me first. Would you agree to do that for me?"

"I will come to see you first if you like," Caroline said a little uncertainly, "but I don't want to bind myself in any way. I quite like coming here and I may come in again whether I want to kill myself or not. I think I'll just go to bed now, if the coast is clear."

Caroline got to the door with a great deal more strength than Michael had supposed that she possessed. There was no-one in sight; the long white painted corridor swimming in its blue night-lights, stretched away empty. Michael heard Caroline's door click safely behind her. He retrieved his eiderdown, and moved his empty glass to its usual position on his bed table. He wished that it was as easy to know what to do next about Caroline.

171

If he did not tell John about her attempt at suicide, he was taking a fearful risk, for Caroline might repeat her attempt.

If John knew, he might not keep Caroline at the Sanatorium; he would probably do what he thought best for the Sanatorium, not what was best for Caroline; it might even be best for Caroline to leave, as well as for the hospital. Yet could Michael betray a soul that had trusted him? Caroline's visits were against a discipline that Michael had whole-heartedly accepted. He must connive at breaking it, if he kept them secret. Caroline was the sort of person out of whom scandals came; and it would cause a scandal if her visits to him were discovered.

Nevertheless, Michael decided against discipline, or rather, he accepted a deeper obedience to a stronger discipline; and decided to run a risk that seemed to him more worth running.

23

Elizabeth's sitting room was the only warm and comfortable room in the regulated, air-flooded interior of the Sanatorium. Easy chairs, soft cushions and bright colours denied it all austerity; and the regal stove and shut storm windows gave the icy nipping air no chance of invasion.

White-painted bookcases shone against dawn pink walls, and only one picture broke against the room's air of homely reality. Elizabeth had bought the picture to take to England with her, when she first left John. A single peak soared into colourless air, stark white, terrible in its rigid purity, above black rock shadows. The artist had felt down into the very depth of the rocks, to bring out their incorruptible solidarity. The cone stood among them, a thin, inflexible presence, stripped to the bone. When Elizabeth had looked at the mountain peak, she felt that she did not need any photograph of John. The strength of the rocks was his, the inaccessibility of the soaring peak; and its coldness.

Elizabeth felt free to look at the picture even in John's presence, since it would not have occurred to him that the white cone had anything to do with his self-isolated heart.

Elizabeth looked at it now, a little doubtfully, before she went to prepare her supper. John, she knew, was on duty, and she would not see him again before the morning. Konrad, since it was his free evening, would be at a Nacht-Lokal dancing.

Since her return from the chamois hunt, Elizabeth was vaguely conscious that something was wrong in the Sanatorium. It was more than a week since Konrad had asked to play with her. Whatever had happened, she told herself, could have had nothing to do with John, and was not therefore likely to be very serious. Still, it was annoying to feel out of things, and tonight Elizabeth felt seriously lonely. She did not want to play alone, nor to read. She did not particularly want to ring up Marie Céleste and ask her to take dinner with her, since whatever was wrong, Marie Céleste was the person who would most naturally have told it to Elizabeth; and she had not told her; but in the end she rang up Marie Céleste, and asked her. Marie Céleste answered immediately that she would be enchanted, and could join Elizabeth in half an hour.

Both women were equally famous for their cooking. Marie Céleste had perhaps the greater flair; in all her dishes there was the element of surprise—a choice but unexpected flavour haunted them. Elizabeth's cooking was less varied, but it had a clear precision of taste that flattered the most exacting palate.

Elizabeth knew that she had the elements of a good meal in her refrigerator, and she put them into instant action. She would give Marie Céleste asparagus soup, ravioli, and a chocolate soufflé; and she would bring out a specially mellow burgundy to drink with them.

Marie Céleste appeared punctual to the minute, in a pea-green frock, crisp as a lettuce, ravishingly plain, but not in the least simple. Her hair shone golden red above her colourless face, framing the queer flattened planes and the shell-like hollows of her cheeks. Her grey-green eyes rested on Elizabeth with laughing kindness.

"Now this," she said, "was a very happy thought of yours, Elizabeth! I was about to drink myself to death

174

on black coffee, feeling too lazy to prepare what I might have liked to eat. Now I shall relax, confident that I shall—with no effort of my own—eat, to the top of my ability to enjoy. And how I like a sensation that I have done nothing to produce! Since you are a woman I need not entertain you and I need not even look as if I were being entertained *by* you—which I find sometimes an even greater effort. The company of men is enchanting to me when I am in tune with life; but in those stagnant pauses—when life does nothing to meet you half way and we have to do all the tuning up required—I prefer the company of a fellow woman, particularly a woman who happens to be my friend. This asparagus soup is excellent: mostly such soups in winter contain only disguised grasses and medicated milk, but this has actually the taste of fresh asparagus —the heads too are mysteriously genuine in shape and flavour. Where do you get it?"

"Only the best grocer in Vienna sells it," Elizabeth explained happily. "He makes it fresh every year, using only the best heads, and he never keeps a last year's tin—at least he says he doesn't! Then I add a little real cream, of course, and a dash—hardly a dash, a lightning flash—of garlic or the hint of a chive—and there we are!"

"And a very good place to be in too!" Marie Céleste murmured. "And of course the Viennese will tell you anything you like to hear—even sometimes what happens to be true! But I will say this for them, they still take the trouble to provide something that beckons beyond cash, because they have the souls of artists—and the soul, we are told, is immortal! It is only their hearts the Viennese have lost. They have been broken so often these last few years that they have found it more convenient to paint imitation ones on their sleeves. They find imitation hearts do just as well as the real ones—and cost far less!"

Elizabeth lifted the basket where the good wine lay flat and still, and poured it carefully into their glasses. Then she said with an intentionally casual air, "Perhaps that is what has happened to Konrad's heart—it has become imitation. I have not seen him since we came back from the Rettenstein—and I thought he would be true to my Bechstein, if not to me! What do you suppose—or should I say 'who' do you suppose?—is occupying his spare time?"

Marie Céleste raised her glass to sniff the delicate fragrance before she tasted it. "Good grapes!" she said approvingly. "This business then about Konrad hasn't reached you? My dear Elizabeth, you should listen a little more to the under-currents of your hospital. Perhaps if you even looked more like listening, they might become more audible to you! No doubt John has told you not to gossip. This is a mistake men often make; it simply means that they don't want to hear what other people want to say. Now I find gossip always worth listening to! Of course there is no need to believe it—nor to spread it if one does *not* believe it. I must confess I avoided telling you this thing myself because of some such reasoning. The thing in itself was a lie; but if one thought too much about it, who knows what fresh hares might spring out under the panic of a good beating? I thought to myself, 'all the noises will die down of themselves'; but since you are wondering about Konrad's absence, it is probable that what happened here while you were on the mountains accounts for it."

"Ah! Then he *did* stay away on purpose!" Elizabeth said quickly. "And what happened *was* to him—Konrad?"

Marie Céleste nodded. "Yes—in a sense. You know that blue-veined, paper-white, wood-anemone, tough as a wireworm, called Caroline? Any girl who has good eyes and knows how to use them can rouse our Konrad, but he is apt to be well in control of his sensations, especially with his girl patients. Caroline felt that she had missed her mouse by a stroke of the paw—he would not come near enough for tossing! So—to give up our metaphor, and to return to this sick girl too long in bed—Caroline slapped Konrad's face and accused him of raping her. You can imagine what screams rang out, what bells were rung, how nurses projected themselves in all directions—wishing no doubt that whatever had happened should have happened to them! The stern, enthralled reaction of our Sister Peckham was a thing apart. Naturally she believed the worst of poor Konrad; and he—well naturally perhaps, since I was his old friend, he gave me the quite unvarnished truth, and then got as drunk as possible while waiting to see how John would take it on his return.

"One can always rely on John in physical or moral emergencies—he took it very well. Nothing but the truth—that the girl had lied—occurred to him; though I still think it would have been better to get rid of her. As a patient, she is unsatisfactory; she is one of those who don't die and seldom recover, while as a girl she is *impayable*! She does not know what she wants and would resent it if she got it. Nor does John wholly understand her. He expects her to conform to some mistaken image in his mind. These waxworks John designs for himself do not all resemble the women he knows; but do not tell him I said so, since I am one of his ingenious waxworks myself, and I rather like the lady-like creature he has made of me.

"John managed by threats to produce a signed confession from Caroline that she had invented the whole affair. I think, chère Elizabeth, that you should begin to take a little intelligent interest in this business—at least that you should be aware that it may still produce some bad effects."

Elizabeth's eyes remained fixed on her friend's face. She did not miss a flicker of Marie Céleste's expressive features.

"I can't see why John didn't tell me a thing like that!" Elizabeth said at last. "After all, it has to do with the whole Sanatorium and especially with my friends in it. Nurse Oliver must know, for instance— and of course Sister Peckham—and then there is Konrad! Don't you think it is rather odd that I shouldn't have been told?"

"Perhaps a little odd," Marie Céleste agreed cautiously. "No doubt we all thought that John had told you; it was kept as quiet as possible; beyond those you have mentioned, no one knew more than that Caroline had had a *crise de nerfs*, and none of us wished to interfere with John's official account. Konrad stayed away because he was ashamed of having been drunk;—and as for John, no doubt with the full denseness of a man's chivalry, he thought it kinder to make no mention to you of Konrad's little lapse!"

"But Caroline," Elizabeth said, "is after all a person I have to see. I take her books; and I don't understand why—for making up such a wicked lie about Konrad and upsetting the whole hospital—John *doesn't* have her sent away!"

"She is a curious case," Marie Céleste replied cautiously. "Her symptoms are far more severe than her lung condition warrants, yet the lung tissue itself is very thin. One bad break might prove fatal. I expect John was afraid of the shock sending her away might cause. Caroline did not want to go—even after the enforced confession."

178

Elizabeth looked at her friend in silence. She trusted Marie Céleste better than she understood her. Her heart told her that Marie Céleste would have told her anything that she thought Elizabeth ought to know, but not something that would give her useless pain. Surely Marie Céleste would not, so late in the day, have wished to hand on disagreeable information about Caroline, unless there was a new danger threatening from John's decision. Elizabeth went into her kitchen and returned with clear, golden-brown coffee tasting as good as it smelled.

"Marie Céleste," she then said firmly, "please stop talking of—what you are *not* thinking about—and tell me the truth. Why does John not get rid of Caroline? Is he too fond of her?"

There were moments when the stern discipline of Elizabeth's eyes must have resembled her father the Admiral's. To flinch before those steady blue eyes was human: to lie to them, without flinching, Marie Céleste found impossible.

"Well," she admitted, "John is a kind fellow—the girl is very young, and fond of him of course, as all his patients are. Once she agreed to confess there wasn't much point in punishing her any further. She must have felt very small indeed having to confess to John—and he would realise that and be sorry for her!"

"I don't think John often allows pity to alter what he thinks good for the Sanatorium," Elizabeth said drily, "and I should think after that humiliation Caroline would want to leave unless she was very much in love with John!"

"Oh! In love—that kettle of fish!" laughed Marie Céleste. "How afraid and uncertain you Anglo-Saxons are when you have to face it! Why *not* in love?—and why do you suppose love is only one kind of fish? It

179

is a *bouillie baisse* composed of at least fourteen different kinds—including octopuses—and though tough, these little black monsters add very considerably to its flavour! Even John might like them in his sauce!"

"Still, you're just as much surprised as I am," said Elizabeth inexorably, "at John's keeping her on here! It is a risk to the hospital and an insult to Konrad. Caroline may die anyway, or anywhere, just as well as here—that is a risk doctors must take—or presumably if she doesn't want to die, get better—anywhere else than here!"

Marie Céleste lifted her eyebrows, her shoulders—and the hand that had just lit her cigarette. "No good doctor I ever heard of," she remarked, "past his adolescence, lost his heart to a neurasthenic: he knows too well what that sort thrive on—the entrails of others! Still, one may not want a patient to die even if her standard of life is rather low. John's feelings are a thing you are a better judge of than I shall ever be, but he has common sense. I don't know myself why I have told you about this silly incident—perhaps because I have a hunch that it has not ended as completely as John believes it to have ended. I do not wish to keep back information that might prevent your being upset by any further of Caroline's antics. I myself have never known a wound to a person's vanity heal so quickly; that kind usually become septic!"

Elizabeth thought this over in silence. Then she said, "I am glad you told me. I think I have known there was something wrong—I mean, more wrong than usual. I don't mind telling you now that our ski-tour was a disappointment to me. I had seen a way in which things might improve between John and myself—but they didn't. They are just the same."

"My dear," Marie Céleste murmured with sudden

180

gentleness, "if I knew a way to help you, be sure I would use it! And perhaps there is a way. I will tell you then that what I do for John—for your sake quite as much as for his own—has altered. I take this for a good sign—since John finds me of no further use to him as a woman, it is because no woman in the world can satisfy him, even momentarily, any more, except you! This business about Caroline is a little red herring of the imagination; we need them—these red herrings —we proud people who cannot give way even to ourselves. But to someone very inferior to oneself, such people as John—even as you, ma chérie—can more easily give way. This is a relief to them, but in the long run—mon Dieu! perhaps they do not enough consider this—the poor red herring is made to suffer rather more than he deserves. Some day I will write a defence of red herrings—but not tonight. Tonight let us both go to sleep early and remember that we need not make the naughty Caroline more important than she is!"

24

After Marie Céleste left her, Elizabeth, instead of going to bed, began to tidy the flat, although it did not need tidying; she arranged separate breakfast trays for herself and John; and then took up a basket of mending. She did all these things in a meticulous, orderly manner, while hot waves of anger broke over her. The long, hidden resentment of years, masked by depression, which she had endured as grief, now flamed up in her suddenly, hard and bright as a weapon. For Caroline herself Elizabeth felt more contempt than anger. It was not surprising that Caroline, if her vanity had been sufficiently stung by him, should have invented this wicked and despicable lie about Konrad. It was, however, surprising and curiously hurtful of Konrad to have allowed sufficient intimacy between them, to get his face slapped.

It was still more surprising and infinitely more hurtful that John should have kept the whole incident secret from Elizabeth, and unforgivable that he had not arranged for Caroline's immediately leaving the Sanatorium. A neurasthenic with a poisoned tongue in a T.B. hospital is surely as dangerous as a cobra; once get Caroline out of her room into the Solarium with the other patients and there would be no end to the mischief she could cause. How dared John of all people keep this girl against the interests of his other patients? How deep must be his interest in Caroline if it could overcome scruples that John had not been able to overcome when his own wife had violated his professional standards!

Elizabeth pushed John's socks away from her as if it was no longer possible for her to mend them. She must think the whole thing out properly and in order, and not get flustered over it.

What exactly had he told her about Caroline in those occasional discussions that still took place between them on the well-being of his patients? The day after Caroline's arrival he had told Elizabeth that he wanted Konrad to take her case, but had changed his mind about it, and decided to look after her himself. He had not said what had made him change his mind. It was Konrad who told her that Caroline looked like Nefertiti. Then Michael was dragged into it. John had told Elizabeth, "The girl saw him in the train—she seems to want to get hold of him somehow—they're next door neighbours—she bombards him with notes; I shall have to stop her." That didn't sound as if John liked her himself; but he had never said if he *had* stopped Caroline writing the notes.

The first few months both Caroline and Michael had been so ill that there was nothing much about them to mention beyond their illnesses. Then one day John had suggested that Elizabeth should take Caroline books, and later still he had said, "Talk to her a little sometimes, Elizabeth!" and Elizabeth had tried to talk to her, but Caroline had only lain there looking desperately ill and extraordinarily pretty, and whispering, "Yes, please!" or more often "No—no thanks." But however ill she might have been, it didn't prevent Caroline from ruthlessly dissecting every movement Elizabeth made, as if she was sure that they would somehow or other be clumsy and injurious to her.

183

Caroline's unscrupulous eyes had wandered over and past Elizabeth, carrying into oblivion the little kindnesses and shy sympathy she was being offered, and disposing of them with arrogant contempt. "She just doesn't like me," Elizabeth had told John humbly. John had said, not exactly reproachfully, but a little as if he thought Elizabeth might have managed better, "Yes—she's difficult of course; but I daresay it's pretty tough, to a girl as ill as that, even to *see* a well one!" Yet Elizabeth had not thought seriously of his defence of Caroline then.

John was observant with all his patients. He saw into this girl's mind as if he himself were suffering her sensations. He had tremendous sympathy, not only with his patients' physical disasters, but with the reactions of their long illnesses upon their weakened minds. "The damage goes straight through them," he had once told Elizabeth, "and it is a very difficult matter to know which is horse and which is cart— whether they're ill because they don't know how to tackle life, or whether they don't know how to tackle life because they're ill. Either way I've got to help them get on to their feet. It's mainly a question of courage."

He could do that, and while doing it could see so well into what had made them ill, that it seemed doubly strange to Elizabeth that he had never made any allowances at all for his own wife. He would have been kind to her, no doubt, if she had been mad—and she really wouldn't have minded going mad to win his kindness; but Elizabeth knew that pretending to be mad wouldn't have been any use with John, he would have seen through her. When he had once made up his mind that she was sane, the only notice he seemed to take of her emotions was to react with mild approval to her

184

unhappiness, and with obvious distaste to her relief from it.

The glorious sense that there was something alive in the world that wasn't John, and that she still had a right to enjoy it, had again failed her. It was still there even after the ski tour; but it stopped—it had abruptly stopped—when she reached home. Unhappiness had seemed to meet her at the door, with Marie Céleste pretending that what she wanted to see John alone about, didn't matter. It *had* mattered—it was this business about Caroline; and they had kept it a secret from her.

Elizabeth found that she couldn't pray any more. No God was in that deep, restraining silence. Even Michael hadn't been able to help her. He was somehow different; he tried to help her, but in a polite and distant way, as if she'd sprained her ankle and he was offering her a footstool.

He wasn't worse, if anything Elizabeth thought he looked better. He could lie out of his balcony now, and he still looked round him as if everything he saw satisfied him—but not particularly Elizabeth—a snow peak did just as well. He was somehow further away from her. Was that because Elizabeth herself was further away from God?

Perhaps Michael knew all about this business of Caroline's. He must have heard her screaming, since he was next door; but if Elizabeth went to him for help about it, he might make excuses for Caroline, he might even have advised John to keep her on at the Sanatorium. That was the worst of religious people, Elizabeth thought, they expected you to put up with things there wasn't any sense in your putting up with. Surely Elizabeth had had enough to bear already—and she was bearing it before Caroline turned up.

Walking up and down the room—for she couldn't sit still any longer—Elizabeth suddenly caught sight of her face, in a round Venetian mirror over the mantelpiece. Her mouth was drawn tight, like a rope holding something down, and her eyes glittered like a bad cat's. She had never seen herself look like that before. She stopped abruptly before the mantelpiece and stared at herself. "There must be something wrong with me," she thought, "to look so plain and disagreeable! Even if it's true that Caroline is as bad as I think her—Konrad as silly—Michael as tiresome and John as cruel, yet if I were different myself, should I feel so bitterly about what they were like?"

This was such a curious idea to Elizabeth that she found her irritation dying down under it. Reason, she knew, was on her side; but reason could look after itself. Need she be quite so angry if only reason was on her side? What was the other urgent, bitter thing—which made her look so ugly? Could it be jealousy? Could it always have been jealousy?

Elizabeth was by nature extremely active. She used the best type of emergency wits, when it was a great advantage both to herself and to others, that she should use them. Yet there were times—including that one dreadful time—when the desire to put her impulses into action had been disastrous, both to herself and others. Before she acted now—if she was going to act—could she not perhaps find out some better way of using the force that was in her? Was it always easier to make things happen than to stop yourself from making them happen?

"In a storm at sea," her father had once told her, "there comes a point when you have to leave things to the elements. Of course you do all you can first; but what you can do, doesn't settle anything: it's what is beyond your control that takes over." He had said this, Elizabeth remembered, with a grave kind of relief, as if being drowned wouldn't be such an agony if you knew there was no way of avoiding it. That looked as if there were times when it was better not to do anything.

But this was different—this new humiliation—Elizabeth told herself. She had taken punishment from a good man who loved his work better than his life or her own; but there was no need for her to go on taking punishment from a man who could put a lying little baggage before his duty to his work—or to his wife. She was free now—free in quite a different, a much fiercer, more reckless way—than that in which Michael had helped to free her. She didn't quite know how she was going to use this new uncertain freedom; but she knew that she was going to use it; and that she did not want to see Michael before she used it.

25

The next morning Elizabeth woke quite calm. She was still angry but in a cool composed manner. She had made her decision. She would say nothing to anyone until she had seen Caroline; from her she would gather, either through plain speaking or by intuition, what the situation really was between Caroline and John.

"I shall expect her to lie, of course," Elizabeth told herself, "but you can feel what's behind a lie, when you once know that a person *is* a liar; it's only when you're not sure, or else expect them to tell the truth, that you get fooled. Then I shall know how to act."

Elizabeth did not worry any further, but carried through her usual routine with no outward change. It was her morning for shopping in the town, so she took the big sleigh and drove into Davos early, choosing everything with expert care, and returning by eleven o'clock. After that she discussed the half week's menu with the cook, and made out a list for the next week's shopping. She would not have time to take her trolley of books round till after tea; but if she wanted to, she still had time before lunch to go in and see Michael.

Sister Peckham stopped her, to say that Michael had asked to see her. This was curious, because Elizabeth could not remember his ever having asked to see her before. He took for granted that she would come when she could and would know that he wanted her to come.

The relationship between them was at the same time deep—and slight; it had answered, without explanation, all Elizabeth's needs; and she believed, without her usual diffidence, that it had answered Michael's.

She told Sister Peckham now that she would see Michael later on, after tea, and that she hoped he was better?

"Well—yes, I think he is better," Sister Peckham said dubiously, "*generally* better, I mean, but I thought this morning that he looked as if he hadn't slept. He had a quick pulse, and I got the impression that he was worrying about something. He didn't say anything and of course I didn't ask, but as he suggested seeing you, I rather hoped he'd get it off his mind—if there *were* anything, of course!"

"I'm afraid I haven't time this morning," Elizabeth repeated, "but I'll look in this afternoon, after tea." It would be quite a good thing, she told herself, to see Michael after she'd once seen Caroline; but it would be a less good thing, she felt, to see him before this interview took place.

Punctually at four o'clock, when the long rest hour was over, Elizabeth knocked at Caroline's door with her trolley.

Caroline was sitting upright in bed, looking astonishingly well. Her eyes were brilliant, her cheeks flushed, her lips bright scarlet. She wore a white angora jacket trimmed with feathery white swansdown.

"Oh," Caroline said, "it's you!" almost as if she had been expecting Elizabeth.

Elizabeth said, "I've brought the books you asked me for long ago," and sat down.

Elizabeth was not in a hurry and she was not at all nervous. She considered the girl before her carefully before she began to talk to her.

"I was very sorry," she said at last, "to hear you had been ill while we were away hunting chamois. I hope you are better."

Caroline said, "I haven't seen you since, have I? I don't know why—somebody else has always brought me my books."

"Well, at first it was because you were ill," Elizabeth explained. "Just after we came back you weren't reading; and the second week I was lazy, and let Nurse Bessie handle them. But now, here I am!—and, funnily enough, you seemed to be expecting me!"

"No, I wasn't," Caroline said incisively, her flush increasing. "I was expecting—John—that's why I said, 'Oh, it's you!' I meant—it wasn't John."

His name, spoken as if she had a right to speak it, struck straight at Elizabeth's heart. To his women patients, John was always the "chief" or "doctor", or more formally still "Dr. MacTaggart"; he was never "John." His spoken name was not a lie on Caroline's part: it was an accustomed familiarity, and it told Elizabeth almost all that she wanted to know.

She said nothing, but her eyes met Caroline's in mortal combat.

"I was ill," Caroline said after a pause, her shallow breath coming faster. "I was ill—partly because I am anyhow—and partly because I was worried about John —I still am. Mrs. MacTaggart, why don't you let him go? Is it fair to carry on this farce of marriage when he no longer loves you, and you must know that he wants to be free?"

"Free—for what?" Elizabeth asked, between lips that felt so stiff, she was surprised that she could open them.

"To marry the girl he loves, of course!" Caroline said without hesitation. She had so often and so clearly

190

gone through this scene with Elizabeth in her imagination, that no actress on a two years' run could have felt surer of her words, or spoken them to better effect.

"He has not asked me for his freedom," Elizabeth said at last. Her eyes had never moved from Caroline's face: they seemed fascinated by it.

"Oh no!" Caroline told her in shocked surprise. "Don't you know him better than that? John would never ask for it—he would die first—of loneliness and misery. He would even let *me* die, I think, rather than break his promise to you! He would only let you divorce him, if it was to release *you*. Surely you know that?"

Elizabeth got up. Something changed in her eyes, and for a moment Caroline felt frightened by the look she saw there. Then Elizabeth put her hand to her throat, and ran towards the door as if she was trying to escape from a physical danger. She was in the passage now with the door shut safely behind her; she had not touched Caroline.

Elizabeth stood quite still and found herself praying. She thanked God for having saved her from killing Caroline; but she wouldn't trust herself to go back and get the trolley. She swayed where she stood. "After all I am a murderess," she told herself, "if I *feel* like a murderess!"

A door clicked a few paces from her, and Konrad came out of it. She did not know that she had moved towards him, till she found herself in his arms.

"Look here—we can't stay like this!" he told her. "I must know what's the matter with you. Come into the bathroom and tell me—there—that's better. I'll shut the door—but I won't lock it—and if anyone comes in, put your finger under the tap, and I'll say you've cut it! I'll get between you and the door, and manage so that they shan't see you haven't!"

His arms were still round her, closer and closer. It was a most wonderful feeling of warmth and kindness. Her body and mind clung to Konrad as if to life itself. She laid her face against his breast, so that she could be blind in this warm, merciful darkness. She was not crying, but her breath kept coming and going in long, shaking, silent sobs.

"Tell me, Elizabeth," Konrad whispered over her bent head. "Tell me what is the matter with you?"

She said at last, "Nothing, now!" and pushed herself away from him.

"But you must tell me," he pleaded. "I can't believe —though I'd like to—that it was just because you saw me in the passage that you rushed into my arms!"

Elizabeth tried to smile. "No, it wasn't," she said. "It was because I knew—I'd just learned—that there wasn't any hope whatever about John and me. Of course I always knew there wasn't; but it's queer—as long as a man doesn't say 'I've stopped loving you'—something in you makes you believe he still does! Now I know he doesn't—so I'm quite free!"

"Yes—you seem to be," Konrad said with tender irony. Sitting on the bathroom stool, he drew Elizabeth into his arms again. "But all the same, I'd like to know how you feel so certain! You were coming out of Caroline's room. If it's anything she's told you, I think you can call it off."

"She may have lied," Elizabeth told him, "but behind her lies, I saw what there really was. It was enough, Konrad, and I couldn't be deceived by it. I don't quite know what to do next—that's the truth."

"Well, I'll tell you," Konrad said, pressing her closer. "I'm going to take you away for some hours anyhow,

192

and give you a little fun. You go straight to your room and dress up—in all your best things; put your dancing slippers in a bag; get the warmest coat you have—and then slip out of the dispensary door, in exactly an hour's time. I'll be free by then, and I'll meet you at the turn into the main road with a sleigh. I'll ring one up now —and just finish my rounds. Don't get there before an hour—nor too much after, for I shall be impatient and the night is cold. Don't think of anything beyond these hours! I'll see to all that—I'll see to everything now! I suppose in a way you trust me?"

Elizabeth gave a sound that was half a sob and half a laugh. "My hands are getting warm," she whispered. Konrad drew them against his bared heart—then he pushed her gently from him. "Now—go!" he said.

There was no-one in the passage. Elizabeth felt as if she were flying along it to the lift. A fierce, fiery joy thrilled her from head to foot. She would go with Konrad—she would be with him all night long. There would not be that awful loneliness any more—no wall stood between her and joy. She would wake again to love and laughter. God had saved both her and Caroline —and it didn't matter any more how much or how little Caroline had lied. Perhaps this was not quite the way in which God had meant Elizabeth to *be* saved; but she couldn't stop to think this out now. Anyhow, she *was* saved—and so was Caroline.

She reached her room and locked her door behind her, as if she were being pursued by someone. She had a fierce longing to be alone, and not to be prevented or held back, even for a moment. She wanted to see her beauty and clothe it undisturbed; yet she behaved with her usual orderliness, drawing out in its turn each thing she meant to wear. She stripped off her clothes for a shower and looked at her body with relief as if she were meeting an old friend whom she had not seen for a long time. She brushed her hair till it had a glittering look, and touched herself here and there with wild geranium scent that Konrad had sent her for Christmas, but which she had never used.

She enjoyed putting on the jewels John had given her, diamond earrings on her small shapely ears, and a lover's knot of diamonds at her breast. She would look as beautiful as she could in John's jewels—to please another man. What John had given to Caroline—pity—tenderness—mercy—ought not these jewels to have been given to Elizabeth?

The face she saw in her looking glass was beautiful, but in a new hard way, like some pretty girl's they were trying out in Hollywood to see if she were suitable for the pictures. It was a face without gentleness or trust. Suddenly Elizabeth thought, "I'm glad Michael hasn't seen me look like this!" Then she remembered that he must be waiting for her now and that he had a right to expect her. Elizabeth frowned at the pretty image in the glass—who when she frowned back suddenly looked much more like her.

The real Elizabeth did not break promises. Sister Peckham would certainly have given her message to Michael. But she couldn't see him—even thinking of him was like a lock on a door turned against her. She would do the next best thing, however: she would write him a note. But when she tried to write she could not get further than "Dear Michael." She looked at her watch: the hour was over. Hastily she caught up her cloak, and her dancing shoes. She was lucky again; no-one was in the lift, or in the long corridor below. The dispensary was empty and the door unlocked. The icy air unfolded her. It was wonderful to taste it against her lips and to be alive and free—as free as the air itself was free.

She knew the way by heart through the trees. It was perfectly still—not a branch nor a pine-cone stirred. The stars moved, they sparkled, shone, and plunged through space with the rush of hurled spears, but they made no sound; nor were they near enough, for all their bright sparklings, to change the darkness in which Elizabeth stood.

Suddenly she heard a voice quite close to her calling: "Elizabeth! Elizabeth!" It was Michael's voice. Elizabeth pressed against the thicker darkness of a pine, to merge with it, so that he could not see her, though she could not understand how Michael could possibly be out there in the wood at night. The voice called again a third time; and then she knew that Michael was not out in the wood at all: the low, clear voice was in her heart. "No, I can't help it, Michael!" she said out loud, "I can't! I can't!" And then she heard the sleigh bells jingling on the road below her; and in a moment she was through the trees—and it was Konrad, not Michael, who called "Elizabeth!"

26

A mere glance at Michael, on his short morning visit, warned John that his favourite patient was less well than usual. Sister Peckham said nothing, but as she handed John the chart her finger rested just beneath the dot that marked the flight upward of his temperature. In the morning it should have been slightly sub-normal: it was now 99.6°.

John told himself he would start his afternoon rounds with Michael and begin early, but he was detained till after eight o'clock in the evening by an important consultation at Davos, and when he got back, even by omitting his supper, he had barely time to wash and change before he started his final rounds.

He had not seen Elizabeth since the night before. He thought of her with a sharp, familiar pang. Before the golden circle of his happy marriage had been broken, she would have been waiting to catch him in his office with something to eat; but even more sustaining than food after a long and depressing day, would be the sense of that inner refuge, that unhindered harmony, which ignored drudgery and disaster. Now that the magic circle was broken, John knew that no matter what he had to face, there would be no hidden refuge. All that was invulnerable had left him—he was alone and exposed, like a single tree on a mountain height.

Michael was his first thought, and, as John had guessed beforehand, Michael was worse. His temperature was now two degrees higher than usual at that time of the evening; and for the first time since John had known him, Michael's eyes looked disturbed.

Before John had had time to speak, Michael asked him abruptly, almost accusingly, "Where is Elizabeth?"

"Elizabeth——?" John said with astonishment. "I suppose she's upstairs as usual in our flat. I've not seen her yet. I've only just got back from Davos or I'd have looked you up sooner. You don't look too good this evening. What is wrong with you?"

"It's nothing!" Michael said impatiently. "But I am quite sure you should find out at once where Elizabeth is! I have a strong feeling that she is in some trouble— perhaps in some danger. I don't think she's here—in the house. She was to have come to see me today—I even sent a message asking her to come, and she promised that she would—but she has *not* come!"

"Well—that's certainly very unlike her," John said soothingly, "but I shouldn't jump to the conclusion that there's anything wrong. Why should there be? If by any chance she has gone out, she will certainly have left a message to say where she is—and when she'll be back. I'll go and find out later, and let you know."

"If I were you," said Michael stubbornly, "I should find out now."

"All right," John agreed to quiet him. "I'll see Sister Albertine and ask her to ring up our flat; and if Elizabeth isn't there, Marie Céleste is sure to know where she is and all about her plans. I'll just take a listen at your chest first."

Michael said no more, but something in his eyes warned John to go straight to the night-sister's office, before he sounded Michael's chest.

John was relieved to find, after his examination finally

took place, that there was no fresh damage to Michael's lungs; but he was dissatisfied with his whole condition. He leaned back in his chair, and looked at Michael steadily for a long time, with his keen impersonal eyes.

"Suppose you tell me what you have on your mind," he said at last. "You've evidently got something on it, that isn't doing you any good."

"I have, what I have already told you," Michael said with quiet firmness. "I am definitely anxious about Elizabeth. My anxiety has not been caused by any rise of temperature—on the contrary, my temperature has risen because I am anxious."

John got up, and went again to Sister Albertine's office. He wished that Sister Peckham was on duty, but she had gone off at 8 p.m. and it was now nine. Sister Albertine was Swiss and fussy, but she was very thorough. She had done exactly what he had told her: she had rung up his flat, but there had been no answer. She had then rung up Marie Céleste: Marie Céleste had said she had no idea where Elizabeth was, but if John wanted to speak to her, she would be on duty in the office for the rest of the night.

Somehow or other John found that he did not want to speak to Marie Céleste. He rang up Konrad, while Sister Albertine twittered around him. Konrad was out. He had, however, left the usual message. John knew that Konrad was not on duty, and that he was quite free to go out. Nevertheless, he returned to Michael's room as disturbed as his patient. "Elizabeth doesn't appear to be in," he told Michael with careful unconcern. "Usually she *does* leave a message if she is going out; but this time she hasn't. She may have gone to a concert in Dorf; if so, she must have rung up for a sleigh: she did not take one of ours. However, there's nothing at all for us to worry about. Elizabeth is a most sensible person; she knows what risks there are in mountain places, and she hasn't taken her skis. I think I have never known her do a really silly thing."

"I am quite sure you have never known her do an inconsiderate one," Michael said gravely. "Why should she have been inconsiderate twice today—once to you —and once to me?"

The two men's eyes met without speech. Each had his own image of Elizabeth—and each looked in his friend's eyes for the reassurance of the other's.

"What is it that you think has happened?" John asked at last, letting his trouble free itself, into his voice. "Had you any warning that she was particularly upset?"

Michael shook his head. "She lives all the time under an almost insupportable strain," he observed, "and I think that today something happened to break down her control. I don't know what it is, but I think it is very important to find out. Have you asked exactly whom she has seen, and what she has done? When was she last seen—and who, if anyone, was with her? Where is Konrad, now for instance?"

Neither of them seemed to wish to break the silence that filled the room after Michael had spoken Konrad's name.

"I don't know," John said finally. "You think," he added heavily, "that they would be together—that she'd *want* to be with him—if she were upset?"

"I think it is at least possible," Michael admitted without further comment.

"I have not done, or said anything to make her feel worse," John said after a pause. "She is my wife—she wouldn't forget that, in order to run off with my best friend behind my back. She left no note—I ran upstairs to look. There was nothing. Besides, Konrad wouldn't take her like that! I don't say I *saved* his life, but he was in pretty poor shape when I took his case over, for a year, it was touch and go whether he would pull through or not. The relationship between the four of us is a rather specially strong and intimate one. Living up here alone in these mountains, we've been very isolated—sometimes in actual danger—surrounded for years by the whole Nazi pack and under their veiled menaces. We've shared practically everything in each other's minds. Of course there've been strains and stresses; and two years ago, this hidden break between Elizabeth and myself; but we've always been comrades —nothing changed that! If she meant to leave me, it wouldn't be like this. Besides, I think you are exaggerating. She must have just gone for a dance with Konrad and means to come back tonight. Marie Céleste is ringing up the night-Lokals in Davos for me now. Elizabeth took her fur coat—she was dressed for dancing —I looked. I know she lives under a constant strain— but I——" John stopped.

Michael said nothing. His eyes meeting John's were still relentlessly questioning, as if John—who felt that he had bared his whole heart to Michael—had told him nothing.

There was a long silence. Finally Michael said, "Very well then—we will accept that she has gone with Konrad to a dance-Lokal. Perhaps not in Davos—perhaps further—where we cannot tell. Marie Céleste will have done her questioning carefully. No-one will think anything of Elizabeth's having gone out for this evening with Konrad. But you and I must think something of it. We know that Elizabeth would not have broken her promise to me, or left you without a message, if nothing extraordinary had happened. Did she take round her books this afternoon?"

"Yes," John said unwillingly, "she seems to have

200

done everything as usual—only one thing was different. I rang up Sister Peckham—and asked her. Elizabeth left her trolley of books behind her—in Caroline's room."

"That would surely be enough," Michael said quietly. "Did you not immediately think so yourself? What did Caroline say to her?"

"What *could* she say?" John demanded with heightened colour. "You know yourself there is nothing she *could* say—nothing that Elizabeth need believe, I mean. Elizabeth *knows* Caroline is a liar!"

"We shall have to find out, nevertheless, exactly what Caroline *did* say to her," Michael persisted. "We cannot tell what goes on in other people's minds, except by the steps they take. Whatever it was that Caroline said, Elizabeth believed enough of it to go away without a word to anyone—even to her easiest friend, Marie Céleste."

"You say her *easiest*," John said sombrely, "you don't say her *best*?"

"I do not think our best friends are always our easiest," Michael answered. "*You* are her best friend, John—but you are not easy—perhaps you are not always easy enough."

John frowned and dug his hands viciously into his pockets.

"Well, it's no use bothering about all that now——" he said irritably. "The next thing to do is to get that cursed little brat next door to tell the truth. Frankly, I don't think I could afford to try. It might kill her to shake her—and shaking her is about all I have left in my locker. Whatever she *did* say—this is the end of Caroline—out she goes. I shall telegraph this evening to her mother to come and take her away."

"There is no hurry," Michael said gently. "Wait till

201

we know everything before you act. Meanwhile I will go and see Caroline for you."

"You aren't fit to move," John objected. "In case you don't know it—by your odd gift for thought-reading—your temperature is 102°—two degrees higher than I expect from your present condition, even at night. Seeing Caroline isn't likely to send your temperature any lower."

"Oh yes, it is," Michael said with a twinkle. "Caroline might relieve my mind very much—even without meaning to relieve it! Stay here till I come back—or go and do some important visit first—and then return. I'll be as quick as I can."

John glanced at him abashed. He felt himself suddenly mocked, and yet Michael's eyes, though they still smiled, were not mocking.

"Very well then—go," John said reluctantly, "and if you're the worse for it, I shall have to shoulder *that* responsibility as well as all the rest!"

Michael shook his head. "On the contrary," he said, "I am not a child of two—nor is Elizabeth. We are two self-deciding adults—like yourself, for instance! As a matter of fact, John, you have only one responsibility to shoulder—and that presumably hasn't occurred to you—you may be just a little responsible for Caroline!"

John swore at him; but he helped Michael on with his dressing gown, and knelt on the floor to put slippers on Michael's feet—while he was swearing. It took a long time, for John was nothing like as good a nurse as he was a doctor. Michael would rather have done these things for himself, and knew that he would have done them quicker, but he let John do them.

He wished there was some deeper way of re-assuring John about Elizabeth. He would have liked to tell John that he himself felt sure that Elizabeth would come back exactly as she went away—but he dared not shrink from letting John bear the full brunt of his long cruelty. The sense of personal rightness which had blurred John's vision would have to be torn off his eyes by pain. John could receive no profit from having given his body to be burned—against Love; nor could Love itself save him unless he was willing to share all that he had—even his stubborn pain—with Elizabeth.

While John was helping Michael, Michael spoke instead of John's self-reproachful anxiety about his own condition, for this, he thought, could be dealt with more safely.

"I shall be all the better," he explained, "when this business of Caroline's is cleared up. You know how difficult it is to reach her. The world she lives in is so very hard to escape from—even for a moment;— and the world she *doesn't* live in—which is more or less other people's world—she hardly notices at all; and I am very clumsy. I have really nothing to offer Caroline but my clumsiness. Still, I think she knows that I'm more sorry for her than I've ever been for anyone in my life—even the hungriest, pot-bellied Zulu child—so perhaps, as she likes pity and never gets enough of it— even of her own self-pity—we may manage to arrive at some of the truth together. I've had this on my mind all day long—wanting to have things out with Caroline —though of course I didn't know what there *was* to have out, till you asked about the books for me! But I'd been busy suspecting it—and suspicion is very bad for anyone even when they're well."

John ignored, although he felt vaguely soothed by, Michael's reassurances. He wanted to give a warning of his own to Michael, about Caroline, but he found it difficult to phrase it. In spite of all that had happened, John did not believe that anyone understood Caroline as well as he did. He wanted to tell Michael that the right way of treating Caroline—in fact the only way—when she was obdurate, was by force; but a curious doubt arrested John. He actually was not sure, until Michael had disappeared into the passage, what force should be used on Caroline.

27

Caroline was pleased to see Michael. It had been a long, exhausting day, and she had not quite known what to do with the last part of it. John had told her on his early rounds that he had an appointment in Davos in the late afternoon, and might not be back in time for his evening visits. Caroline made up her mind that she had nothing to look forward to, and that the day would be dull; but the day had not been dull.

Caroline had had exactly the kind of scene with Elizabeth that she had time after time painted for herself in her vivid imagination, an even better scene in some ways. Elizabeth, not having a great deal of imagination—and what she had being unhaunted by Caroline—had been taken entirely by surprise. She had made no real defence, and had run away like a frightened school-girl.

There was one curious moment, just before she ran away, when Elizabeth had looked frightening, instead of frightened; but it had led to nothing; she had gone and left her trolley of books behind her. Caroline had had nothing to face beyond her own physical reactions to excitement. Her heart behaved for an hour or two like a skittish horse that won't make up his mind whether to go backward or forward, her head ached as well; and Caroline asked Sister Peckham for an aspirin. Sister Peckham had given her one, in a churlish manner, after having made an unpleasant reference as to why

Elizabeth had left her books in Caroline's room. "Are you sure," she had asked acidly, "that you said nothing to upset Mrs. MacTaggart?"

Caroline looked at Sister Peckham scornfully and replied, "Surely *I* am the person to be upset if anyone is—not a perfectly well woman like Mrs. MacTaggart, who could run a mile as soon as look at me!"

After this fleeting triumph, Caroline's temperature went up, and she felt for a brief, excited hour on top of the world. But then the exultation gradually died down and she began to feel rather flat.

It was a great relief to see Michael, who was a person with whom Caroline felt that she could confidently share the emptiness of space. She had often told herself that she could turn Michael's head if she wanted to; but curiously enough she had never felt any inclination to turn it.

"I'm terribly tired, Michael," she now told him, "but I'm very glad to see you all the same. I know my temperature has been sky high by the way Nurse pretended it wasn't, and I've had a racking headache and some kind of heart upset. It's funny what a lot of things can happen to you when nothing is supposed to be happening at all! Well people can even think your life is dull when you're ill—but that's just the one thing you can't be—any duller than if you were clinging to a lobster pot in the middle of the Atlantic!"

Michael smiled at Caroline; but his eyes reached beyond her words, and were graver than usual.

"Did nothing happen today except feeling ill?" he asked her.

"Not really," Caroline told him in an airy way. "I mean, I don't need things to happen, to start me off feeling ill. John isn't trying any new injection on me, or anything like that, just now; but he lets me sit up to have my bed made, and I can have visitors if they aren't tiring ones. I like having you because I feel as if I don't have to say anything to you unless I want to!"

"No, not unless you want to," Michael agreed, but his eyes went on asking her what had upset her.

Caroline hesitated. It occurred to her that she had done a brave and good thing in asking Elizabeth to set John free,—perhaps just the kind of thing that might persuade Michael to give her absolution. She had been rather glad to think she needn't see John till tomorrow, because although of course John would like being free, he might not like Caroline's having set him free. But surely Michael would take a more enlightened view? He knew that very ill people fight at a grave risk, and Caroline had fought Elizabeth in order to save both herself—and John."

"Well," Caroline said at last, "in a sense something *did* happen! I have known for a long time that there was something wrong in this hospital, and though it was hard for me to do it—I had to work myself up over it for a long time—today I tried to set it right. I suppose that's why I felt ill afterwards. It was like Christian fighting with Apollyon. There seemed nothing left to breathe with—after Elizabeth had left the room."

"Elizabeth then—was Apollyon?" Michael asked a little drily.

"Yes—but I'm not altogether sure it was a *final* victory," Caroline went on after a pause. "I'm not *sure* that she meant to do—what she now sees she ought to do! I should rather like to have your opinion about it— if you could give it, I mean, without being a clergyman or anything of that kind?"

"I could try," Michael suggested. "But I think you would have to tell me a little more about it first—what actually happened, I mean, and why you think Elizabeth is your enemy."

"I don't look on Elizabeth as a personal enemy at all," Caroline told him with generous kindness, "just as a power for evil. I'm really quite sorry for her in a way. She never seems to know what to talk about, and sits on the edge of chairs. I expect John liked to play outdoor games with her. Of course you know all about their marriage? It was a cruel mistake from the first. Actually Elizabeth is rather fond of Konrad now—at least, Nurse Oliver seems to think so—but perhaps that's only because she's got a crush on Konrad herself —quite uselessly; he's a terrible flirt, and just likes to play about with any girl who'll let him. You know that kind of man—the very opposite of John, who's marvellously loyal and constant.

"I knew John would go on for ever with Elizabeth— both of them breaking their hearts about nothing—if no one helped them out of it. So I prayed for quite a long time about it, and then I made up my mind to tell Elizabeth the truth; when she came in with my books— I told her!"

"You told her—exactly what?" Michael asked in a low voice. He turned his eyes away from Caroline, while he waited for her answer.

"Naturally I told her that John wanted to be free again," Caroline said a little impatiently; fond as she was of Michael, she often thought him rather slow in the up-take—slower than John—and far, far slower than Konrad!

"But how did you know this was the truth?" Michael stupidly persisted. "Had John told you that he wanted to be free?"

"You don't need to be *told*, when you love a person —you just *know*!" Caroline explained kindly. "I know that John would never ask to be released, so I asked for him! I made a tremendous effort—I should think you would want to absolve me from that other thing, now you realise what an effort I've made to help things all round. Elizabeth quite took it in; she didn't answer me exactly—she simply got up and ran away. I expect she was astonished at my courage."

Michael got up; he held on to the chair he had been sitting on, as if he wanted support. Then he turned towards the balcony door, which opened on the dark. It was a relief to him to look into the starless, untenanted night.

"Caroline," he said over his shoulder, "when you had that trouble with Konrad, it was because you imagined things in his mind that weren't there. You were angry with him—and punished him—for things that had never happened. You suffered very much yourself afterwards, because what is not true often has very painful results. That is why I could not give you absolution—you had not got to the point where you saw what you had done—and I still think you have not reached that point, because you are still inventing things in people's minds—that are not really there—and acting upon your inventions. This has happened now. You are imagining what is in John's mind—and you have told Elizabeth what you think it is. You may have to suffer for this very severely as well as John and Elizabeth. It is true that you have courage; but perhaps other people's lives are not very good material for our courage. Our own lives need all the courage that we have got. John is your friend and your doctor: I do not think he is your lover, or that you have any grounds for thinking so. Elizabeth is his wife. Whatever wrong they have done each other—if they *have* done each other a wrong in their married lives—is strictly their own

affair. We must not speak of it or—if we can help it—
even think of it. We must accept them as they are."

Caroline was not as angry as she expected to be with
Michael's long speech. She listened quite quietly to
what he said, without interrupting him. The words
he used did not seem to be particularly about her. It
was as if Michael were sharing with her a difficulty
common to them both. When he had finished, she felt
that he needed instruction rather than reproof.

"But Michael, it would be very selfish of us—surely
—not to try to help them?" she said. "About Konrad—
I think I know what you mean. I did rather put on an
act, though there was far more basis to it than John
thought! It was so dull with John away—and you were
too ill to come and talk to me—but I couldn't have
flirted with Konrad if he hadn't wanted to flirt with
me! Still, none of all that was quite real, but what is
between John and me *is* real! I'm not pretending at all
about John!"

For a long time Michael was quite silent. Caroline
had a funny feeling as if he had gone a long distance
away from her, and could not come back very easily.

At last he said, "You are responsible for what is in
your own mind, Caroline, but not at all for what is in
John's. It is there that your sense of reality breaks
down. You must not invent what he is thinking, nor
act upon your inventions, or you will lose all he has
to give you! Don't you remember how very nearly
you lost it once before?"

"You think I shouldn't have told Elizabeth the truth?"
Caroline asked incredulously. What seemed even more
incredible to Caroline than Michael's obtuseness was
that he never answered her last question. The door
closed after him very softly; and the word "truth"
seemed to remain in the room, long after he had left it.

28

The moon was not yet up, but a faint pool of light heralded her rising, cutting the jagged edges of the peak above her away from the massed darkness. Where Davos lay, a troop of dancing lights spread flat on the valley floor, sparkling in vain against the heavy layer of night that lay between them and their fellow stars. The jangle of the sleigh bells sank into the frozen silence without changing it. The air was still, but every breath they drew had the shock of a separate experience.

Konrad had what he wanted at last. Elizabeth was alone with him; and he could concentrate all his heart and mind upon making her conscious of nothing else but him. She would never see the stars again as she saw them on this night. They were no longer distant or incommunicable; they were close above their heads and shone with her lover's longing.

The narrow track of desire closed in upon Elizabeth without expanse or turning. Rapture drove her along it; but she knew that she was being driven. No voice could speak in her heart now but Konrad's; an intemperate, blind ecstasy ran between them, like the magic draught Iseult drank with Tristram instead of with the King.

"Konrad," Elizabeth whispered, with the last stab of her retreating conscience, "why do I feel so strange?"

Konrad laughed at her tenderly. "So did Cinderella," he reminded her, "when the pumpkin turned into the fairy coach. You have lived too long in the kitchen,

Elizabeth, among the ashes. *You* are not strange—it is joy that is strange to you—you have forgotten it!"

The new born Elizabeth was silent, but she still kept a little of the old Elizabeth's discipline; she knew that she must not disappoint her new lover who depended on her joy for his happiness. She gave herself up to Konrad's eyes and hands; she laughed back at his words, and surrendered to his kisses; but she still felt strange.

She saw that they were dropping away from Davos far down the valley; and asked no questions. She felt that she would like to drive forever, to the sound of sleigh bells, through the icy air; and never arrive.

"This place I am taking you to," Konrad told her at last, "is a good Lokal; it is gay but not at all rowdy. People go there who know how to enjoy themselves properly. The Swiss themselves don't frequent it—but they run it. They provide good food, good wine, good music. They have hired a band of Hungarian gypsies too—refugees who no doubt come cheap—but to listen to them is not cheap! Hungarian music—as the gypsies play it—is as light as a Salsburger-Gnöckel, but it is not only light, it grips the heart. You can't get away from it. It tells you that there's nothing in a man's life as sweet as love—or as dangerous. You are not afraid of love, are you, Elizabeth? You have courage?"

Elizabeth thought this question over very carefully. She had been brought up on courage. Her father had taught her to take whatever came without flinching. "You must go on till you drop," he had told her, "and then drop as quietly as possible." But to go out into things, Elizabeth thought, was perhaps different from going on with them. It might require a different kind of courage. She knew she could resist, that she discounted pain, that she would not give up easily what she believed in. Elizabeth had—and knew that she had

—what is called 'back to the wall' courage; but what if there were no wall—would she have courage then? As long as John had been with her—however hard what he expected of her was—there had been a wall. Now she was running away from the wall. Was she running away because the wall itself had fallen, or because her courage had depended upon it, instead of upon what was in herself? Was it not courage to escape from a smaller life into a larger, from emptiness into something tingling with life? Wasn't the real question what were you using your courage *for*? Or was running away—wherever you ran to—always cowardice?

She said after a long pause, "I don't really know, Konrad, if I have courage or not."

"Well," he said, drawing her closer, "then tonight you are going to find out! But Elizabeth, before we find this out, and the Slav music gets into our blood, I have something I ought to tell you. I cannot ask you to join my life without telling you I have been—perhaps I still am—corrupt. I drink at times like a fish—and unfortunately I have not a fish's aptitude for drinking, however, I am not a drunkard. I am only a man who is very easily shaken out of his wits—a pretty face will shake me—disappointment shakes me—fear of any kind shakes me. I suppose I am a light man—I have always enjoyed whatever I could get hold of to enjoy; but I want you to believe that when it comes to serious things, I can be serious. Marie Céleste will tell you that I kept my wits when other people depended on them; and when it comes to a serious love affair, I can be serious too! I loved my wife seriously—just as I love you, Elizabeth. She is gone—the war took her—but I did not throw her away. I need not be ashamed of the love I gave her—and you need not be ashamed of it either!

213

"Because I am—what I am—I may disappoint you often; but I shall not change to you—the deepest thing in me will always be yours."

Elizabeth was silent again, and for a still longer time; then she said, "I don't know that I mind risks—about you particularly; after all, I've known you pretty well for four years—and I've always liked you. But you see I might be afraid that you would not trust *me*. Why should you—or any man trust me—after tonight?"

"Do you suppose," Konrad asked her with a gravity she had never heard in his voice before, "that I don't know what happened to your marriage—or that I blame you for it? You do not need to tell me anything at all—and I shall always trust you. I am quite sure you were never unfaithful to John. Yet I know you did what John calls 'wrong': Marie Céleste and I have often talked of what it might have been—forgive me, darling—we have even laughed about it, because we knew it must be a thing we *could* laugh at!"

"No—no—it wasn't!" Elizabeth said quickly. "I felt exactly how wrong it was. I agreed with John. You could not laugh at what I did. I did not take a lover— what I did was out of hate. I have sometimes thought John might have pitied me for doing it, but perhaps pity would not have been quite fair either. I should not do it again. I am sure of this—because when I wanted to—I didn't. But that does not mean that I might not make very bad mistakes—too bad for me to trust myself, or to ask you to trust me. Perhaps what I am doing now is one of these mistakes. I want you to *understand* this, Konrad, and not just admire me! I spoilt John's happiness—he did not spoil mine. I do not think it would be nice to spoil anyone else's happiness."

Konrad drew her closer against his breast, and between his passionate kisses he told her, "I shall not let my happiness in you be spoiled!" But although she returned his kisses, Elizabeth was not sure if she believed that Konrad could prevent their happiness from being spoiled. She was not even sure that it was happiness. Would she have courage enough to face another desolating surprise? If their happiness were only pleasing each other, would it not die of its own greed and selfishness?

Elizabeth had always been deeply aware of Konrad's subtle understanding of her as a woman. She had realised throughout their whole relationship that he eased her life by the homage of constant little services. But could they not be taken away from her?—and if they were ever taken away, what would be left? When John's love had been withdrawn, Elizabeth had had something left. She did not want to think of it now—it hurt her like a fire scorches—but she knew that she had had respect. Her respect for John remained; and even—though he denied her love—John's respect for her. He had not quite lost his confidence in Elizabeth. He still talked over his patients with her; he thought she did her work very well. He would not have thought that she would run away with Konrad.

The clear darkness was suddenly broken up by a cluster of dancing lights. "There is 'The Quiet Lizard'," Konrad told her. " 'The Quiet Lizard' has all that I think a good Nacht-Lokal should possess—a French cook—Hungarian music—and anonymity. No-one here is likely to recognise you. They will simply say, 'Our good Konrad has a lucky evening!' They have something on their minds besides other people's business; and since everyone pays enormously highly for their evening's pleasure, they are likely to mind their own business, rather than ours."

"He will be very considerate of me always," Elizabeth

thought, "but I shall have to get used to having to be considered."

Konrad looked long and appraisingly at Elizabeth, as she passed before him, down the icy steps into the light above 'The Quiet Lizard's' door. She was, he thought, beautiful, but not at all conspicuously beautiful. It was not enough to look at her: she had to answer your look, before you realised that it was supremely worth while to go on looking at her; and Elizabeth would not look at any other man but Konrad in a Nacht-Lokal.

The hall was dark, but it was warm and flower-scented. Music thrilled through the air and stirred the senses. 'The Quiet Lizard' had its own laws and its own world, and knew just what to make of both.

Elizabeth was guided away from Konrad into a beautifully lit and scrupulously cared for dressing room. The girl who took her cloak from her gazed at her with ravished eyes. Elizabeth saw a half familiar figure flashed back at her from a dozen mirrors. She was a little surprised at her own image. Did she really look so astonishingly well? Were her cheeks so light and firm a pink, her eyes so shining and so deep a blue, her sea-green dress—with its embroidered silver lilies on the panels of her swinging skirt—so becoming to her rounded slenderness?

"I hope it has a strong clasp, *Gnädigste*!" the girl said, her fascinated eyes intent on the diamond knot between Elizabeth's breasts.

"Yes," Elizabeth said smiling, "it has a very good clasp. It would have to be torn off me; and as my father taught me how to box, I should not make it very easy for anyone who tried to tear it off me!"

"*Unmöglich!*" the girl murmured respectfully. "But foolish," she thought to herself, "when you look so that any man would box for you!"

216

Nevertheless the girl liked Elizabeth, and all the more that she thought Elizabeth did not know how to use what she had got.

Konrad was waiting for her under an imitation bread fruit tree. The Swiss felt that with a temperature apt to fall twenty degrees below zero, a tropical outfit would appeal most to their clients.

It was evident that Konrad felt very much at home in this half-lit, nerve-stirring place.

The dance room into which he took Elizabeth was painted to look like a South Sea Island. Sheets of artificial bougainvillaea hung in curtains of apricot, purple and bright crimson from painted trees. Scarlet 'Flames of the Forest' reared above a bar that shone like an altar. Banana leaves in long green ribbons stood out from shadowy walls. Each carefully alcoved table had its own glass tank full of iridescent fish. There was even a painted turquoise pool, above which the gypsies played.

"Soon you will be as warm as you are meant to feel," Konrad told Elizabeth, "but these transformations depend a trifle upon the stimulants that you consume! A little hot Glüwein is advisable before we dance."

The music poured over them like water, melting them into each other. Elizabeth had often danced with Konrad before and she knew that there were very few physical pleasures to match dancing with him. Every muscle in her body released itself into fresh movement. Konrad could make any woman dance well, but when a woman was already a good dancer he could make her feel as if there was no difference at all between her senses and what stirred them. But they had not danced together to gypsy music before: it was like swimming in water so alive with salt that you cannot drown.

Elizabeth plunged deep into the strange, intoxicating

217

sea of sound. The rapture of the depths took hold of her as it sometimes takes hold of deep sea divers, so that a man has been known to throw away the mouthpiece through which alone he can breathe and live.

Elizabeth and Konrad danced until she did not know in what world or through what element they moved, nor did she know which was Konrad and which of them was herself.

"We must stop dancing," Konrad whispered. "You are trembling all over with exhaustion. Such music uses all you have!"

They sat in silence in their sheltered alcove between the long swaying ribbons of the cleverly pretence-banana leaves. Konrad's eyes meeting Elizabeth's knew that she was drunk with acceptance. For the first time he felt sure of his hold upon her future. He began to ask her tender, teasing, intimate questions. Elizabeth's simple, straightforward answers delighted him like wit. She could be as stupid as she liked tonight: her least expression pleased him. She could not make a mistake. She was successful without, she thought, anything to be successful about. There was no question of a flying trapeze whose rings she had to catch. Konrad asked nothing of her—beyond acquiescence. Gifts fell from the skies into her open hands.

No-one was dancing any more. Once in the evening the Leader played, accompanied only by the piano; and everybody in the room sat still, drinking and listening. Elizabeth's eyes left Konrad's. The Band Leader, still under the spell of her beauty, was playing for Elizabeth alone; she knew the music—the opening bars of the Kreutzer Sonata. She and John had heard it separately in the great Toronto concert hall, in the early days of the disastrous unequal war, between the distant small Island they loved and its tremendous enemy. Hitler's invincible army held all Europe in its grip except that one small Island. Their eyes met across a sea of faces and locked together in stern sympathy—and the music drove them on—beyond sympathy—into conscious love. After that long look, the music was no longer a single experience; whatever happened in that stormy sea of sound—ecstasy—conflict—release and ultimate harmony—happened to them together.

Elizabeth knew now what courage was: it was the acceptance of this partnership. She could not decide alone, what she would do with her life, since it was part of John's. They had accepted this togetherness—its storms, its agonies and ecstacies—even at the end of it—its loneliness. There were no decisions she could make without him. Once and for all—she must go straight back to John, and tell him that if he wanted his freedom it was his; but he must accept it from her hands—she could not take it away from him without his acceptance. What she had given to Konrad already had not been hers to give—it was stolen from John. She must give Konrad no more; she did not need to meet his eyes, to know that Konrad would take all she had. He would break her down with his ruthless longing —with his logic—with her own remorse for the pain she gave him. These were things Elizabeth knew, without thinking about them. She was too poor and starved a suppliant in the court of love to keep her integrity against Konrad's pleading mastery. This was the answer to his question. She had courage—the courage to run away and face John. She knew now that it would be the ultimate cowardice to run away without facing John.

Elizabeth sat very straight and still with her eyes turned away from Konrad's. She saw the other faces in the room now. All of them were sad—the Band Leader's was perhaps the saddest face of all. Why should he not be sad? He had been bereft—by the time it took to ring a bell and enter a house—of his country, his speech, his friends, all his little homely habits and traditions. It might be that he also lost—as Konrad had lost—his wife and children. It was lucky for him that he still possessed music and the knowledge of how to make it for others.

This was the haunt of pleasure, the expensive, beautiful haunt, and the taste of it was bitter as salt—even to the pleasure makers. Those sitting there simply to take pleasure, or who were trying to escape by it—were alike prisoners. The business of living had, for one reason or another, proved too hard for them; but Elizabeth had no such excuse. She liked the business of living. She had got into the wrong world and was not at home in it.

Konrad did not feel her slipping away from him. Yet Elizabeth thought that it was a cruel thing to leave him now—though far less cruel than if she stayed. Counterfeit loving, excitement and a desire to escape, were not what you gave to an honest lover, who gave you all the heart he had left in him to give.

The Kreutzer rose to its peak—shattered all its glory—and fought its slow way back to peace. Elizabeth turned her eyes back to Konrad's. He saw nothing in them but their beauty. "I am going to tidy up," she told him. "Wait for me—here—I may be a little long, quite ten minutes perhaps. I danced something loose that I shall have to mend."

The same girl was still in the lovely little scented empty room. "I am in trouble," Elizabeth said quickly. "I am going straight home by myself. Is there a train I can catch?"

"There is only the milk train left, *Gnädigste*," the girl said breathlessly. "It runs up to Davos at four o'clock. I don't know if you can catch it. The station is nearer by the back way."

Elizabeth already had her coat on. They slipped down a half lighted corridor—the music following them—and stood for a moment under a dim light above the door.

"Wait ten minutes," Elizabeth told her urgently. "Misdirect him when he asks where I've gone; and then give him—the man I was with, Dr. Rainer—you know his name—this card!" "I can't go on," Elizabeth had written on a card snatched from her handbag. She wanted to add, "Forgive me!" but she thought perhaps it would be better for Konrad not to forgive her.

"The station is across the way, you can't miss it!" the girl told her. Elizabeth took up her skirts and ran: it was almost as if the girl watching her, ran with her.

Elizabeth had forgotten to change her dance slippers; but if her feet had been bare, she could have run through the snow without noticing it. She caught the milk train while it was already trying to clank its way out of the station.

"You damned fool! Is your life worth nothing to you?" the guard shouted angrily, as he dragged Elizabeth from the footboard into the rocking train. He thought he might be going to have some fun with her after she'd settled down; but Elizabeth looked at him with eyes sharp as icicles, and said, "Nothing at all!" He let her arm drop and muttered, "Unheimlich" as he watched her step, poised and alert, through the rocking cans.

Elizabeth sat on the hard seat of a third class carriage perfectly erect, and still. Her head was as empty as her heart; but though she could not think or feel, she was aware, while the little train rattled and banged its way up through the hidden mountains and under the last stars, that she was going home to face John; and she was even aware that there was more of her to face him than there had been—of the Elizabeth who ran away from him, and had taken shelter a few hours earlier in Konrad's arms.

29

*E*lizabeth came out of the dense mist of the valley into the grey visibility of the dawn. Pin points of stars quivered without hope against the retreating shelter of the night.

The Sanatorium had reached its last lap of sleep. Those who had not slept all night, slept now; and those who could only sleep restlessly, sank into rest. The pine woods slowly cut themselves away from the wall of snow mountain that rose above them. Colourless peaks soared into the less solid pallor of the sky. The silence was so complete that Elizabeth thought her heart-beats were more audible than a footstep. She had not felt conscious of the cold until the door behind her closed, and she found herself in the hall. She saw a faint line of light under John's office door, and heard voices behind it.

Although they had been listening and watching for her all night, they did not hear her light footsteps, nor for a moment see her, as she stood in the open doorway.

John stood with his back to her, his hand on the telephone. "I must ring up the police whatever you say!" he told Marie Céleste in the angry voice of a man who is desperate from inaction. "We don't know where she is: anything may have happened to her!"

"And how do you know that she *wants* to be found?" Marie Céleste answered accusingly. "What is in other people's minds you never think of!"

Marie Céleste sat inert, her hands in her lap. She had a dishevelled look as if she had been travelling for so long a time that she had ceased to care what she looked like when she arrived. The fire and zest of life had gone out of her. She was the first to see Elizabeth.

"Alors, c'est toi!" she said, lifting her hands from her lap. "Qu'est ce que tu as fait avec notre cher Konrad?" She did not move, and her tragic eyes fixed themselves on Elizabeth with bitter irony.

Elizabeth found she could not move her mouth easily: her cheeks closed in on it as stiffly as walls.

"I left him," she said between little pauses. "I caught the milk train from Klosters. I don't know where he is."

Elizabeth answered Marie Céleste but she looked at John. His head had turned in a flash at the sound of her voice, but not too quickly to have shown the relief in his eyes—if there had been relief. He looked at her instead with fierce exasperation.

Adoration and delight were gone. Elizabeth had left the world where she was a queen who could do no wrong, and whose every wish was law. She need not have returned to these middle-aged people who had sat up all night waiting for her—like enemies.

Marie Céleste got up with a brisk movement. "You don't know where he is," she said, "and does he by any chance know where you are? You seem to have a gift for disappearing without a trace!"

"No—I don't think he does—there wasn't much time," Elizabeth faltered, "but I left a note."

"Ah!" Marie Céleste said on an indrawn breath. "I see exactly how it is—he sits there at Klosters by himself. There is no train—no sleigh. He is aware you have stood him up—and that he may now drink himself to death at his leisure—hein? *Je m'en fiche de tous les deux*—I go after him!"

Marie Céleste's voice cut like a whip lash, and she was out of the room before Elizabeth could think of an answer.

"Take the sleigh," John said before the door shut. He had not taken his eyes away from Elizabeth; nor had he spoken a word to her; he looked at her as if he saw her in her lover's arms.

The door clicked sharply behind Marie Céleste. The falling wood moved in the big yellow stove that warmed the room. Elizabeth felt the weight of her fur coat dragging her down to the ground—and yet she did not open it; she did not want John to see the diamonds on her dress.

"I couldn't go on," she whispered.

John's heavy eyelids shot up till they reached his thick, untidy hair. "Why did you go away at all?" he demanded. "No doubt you'll tell me it was because of what Caroline told you. I sent Michael in to find out. But you must have known she lied!"

Elizabeth, not being able to move her lips again, said nothing. She looked about her for a chair but they seemed to be too far off. John, his eyes racking her from head to foot in merciless condemnation, suddenly said, "There's blood on your shoe! God damn you, Elizabeth, do you mean to say you walked three miles in dance shoes through the snow?"

He moved before she had time to speak, picked her up, and laid her with extraordinary gentleness, on the couch, where he should have slept.

Elizabeth said nothing: she knew now there was nothing she need say. Her eyes followed his every movement with relief.

John brushed away his night of a thousand knives as if it had never existed: he thought only of Elizabeth's needs. With infinite care, he cut away the frozen fragments of her dancing shoes. He opened the window,

224

shovelled snow into a bowl, and began gently to manipulate the numb wooden things she had been using as her feet. It was the hill that had mattered, after the freezing valley mist; she had run through the valley, but the last part of the hill she had feared she might not be able to make her feet move any more. But then she thought she would still have tried to reach John, if she hadn't had any feet. She had seen the faint night lights of the Sanatorium through the trees; and now she had got back. This was John. He had put on an electric kettle to make her tea; he drew off her coat and pulled the blankets over her loosened dress. He did not seem to mind, or even to notice, the lover's knot of diamonds he unfastened, nor the shining earrings that he took off with exquisite gentleness, so that her head might rest better, against his rather hard night pillow.

"There," he said, "don't talk! I daresay you couldn't if you tried—your chin's too stiff! This other foot isn't so bad: I'll just rub the toes a bit; moving along fairly fast as you must have done, has helped them from getting too badly bitten. Still they're both a little on the frozen side. I'm just going to make sure of getting hold of some pretty good stuff those mountain expedition people used last year, for anti-frostbite injections. I've got some in the dispensary. The water'll be boiling by the time I get back, for tea. I can't put anything warm near you just yet, but drinking boiling tea will do the trick."

He moved with such speed and certainty that everything he touched seemed to meet him half way. Elizabeth lay still and watched him with a joy that was like warmth. The heavy unrelieved lines of his face that had set like a mask seemed to have receded; he looked young and lively, and his eyes that had been so hard and hot with anger, smiled.

He lifted her head, cupping it with one big hand, as if she had been a new born baby, while he fed her from the other with a feeding cup.

"It's not very comfortable here, I'm afraid," he murmured apologetically, "but as soon as I get these feet dressed I'll carry you upstairs to your room. You must drink a lot—all you can. Go on! Show me your hands! You wore gloves? Well, that showed some sense —but why the hell didn't you go into a hotel at Davos —ring up one of these night porter fellows—and get a sleigh to bring you out here?"

The hot tea eased her frozen jaws, and she said, "Well——" quite easily. She did not know whether it was heat or cold that ran burning through her veins— but something ran—and she did not feel like Lot's wife any more. "Everything was asleep," she explained. "I did think of hotels, but then I'd have had to say who I was, and at the station I just got out—I had my coat on and everything—and somehow I felt in a hurry— and so—I ran."

"And I told Michael you were a sensible girl!" John said drily. "By-the-bye—I ought to ring up Sister Albertine and give her a message for Michael. You can hold this cup now—with both hands—they're still shaking! I expect Michael's been praying all night—or something of that sort. It seems he'd been expecting you all day and got awfully fussed about it—thought something had happened to you. Queer chap, though likeable! I don't believe in second sight of course, but the senses can play tricks with these over-sensitives. Don't drink too fast or you'll choke. Can you feel the big toe of your right foot now? 'Pins and needles'? That's just what you ought to feel in it—they'll get a damned sight sharper in a minute or two."

He moved to the telephone and gave his message,

but he did not turn his back on Elizabeth even while he spoke. His eyes rested on her with kindness but not with love. She had enough to bear, he thought, without fresh emotion. Perhaps she had not even got this emotion—for him. She might very well have lost it, and come back only from loyalty. In spite of his pride, John was, in some ways, a humble man. He put into the lucid instructions that he gave to Sister Albertine, the love he kept out of his eyes.

"We'll have hot water bottles soon," he told Elizabeth, coming back to rub her feet with his sure, determined hands. "However much it hurts we must get life back into them. This injection I'm going to give you won't be very comfortable, I'm afraid. Would you like Sister to come, and help with it?"

Elizabeth shook her head. She found that acute pain was nothing at all compared to remorse. What happened to her feet didn't matter—but what had happened to her straying heart was too terrible to contemplate.

"Has Marie Céleste taken the sleigh?" she asked.

It was the kind of unfortunate question that Desdemona might have asked, and John's face promptly hardened as if he had been Othello.

"I'll find out," he said, rising from his knees as if he would never come near her again; and this time when he took up the telephone, he turned his back on Elizabeth.

"She's taken the sleigh—it's all right," he told her without turning round. "She'll get hold of him—one way or another—and fetch him back. You know she's pretty fond of him. Not that it matters. I mean, you're perfectly free to do what you like. There's nothing to prevent it."

He went out of the room, and returned with the injection. It took a long time to get the needle into the frozen vein, and hurt her so abominably that Elizabeth wondered if she could bear it; but she did bear it, and when John drew out the needle, he said, "That's a good girl" as if he had found something he expected in her.

Sister Albertine rang up to say that Elizabeth's room was now warm and ready; everything had been thought of and attended to. She made various fresh offers, which John apparently and not very graciously, refused.

"No, I don't need any help," he finished crossly, but greatly to Elizabeth's satisfaction. "Only remember where I am, and see that the extension is on. I shall stay with Mrs. MacTaggart, for the time being; her feet may need further attention."

The Sanatorium had begun to waken. The windows at the corridor ends gave more light than the blue lamps, which were never turned off.

Sister Albertine and the night nurse in attendance drank their last cups of tea. The day nurses began to get up. The early wakers, who were convinced they had not slept all night, impatiently rang their bells. More lights went on.

John carried Elizabeth to the lift as if she were very precious china; but Elizabeth did not feel precious. It was impossible to be in John's arms, and not feel worthless. He looked away from her, and did not make it any harder for her than he could help. What he could not help, was that he held in his arms the whole meaning of his life—and knew that he might have lost it.

Elizabeth's room was warm and brightly lit. It was, Elizabeth thought, a very pretty room to make a person's heart ache quite so much. He laid her carefully on her own bed, and said, "You'd better take your dress off now. Shall I help you?" Then when she said he needn't, he left her for a few moments. "You mustn't move off your bed," he told her.

If he hadn't noticed her dress before, he must notice it now, Elizabeth thought, flung over the chair beside the bed—the lovely brocaded sea-green stuff with the silver lilies, they had bought together in Paris three years ago, at a fabulous price from a fabulous French house. She hadn't worn it very often, and this made it worse that she should have worn it, just this night.

It seemed a very long time before John came back again with another drink.

"Now you can stand something a little stronger," he told her. "It's a pick-me-up. That foot's a better colour now. I daresay you haven't done yourself much harm, in spite of having tried to!"

His mouth twitched as he spoke, and Elizabeth saw it was almost a smile, so he couldn't have minded the dress as much as she had thought he might.

"I had to come back," she said, after the lovely fiery drink gave her courage to speak. "You see—I wasn't quite sure!"

"What seems odd to me," John observed, "isn't your coming back—though I don't care for the method —but I still don't know why you ever went away—I mean, without letting anybody know where, or—if you meant—to return?"

He stood a little awkwardly at the end of her bed, trying not to remember that he had not been in her room for two years.

"Everything was, as far as I was concerned, just as usual," he added, "and Caroline's lying wasn't out of the way either."

"It was what you hadn't done about it that—that unsettled me," Elizabeth explained. "She had done that dreadful thing—while we were away—and yet—you kept her on. So when she told me what she did— although I knew that it couldn't be quite true—I felt she knew too much about us. She called you 'John'. If there had been nothing—nothing whatever between you—would she have called you 'John'?"

"She might have—she has the cheek to do any damned thing," John answered after a pause. "Still, I'm not denying that there was a sort of—well—tenderness between us. I wanted her to get better more than I wanted most of my patients to get better—and that's, as you know, enough. Still, I must say, you're pretty strict, aren't you, if you insist that there shouldn't be anything—anything at all between me and another woman? There's Marie Céleste, for instance—she means a lot more to me than Caroline ever could—but you pushed her down my throat yourself. Don't you count her?"

Elizabeth considered this fact in silence. "Yes—but I trusted her," she observed finally. "Besides, she's French. She knew what I meant—and she liked us both. This girl I didn't know—and she didn't like me—so it was quite different. It made me feel—an outcast."

"It couldn't have made you feel any more of an outcast than I already felt," John reminded her. "What about Konrad—or for that matter—Michael? One you gave a piece of your soul to—you can't think I enjoyed that confession stunt! And the other may have had—anything—how was I to know? And I did a considerable amount of figuring out too!"

"But neither of them had both!" Elizabeth said quietly. "You knew that—I showed you—that *you* had both! That's why I went up to the hut. You knew then, but you wouldn't care!"

"Oh! I cared all right," John told her morosely. "But the way I looked at it then was—that I had to put up with caring! We'd decided—both of us together—

what was right to do and we were doing it. I didn't
see why you had to change when I didn't."

"I changed because I found I could," Elizabeth said
quietly. "I daresay it's all right *not* to change—if you
can't—but I was very glad to find I could. I think I'd
minded enough."

John raised his eyes, and looked at her, as a man
looks at another man, in whom he trusts. "Yes—
perhaps you had," he agreed. "I really hadn't been
thinking about the way you minded it. I see that now;
but you needn't think I've changed because of the
merry hell you've given me tonight—nor because of
what this nice chap Michael has up his sleeve about
God. I've changed because I found I daren't go in and
see Caroline after I knew she'd lied to you. I had to
send Michael to find out what she'd said. I didn't trust
myself to go in because I knew I'd have killed her.
You can kill a girl . . . as ill as that, very easily. That
showed me—what you'd done about Brandt. Before I
couldn't understand it—now I can."

"You mean—you *have* changed?" Elizabeth said.

"Yes," John repeated, "I've changed. I'm never
going to let you out of my sight again—unless you
want to be let out! It's no use trying to give parts of
oneself away to other people—when the whole of
yourself belongs to one person. Besides, I don't see
anything the way I did—how can I? Caroline is my
patient. I've done her far more determined harm than
you ever did Brandt. It's much worse to like what
you don't respect out of vanity—than to hate what you
don't respect—with perfectly good grounds for it, as
I must admit you had! But you needn't worry; I'm
really going to act now. I'm sending Caroline away,
though I know it may cost her her life—and that it's
my fault if it does. I don't know how you feel about

Konrad—and I don't want to know. I'll give you all the time you want to come round—and if you don't come round I'll make it easy for you both to go. But I know you came back—just as Michael said you would!"

Elizabeth nodded. It was on the tip of her tongue to say that had she seen Michael, she would never have gone with Konrad; but she decided that since John was jealous where he had no need to be jealous—as well as where she had given him cause—she could spare him best by holding her tongue about Michael. She wanted desperately to reassure John; but she could not put Konrad out of her heart and mind so easily, nor her remorse at what she had done to him. She looked at John for a long time without saying anything to him, except with her eyes.

Something indestructible had come back into her life again. She did not think it was only John himself, but it was something that came back to her through John; and of which John himself was a part.

"You'll be all right now," John said to her at last reassuringly. "I'm still on duty, so I must go down to the office again. Try to get some sleep. I'll tell them not to send your breakfast up to you till you ring. You mustn't put your feet to the ground till I've had another look at them."

He was gone; but the strangeness that she had felt with Konrad had gone too. Elizabeth was no longer an intoxicated fragment of herself on an unknown road; she was a real person in her own home; and when she was left alone, she found that she did not feel lonely any more.

30

Marie Céleste slipped inconspicuously, by a side door, into the waiting sleigh. She did not look like a woman dressed to charm, on a mission of rescue; she looked like a neatly made male acrobat about to perform a feat of some severity.

She stopped the sleigh at the entrance to Davos Dorf.

"Now, Pierre," she said, fixing the driver with her laughing eyes, "you were to take me to my destination —were you not? You must know then about what time you were expected back from Klosters? It was understood that I should return later on by train. But you will not be driving back from Klosters, because you will not take me there! For you—this *is* my destination. But do not return to the Sanatorium until the time arranged for—nor mention that you left me here. Meantime the less visible you are the better for both of us! 'The Eye of the Holy Ghost' is in a back street —and has a stable behind it. The wine there is a tolerable *Magdalena*—do not drink too much of it. To any questions that you are asked on your return, you will know very well what to reply."

Marie Céleste gave him a handsome tip, and a conspiratorial twinkle, and vanished up a side street. It was time for an early breakfast, but she was not going to eat any breakfast. She knocked instead at a well equipped sport shop, kept by a friend of hers.

"Good morning, Herr Wilhelm," she said. "I want very quickly a well seasoned toboggan and a pair of trustworthy rakes. Can you supply these on hire, and are you prepared as well to do me a favour that has a slight soupçon of privacy about it?"

"If I am to be let into a secret, I can keep a secret," Wilhelm told her. "Have I not lived surrounded by Nazi sportsmen—who were also officers for five years on the look out for secrets? Still, I should like to know how illegal you want me to be!"

"I am in a hurry," Marie Céleste reminded him, "and my quickest way to reach Klosters is down the Bob run on a single toboggan. I want you to remove for a few minutes whoever is guarding the run."

Wilhelm Buchs scratched his flaxen head as if that was the way to bring ideas out of it.

"I know the guard," he admitted. "In fact, he is a cousin of my wife's. We curl together—he has a good swing to his arm. The run is far from easy for a single toboggan—a long, steep run—with corners like the Matterhorn. You have been on ice runs lately? You know the risks?"

"Naturally I know them," Marie Céleste said impatiently, "but there is also a risk if I don't get to Klosters in time. I know that still better. Now, if you will help me we will get started."

Their eyes met, sounded each other, and approved of what they had sounded.

In less than ten minutes Marie Céleste stood behind a pine tree, watching the retreating backs of Wilhelm and the run's guardian. She kneeled on the snow, fastened her rakes with meticulous care, and rising, looked carefully about her. The visible world was empty. The first shadows of the pines lay cold and grey against the snow. The mountains rose featureless—a toneless white against a sky that was not yet blue. The frozen air was still. At her feet lay the congealed and sinister ribbon of the run. The first corner rose up a menacing blue wall, dropping almost vertically back into the knife blade beneath it. "Yet it is when I swing for the second corner that I must pray my grandmother was a limpet!" Marie Céleste told herself. "I must not die yet if I can help it or I shall get those two nice young men into trouble; but if I cannot help it—they will just have to face their difficulties for themselves, and I shall die less painfully perhaps, and certainly more quickly, than if I die in bed. Is not Konrad worth a risk? I thought so once—and I think so still."

She crouched, tested her rakes, and plunged forward. For the first few seconds her eyes blurred, the breath ran out of her lungs like water from a sieve; the sea roared in her ears, and every bone and muscle shook and strained in the narrow frame of her body.

Faster and faster she shot between the icy banks, her strong hands gripping the runners, the rakes biting into the ice, to give the split seconds she needed for the desperate swing of the first corner. She was up it, and dropped, slithering into safety by the turn of a hair, once more into the strait. Her body felt astonishingly limp and small, like a leaf that the wind might pick up and drop wherever it would, against the whole of her taut resistance. The uncoiling ribbon of ice ran before her eyes with inconceivable rapidity. The air roared in her ears, her eyelids stiffened and froze towards each other. She passed up and over the next corner without seeing it, feeling as if a giant hand were tearing her clenched arms from her shoulders.

She must slow now, at any cost, for the great swinging turn of the run when the whole hill side turned with her, to plunge into the apricot mist beneath it.

The toboggan lurched hideously, but the turn was over, the ice changed and softened. They were crossing the road to shoot through a tunnel, with a flick like a shutter, between light and darkness. The smooth ice turned to the softer unevenness of snow. Marie Céleste caught a strange glimpse of blue sky hurrying over the world's edge. Now nothing lay before her but the strait with its ding-dong swinging of terrific speed. A hill rose in front of her, without perceptibly altering her pace; she shot up it, a spray of flying snow broke over the leaping toboggan; and it crashed down on the hard surface of the snow as if it meant to burrow underground. This sudden silence was the end.

Marie Céleste sat on her toboggan, her head bowed, her breath whistling through her—limp as a rag doll —while the rocking world sobered into stillness. It had been good timing. The next thing was to find Konrad.

The yawning, dishevelled Nacht Lokal knew nothing of him. There had been a young man who, at four o'clock, had made a fuss about which way a missing young lady had gone. On the whole, Marie Céleste gathered this was rarer there, than a young lady who made a fuss about a missing man. Anyhow, there had been no trouble, since their bill had been paid.

Marie Céleste went through the little town house by house, till at last, on the outskirts, in the back room of a wayside inn, she discovered Konrad. A child with a good memory for strangers located him for her, and showed Marie Céleste where she could climb into the house by an unlatched window. The door was locked and barred, and Konrad would, Marie Céleste knew, have bribed his host into silence. No-one would come near them; they were alone, in a cold, stuffy little room smelling of manure and sour milk.

Konrad had already drunk half a bottle of bad brandy, but he was still startlingly sober; and had reached an abusive and rather dangerous stage. He cursed Marie Céleste for having found him—for being a woman—and for never leaving him alone. He threw a plate at her; and became obscene on the subject of John and Elizabeth.

Marie Céleste took off her leather helmet, shook her ginger hair free of intensive particles of ice, and unwound her tightly bound leggings; then she took Konrad's glass out of his hand, and drank a neat thimbleful of the remaining Cognac.

"You have only drunk half the bottle," she told Konrad incisively, "so that you can perfectly well hear what I have to say to you—and it is high time you listened. Your vocabulary of curses is used up, and has become monotonous. Your opinion of John and Elizabeth is only a more highly coloured version of my own. I do not admire them for having preserved their exasperating principles, at your expense, though Elizabeth —it seems—has been even more expensive to you, by *not* preserving hers, strictly enough! The virtuous should never have lapses. You must, however, allow for Caroline's skilled poisoning, and your own persuasive charms. Elizabeth very nearly imagined that she had a right to behave as badly as she felt like behaving. In her place, I should have thought that I had no right to behave *well*—if by behaving well I meant retaining the technicalities of virtue. But Elizabeth is human—she fell into the temptation of morality too easily! What is ridiculous is that you do not understand how unfortunate it is for you to kill yourself with bad brandy because Elizabeth turns out to be as good a wife as we have always known her to be!

"I do not for a moment say that the world is a very

237

nice place—or that the human beings in it are an engaging lot—but so long as there is work to be done and we know how to do it, only a coward leaves it by his own volition. Besides, is Elizabeth the only woman in the world? A good little girl, with skin the colour of a peach and eyes like a gentian—that I grant you—but have you ever thought what would be left for you to talk about, once you knew that you could sleep with her, whenever you liked? Yet three parts of life is conversation, and does not take place in bed. I am myself very fond of Elizabeth. She is a nice child—good as bread and clear as sunshine—but for how long would you find these qualities thrill you?"

"You don't know what you are talking about," Konrad said heavily. "For me, she has magic; when she goes away my blood goes with her. For nearly two years I have tried to win Elizabeth, and to-night I thought that I had won her! When she first married John, she meant no more to me than a china shepherdess —she was invulnerable because she loved him. I have never yet tried to win a girl away from her lover. But when John threw her over, it was entirely different. Elizabeth was then a hurt child, and had I no right to try to comfort her? She felt like dust, and my homage and devotion did her good. You must admit it—and you have often urged me on. But she had so strong a determination to remain virtuous that I could do nothing but play the piano with her! She told me twice—and I dared not risk asking her a third time—'No matter what I feel for you, I cannot do what I think wrong. I am married. You must not forget this—for I never shall!' I almost came to believe that Elizabeth *would* never forget it, and then suddenly with no warning whatever—not the lift of an eyelash—she bounds into my arms like an antelope! I admit she is seeking shelter from her broken heart—but it is in my arms that she seeks it. I had her willing lips and eyes. You know whether I am a good judge in these matters! A man on fire knows whether he meets ice—or an answering flame. He cannot be mistaken. Elizabeth was mine— and then——" he pushed towards Marie Elizabeth's blurred little card. "I can't go on."

Marie Céleste read it gravely. "Poor child," she said. "Poor you! What power we have to hurt each other—we who seem to have so little power to help! Perhaps it is because we do not understand ourselves and so have never learned how to understand others. Ah! here is my breakfast that genius of a little girl— who no doubt belongs to the inn—has had the wits to order for me! You can hardly believe how hungry I am! My stomach, which was flapping against my back the whole way down the run, has at last settled where it can function properly. Only it has never in my life felt so empty as at this moment. Fear is, I suppose, good for the appetite, and frantic fear is what I enjoyed for—how long was it?—a pocket eternity—perhaps a quarter of an hour! Now it is my appetite that is frantic instead of fear."

"Marie Céleste!" Konrad cried aghast. "You came down the Bob run—*iced*—on a single toboggan?"

"But certainly," Marie Céleste asserted, calmly swirling coffee and foaming milk together simultaneously with a flick of her wrist into their two cups. "You chose the worst inn you could find no doubt, but even the poorest Swiss cow produces milk and butter fit for angels! The bread, of course, is stale, but had your landlord offered me a stone, I should have accepted it."

"You risked your life to reach me," Konrad said slowly.

"Pooh!" Marie Céleste laughed. "What a thing to risk—a half lived life at that! I must have sampled all the sensations I need by thirty-five! Besides, I was never a very valuable specimen of womanhood. A woman should be patient, gracious, a little deceitful and agonisingly unselfish—and I am none of these things. I had to get to you before you had time to drink away your wits. But do not think I came simply to scold, and annoy you—or even to show off my skill as a toboganner! I came because I had a plan that might suit us both. You know that my parents are not too badly off, and that I am their only child? They have a little farm in the wine country, and possess good vineyards. They are growing old, and my father has often said to me that if I would care to manage them, I might have the vineyards; and he and my mother would retire to a flat in Paris. The house is big enough for guests. I can imagine we might run it together—you and I—as a convalescent home for T.B. patients. Such work in the open air is the best possible therapy for convalescents. Our partnership need have none of the *longneurs* of marriage, but I should not refuse you a little of the *aisance*! A mutual name and the wearing of a wedding ring on my part would not be out of place."

"It is nonsense—what you are offering," Konrad told her angrily. "You need for such a scheme—which you are suggesting out of pity—a young and eager man, not a broken, drunken sot!"

He turned his bloodshot eyes on the half bottle of brandy. He had only to wait a little, he told himself. He could get rid of Marie Céleste somehow—for he must keep his bottle. The Nacht-Lokal had cost too much—he could not afford to buy another.

Marie Céleste took out her compact, and with a few

deft, business-like touches restored her shaken complexion.

"A broken-hearted vamp!" she thought. "Trying to win the attention of a compulsion-driven neurotic—what a type—and what a destiny!" Then she said very gently in a voice that was made of music, "Konrad, do you think it was pity that held us together those winters in the rain and snow above Grenoble? In woods —chased by dogs—through the *bise*, without shelter? When the Germans caught us at last, separately, and confronted us, while each denied the other? When they beat you in front of me, and outraged me in front of you?—so as to get our names—and the names of our comrades—but we gave them nothing but our broken bodies? We kept silence for each other and for them! You think that was pity? You know it was more than pity! We had no dignity left—the walls of our self-respect had fallen—we could not separate ourselves from each other any more. Your pain was mine—my fierce shame burned in you! We were, I think, united in those hours of torment as few married lovers have ever been united. I do not know the name of what united us— but I know it is still there! For when Elizabeth deserted you—it was me also whom she deserted!"

Konrad said nothing; but he turned his unwilling bloodshot eyes away from the brandy bottle towards her face. He let her look into his defeat at last. A wave of compassion deeper than anything she had ever felt carried Marie Céleste into the depth of his misery. With what anguish she remembered the firm thread of his courage through long months of emergency and squalor! How she had leaned on his laughter, and been saved by his agility from disaster, and had in her turn saved him by the quickness of her answering wits! Her eyes shone back into his with the light of her memories.

"It was not pity," she said quietly, "that I felt for you then, Konrad—when you were beaten into a bloody pulp on the stone floor—it was admiration! And it is admiration that I still feel for you!"

Her beautiful low voice stopped, but her shining eyes went on speaking to him. She would not believe in his hopelessness, and hope shook him again, through her, like torture. "If we had wanted this," he said with sad lucidity, "should we not have chosen it long ago? Are we not being driven—or are you not driving me—into this mere shell of living, from disappointment and fatigue—perhaps from fear? It is John, not me, whom you admire now—and rightly—for I have no strength left—no dignity—no fortitude. Do you think I could build a life worth living from the ruins I am lost in? And do you suppose I can bear not to do honour to such a comrade as you are?"

Marie Céleste pushed back the thick waves of her ginger-coloured hair with a quick, impatient gesture. "This John," she said, "I see I must clear up the image you think I have in my heart of him! His life is not my business any more, whatever it once might have been! Have you forgotten that I knew him before his marriage—and well—so that I brought you to him after our escape? You were then, as we both thought, hopelessly ill, and we worked together for your life, as we had worked before together to save other lives. I thought John cared for me then: I did not see that it was the vision of his work with which he was in love. I had a function in this vision—I was useful to him, perhaps he even thought of me then, as his future partner. It is difficult to know what an Anglo-Saxon really feels for a woman whom he respects and admires, but does not want—or perhaps does not let himself want—because he does not know that you can respect a woman that you take, as well as one you leave! He went back to Canada, to complete his plans, and fell in love with Elizabeth, a British girl so young—so innocent—but not at all helpless!—a strong, efficient girl, just the wife he wanted—not a woman with nerves broken by outrage, but a mother for the children he desired!—a virgin—immaculate—faithful! And where do you suppose I came into this bright, wholesome picture? Nowhere at all! The war by now had changed: we could foresee victory. Perhaps it would have been wiser to cut myself adrift, and to return to my nerve-shattered country—refusing the post John offered me, ignoring what I then felt was your need of me. But women have an indelible failing—they want always to be indispensable to some man! I was still greedier—I wanted to be indispensable to two men—and perhaps also to Elizabeth—for you must remember I liked Elizabeth—that I still like Elizabeth! John said, when I spoke of leaving after his marriage, 'I cannot do without you, Marie Céleste.' As a matter of fact, he could have done perfectly well without me, although X-ray experts, at that moment, were hard to get. You, too, implored me to stay. You were still in danger, and at this time you were not in love with Elizabeth. These things appealed to a proud woman who suddenly found herself without any reason to be proud. If I went away, people would have said—or so I thought— 'She had to leave because John preferred Elizabeth!' Well—I stayed—and you see John still prefers Elizabeth! I have spent the night arguing with him, while I watched his jealousy tear his common sense to pieces. He wanted to ring up the police to search for you and Elizabeth. Poor John!—it is always the police he thinks of in any emergency! Law! Force! Order!—and you and Elizabeth were dancing at a Nacht-Lokal. I knew that you were dancing. But my dear Konrad, I also knew that Elizabeth would stop dancing!"

Marie Céleste pushed back her chair with a brisk movement, and walked to the window. He could take the bottle of brandy while her back was turned. Marie Céleste would not interfere even if she saw that it was gone. This scheme of hers would fade away. He would of course leave the Sanatorium. He might kill himself, perhaps, in some quicker way than drink, or he might— not wishing to upset good comrades by being dramatic over his final defeat—just slink back to his married sister in Vienna, who would see—though reluctantly— that he did not starve.

"There is that young patient of yours, Gustave Arnaud, from Geneva," Marie Céleste said over her shoulder. "He depends very much on you. Has he not to have a phrenic nerve cut tomorrow? He would do very well in this scheme of ours, if he gets through the operation satisfactorily; but he will need all the help he can get—a ticklish operation for a high-strung boy. If he gets frightened, and his breath goes too quick, you know what happens? Myself—I dislike these operations under a local anaesthetic. They depend far too much on the human element—and this, John does not understand. He thinks of what can be done with what is in his hands and his brain, but the player behind the instrument he is mending—he forgets."

Konrad moved restlessly. He did not make any decision at the moment, or if he made one, he did not know what it was. He put the brandy bottle in his pocket, as a gesture of reassurance to a self he had already discarded.

"I forgot about the boy," he admitted. "I must go back and see him through, but I shall let John operate. As for this scheme of yours—it might suit me very well, of course—but why should *you* leave *now*, more than at any other time—just because I must? If I ever agreed to it—you would find me a bad bargain."

Still Marie Céleste stood with her back to him.

"My dear," she said at last, "I go away now because I find myself a little meaner and more greedy than I thought. If I stayed on I should be in the way. I might nibble at those good lives—that may come together and satisfy each other fully at last, if they are left to themselves. I shall go now—whatever you do—as soon as John finds someone to take my place. Whether I go alone—or whether you go with me—is for you to decide. I have told you my preference."

She turned round, and saw that the brandy bottle was no longer on the table; but the smile in Marie Céleste's eyes remained unaltered as she looked at him.

31

It was some time before Caroline recovered from the uneasy feeling Michael's last words had left with her. It is one thing to know that you sometimes manipulate the truth to suit your own purposes and it is quite another, and a far more painful thing, to realise that you are losing the power of knowing what the truth is.

Caroline had to depend on her knowledge of John, in order to bring about her wishes, and if she were mistaken in this knowledge, then her wishes might fall to the ground; and her dreams with them.

She pushed the thought of John's possible displeasure, at her bid for his freedom, as far away from her as she could push it. No detective story would do it for her to-night. She did not care who was murdered by whom, until she had seen from John's face—that she had not betrayed him. If John had been in the Sanatorium, Caroline would have got to him by hook or crook; but she knew that he had not yet returned from Davos.

Caroline ate her supper mechanically; turned on her radio for the nine o'clock news; and permitted herself to be slowly and methodically settled for the night by Nurse Agnès. Sister Peckham and Nurse Agnès vanished. There was very little actual nursing to be done during the night. If anyone wanted anything they rang their white bells and Nurse Clothilde answered them. Anything innocuous she did for them; anything serious she reported to Sister Albertine. Sister Albertine saw each patient once, after she came on duty;

then she sat in her office on the second floor, in the middle of the Sanatorium, knitted, prayed and read devotional books, and drank tea brought to her by Nurse Clothilde at stated intervals throughout the night.

Caroline had long ago taken Sister Albertine's measure. She was too stout and too holy to be always on the prowl. She didn't want to find anything wrong, though if she knew anything *was* wrong, she would attend to it quite efficiently.

Nurse Clothilde was even less to be reckoned with; she wrote long letters to her boy friend during the night; and only answered bells.

Things were not exactly as usual, Caroline thought, although she could not quite put her finger on what was wrong. She thought she heard sleigh bells a long way off, but they could not have been John's returning sleigh bells, for they did not come up to the door. An hour later she heard the real bells of John's own sleigh, and questioned Sister Albertine, who had looked in to say good night, upon his arrival.

"Yes, it is the Chief," Sister Albertine agreed, "but far too late, of course, for him to do any rounds tonight. He is on duty, and will sleep as usual in the office. Not that he sleeps much, for it is then that he attends to his letters to relations, makes up his accounts, and arranges his files. With our system of telephones there should be complete relaxation for the medical staff, between calls, but I cannot say that Dr. MacTaggart takes great advantage of it. Now, if you do not feel inclined to sleep, here is a nice little pill for you!"

Caroline despised Sister Albertine's nice little pills, but she took one to get rid of her. She tossed restlessly from side to side, and if she had had a thousand sides, Caroline concluded, she would have tossed them, a thousand times. One instant after she had changed her pillow, it was as hot and flat as ever, under her burning cheek. She was quite grateful to the night sweats when they came, much later than usual, since they gave her an excuse to ring for Nurse Clothilde to change her nightgown and sheets.

Nurse Clothilde, when milked dry as to news—produced two interesting items. Dr. Rainer was out for the second night running. Dr. MacTaggart would dislike this second late night very much, though no doubt Dr. Rainer was free to spend his evenings as he liked when not on duty. It was odd too that Mrs. MacTaggart, who seldom if ever went out at night, had apparently gone out with friends. Their own sleigh had not been ordered—so somebody must have come for her; and without leaving any message. After this information, Caroline found it still more impossible to sleep.

The whole house seemed haunted with expectation. There were no sounds, nothing moved; the air was so still, it might have hushed itself to listen.

Caroline's watch was immovable between two and four o'clock. Then she heard the hoot of the milk train from Klosters, puffing its slow way up the mountain side to Davos. Caroline wished she could have visited the minds of all the other patients who were awake like her. What were they thinking of? Or if they slept, what dreams reassured or tortured them? There was John himself, for instance. Did he know that Elizabeth had not come back? There had been no more sleigh bells; and if he knew, did he care?

Caroline herself had instantly put two and two together and she was quite sure that Elizabeth was dancing at a Nacht-Lokal with Konrad; and did not this fact entirely justify and substantiate Caroline's few sound words to Elizabeth?

If Caroline herself had been dancing with Konrad,

248

she would, she thought, have worn scarlet, and looked like one of those slender, wild tulips that dance like flames in the spring, under the early vines in Italy. Caroline's mind brushed aside the thought of Konrad with a mingling of exasperation and regret. How badly he had behaved—but how amusing it had been—and if he had behaved a little worse—how more amusing still, it would have been! What did he see in Elizabeth? What *was* there in Elizabeth *to* see, that Caroline had not got—except her health? Except her health! Elizabeth could dance all night long, and in the morning her skin would be as fresh, her eyes as bright as if she had not danced at all. How stupid it had been of Job, not to curse God and die, as his friends suggested! Dying was, of course, not so easy—but cursing at least was well within anybody's powers.

Caroline turned off her bedside lamp to look at the reluctant dawn. She could see nothing but one pale star, like a tear upon the shadowy face of the retreating night.

Caroline decided that she could bear her solitude no longer. She would get up, and go out into the corridor. There must be something she could see or hear, outside a hundred people's doors, even if they were shut. She drew on her pink shetland dressing gown and warm feathered slippers. She had sent her mother all over war-impoverished London to find pink feathered slippers. The corridor was warmer than her room, and at either end, through the tall windows, there was a vague, colourless light, as if someone were pushing back the night before day could be born. There was a sound of tea-cups clinking in the Block kitchen. Clothilde was no doubt making Sister Albertine's latest, or earliest, cup of tea.

Caroline wandered like a ghost down the long corridor, stopping outside the door of any patient whose history she knew. Michael was awake too; his light was fully on—but she wasn't going to go near Michael. He had been quite rude to her about the truth. Besides, he believed that John still loved Elizabeth.

Caroline thought that she heard a faint sound coming up from the doors of the lift: she stood nearly opposite them. She could see whoever was in it now, if it rose; but anyone in that bright golden cage could not see Caroline standing in the darkness. The light above the lift door sprang on, and a faint click heralded its approach. Who would be in it at this least-tenanted hour of the whole night? The light rose up ahead of it, and shone full through the iron-work gate.

John stood in the lift, holding Elizabeth in his arms. He was carrying her, because although she wore an evening dress, her feet were bandaged. Elizabeth did not, however, look as if there was very much the matter with her. Her eyes were wide open, and her lips just parted, as if she were going to smile.

They were not speaking or even looking at each other; but as they shot past Caroline into the further darkness, they seemed to carry with them all the light of all the world.

Caroline had never faced facts so convincing. Elizabeth belonged to John; and John was glad that Elizabeth belonged to him. All Caroline's arrangements came to an abrupt end. She felt like a producer, who, upon the eve of a great performance, finds his props irretrievably missing. Nothing but solitude stretched before Caroline—and it was through this solitude that she found herself moving to reach her empty room.

32

When Caroline reached her room, she looked round her carefully, as if she had mislaid something important to her. It was light enough for her to see the shapes of all the furniture quite plainly; but there was nothing in the room that she was looking for.

She sat down in the big armchair by the balcony door; but she soon got up again shivering. "I don't know why I should go on living," Caroline said to herself bitterly, "but I shan't throw myself into the snow again —it's much too cold!" She went back to bed, and for a time found that her hot-water bottle was quite a comfort to her. She went on thinking about how to kill herself; but there seemed to be a space between the inviting idea of death, and the actual brutality of dying, which Caroline's reluctant mind could not bridge.

"There isn't any way that I can get hold of sleeping draughts," she thought, "or any quick, easy things— like prussic acid. John keeps even constipation pills locked up. I shall tell him that he's ridiculously strict!" But she suddenly remembered that the John to whom she could tell things had gone. The man who held Elizabeth in his arms was a stranger.

Her mind moved uneasily from image to image of the people she had learned to hate. She hated Elizabeth: she hated her mother and Sister Peckham: Konrad and Marie Céleste: and of course John—and God. It was no use thinking about any of them, because whenever their images recurred, she found herself flinching from her former contacts with them, without being able to envisage any other contacts. She didn't think about Michael; but if she had thought about him, she would have hated him worst of all. Had he not been unendurably right about Elizabeth and John, and is there anything so unforgivable as a person being right against the chief wish of your heart? Death was the only shot left in Caroline's locker—the only statement she could make, that would make her world sit up.

For every one of these torturing jailers would attend to a dead Caroline. People might say what they liked about putting an end to capital punishment—they could never put an end to the capital revenge of suicide. Her London doctor, a more confidential one than John, Caroline reminded herself, had told her that it might be fatal for her to laugh or cry, or take any sudden exertion; "above all," he had added earnestly, "you mustn't *lift* things!" That was an idea! Lifting things! Caroline had tried crying more than once before and nothing had happened except that the last time Sister Peckham had held her jaws tightly together till she stopped. Caroline didn't somehow feel like crying again now— and certainly not like laughing; but lifting things sounded an inviting idea. Caroline thought she would rather like to go round the room, lifting things. She started with the bed table, and a little chair; they were both easy matters. She was breathless after lifting them, but they were well within her capacity and they increased her appetite for more spectacular efforts. There was the armchair by the window; even Sister Peckham spoke of it as a "heavy" chair. Caroline set to work upon it, but found the chair impracticable as a whole—she could strain and strain but it did not budge. However, by crouching on the floor, and putting the whole strength of her back and shoulders into it, she could just lift one of its legs; by terrible straining, she lifted both legs; then she had to let go of them again, and still nothing happened.

There was only the wardrobe left, and if she tried to lift the wardrobe—painted wood and rather ramshackle —it might fall on her; and the idea of being smothered under a wardrobe struck Caroline unfavourably. Besides, in spite of her heart bumping intolerably hard, she had begun to feel sleepy. She did not give up her plan, but she decided to postpone it till tomorrow; and got back into bed. She must have fallen asleep, for when she woke up, her little white room was full of golden light. It was going to be one of those days which well people call "perfect" and expect invalids to enjoy, when they can't do anything with its perverse loveliness but lie in bed and look at it.

There was rather a funny taste in Caroline's mouth, as if she had been sucking a piece of rusty iron. Her mouth seemed filled with this peculiar liquid. There was nothing painful or sudden about its flow, but Caroline supposed she had better get rid of it; and when she got rid of it, she saw that it was blood, bright, arterial blood.

Caroline knew exactly what this meant, but she rang the emergency bell without undue anxiety. "Now," she thought, "I'll see for myself whether they can reach us in thirty seconds as they all say——!" But Caroline did not get to the end of her methodical reckoning, for all of a sudden so much of this disturbing fluid rushed up into her mouth that she was quite unable to deal with it. She felt as if a cataract was sweeping through her. If she wasn't very careful she would choke. However careful she was, she *might* choke! She *was* choking! However, Sister Peckham was suddenly in the room in her usual silent way. "It's not so very dreadful!" Sister Peckham said severely to the haemorrhage.

Caroline's panic receded. At last John got there. He said: "It's all right, Caroline, it'll be over in a minute!" She was in his arms—like Elizabeth had been. He seemed to know the right way of holding her—so that she stopped choking. He went on talking to her in a most friendly and gentle manner, so that he couldn't possibly have minded what Caroline had said to Elizabeth. He was explaining haemorrhages, as if they were better when you had explained them. Caroline lay relaxed against his shoulder. She hardly noticed the prick of an injection needle in her right arm; but everything had become suddenly less frightening. The flow of blood came differently, no longer as if it were being pumped up out of her by a giant hand, but as if it just ran gently of its own accord. It was still running, however; it ran all over the snow-white sheets and immaculate blankets that Sister Peckham always made such a fuss about, if the least little thing was spilled off a tray on them, and now she was making no fuss at all.

"We'll tidy up later," John told Caroline. "It's wonderful what a lot of blood you can lose without it doing you any particular harm. Now you can see for yourself it's stopping beautifully. I'm going to ask you to lie down now perfectly flat and not move. I'll put you just the way I want you to lie, and I'll stay with you, just the same as if I were holding you. You won't choke any more. A little chopped ice now, Sister—and we'll have the oxygen cylinder up here to use if we want it. Caroline, if you notice your heart beating rather fast, don't worry. I shall know about it and give you something to control it. Meanwhile we'll get the light out of your eyes. I want you to rest, and you will rest better with the shades down."

It was better, Caroline found, in this shadowy room; it was better when the ice came; and it was much better

254

when, except for a little mouthful or two, now and then, the bleeding stopped.

In no time at all, and without the slightest trouble to anyone else, Sister Peckham made the room look as if no-one had ever thought of a haemorrhage.

John sat close to the bed holding Caroline's thin wrist between his fingers, smiling at her, talking to her as if there had been no endless night, no cruel dawn, and yet there had been both the night and the dawn. Nothing could obliterate them. The brilliance of the light was lessened by the drawn curtain, but the room had still been very full of light. Now, unaccountably soon Caroline thought, the light was growing dim. She wanted to ask John if the sun was going down, or if it was her eyes that no longer saw so plainly. She could not see John's face except through a vague mist, nor Sister Peckham's resolute figure. But both of them seemed to know quite well what Caroline wanted. Caroline thought—though she knew the balcony door was wide open—that there was singularly little air in the room. It was as if she could not use air any more in the same way—but now the air came all round her, and instead of her having to catch it, the air itself caught Caroline. It stirred her hair, and streamed through every passage of her being; but it brought her no real relief; she was still unsatisfied. Her eyes began once more to look for something in the room that was not there.

"Michael—I think," John said to Sister Peckham.

Michael was kneeling beside her now, and Caroline heard his voice and knew that it *was* Michael whom she had been looking for—looking for—at dawn when she had found the room so empty—and perhaps ever since she had first seen him in the train. She wanted to explain this to Michael, but she could not find the words;

besides, since he was there, the words no longer mattered. She felt herself hurrying, hurrying at a terrific pace that was not doing her any good; because however fast she hurried, Caroline could not guess when—or even where—she was going to arrive.

She felt a little prick in her arm again, and, as John had promised her, the dreadful pace slowed up a little. She saw Michael's face quite plainly now. His eyes were full of a peaceful, friendly light. He said, as if they had simultaneously come upon a secret that was the key to everything: "You see, there is nothing else but love!"

His words struck through the stumbling confusion in Caroline's mind. She felt as if she were joining something that she had always wanted. It belonged to her, perhaps it belonged even more to Michael; but he was quite ready to share it, because it belonged to everybody. He spoke again, and a little thrill of triumph shook Caroline. He was saying the words of the Absolution which he had refused to her before. She could not quite follow the short, releasing sentences; but she knew that they were releasing. Only now she felt as if she wanted something more—to be released—wasn't quite enough. It did not tell her where she was going. Each moment seemed more important than the last. Yet it no sooner came, than it was gone; and with its passing came the warning feeling—that her destination was still unknown.

It was quite dark in the room now, but Caroline could still hear Michael's voice. It was as if her heart heard his words, without her having to take the trouble to listen to them. Michael said: "Our Father . . ." They were the last words that reached Caroline, for her heart, having done its business, stopped hurrying.